SESSIONS

The Purrfect Accident

E. VICTORIA

authorHOUSE®

AuthorHouse™
1663 Liberty Drive
Bloomington, IN 47403
www.authorhouse.com
Phone: 1 (800) 839-8640

Published by AuthorHouse 04/14/2016

ISBN: 978-1-5049-7487-5 (sc)
ISBN: 978-1-5049-7488-2 (e)

Print information available on the last page.

Any people depicted in stock imagery provided by Thinkstock are models, and such images are being used for illustrative purposes only. Certain stock imagery © Thinkstock.

This book is printed on acid-free paper.

Dedication

First and foremost, I would like to give thanks to my maker, despite my obstacles each and every one of them was set in place for a reason and I can't be anything but grateful. Which brings me to the love of my life; if it weren't for you, I'd be obsolete. You are the best thing that could have ever happen to me. You are my reason for being. I love you son with every breath, ache and inch of my body and soul. You are my heart and for that I dedicate my life and this book to you.

Our deepest fear is not that we are inadequate. Our deepest fear is that we are powerful beyond measure. It is our light, not our darkness, that most frightens us. Your playing small does not serve the world. There is nothing enlightened about shrinking so that other people won't feel insecure around you. We are all meant to shine as children do. It's not just in some of us; it's in everyone. And as we let our own light shine, we unconsciously give other people permission to do the same. As we are liberated from our own fear, our presence automatically liberates others.

~Marianne Williamson

OPENING UP

MY DREAMS ARE HEAVY, MY THOUGHTS ARE STEEP.
DISTORTED Memories UNFOLD I FEAR AS THEY CREEP
UPON ME…
RELENTLESS.
MY STORIES…are UNTOLD.
BOLD and EXGGERATED,
And yet THEY still PIERCE right THROUGH MY SOUL
But Oh to know…
About THE LIES, THE AGONY and THE DEEPNESS OF THE PAIN.
I WOULDN'T BE SURPRISED IF They'd,
LABELED ME MENTALLY INSANE.
Cause Damit,
I'M DRAINED.
I'm CONFUSED
STRUGGLING WITH MY inner THOUGHTS
The abuse,
From All the YEARS
now stirring away, and
boiling in my dark little pot.
These DREAMS
I've tried to keep them
SEALED AND BOTTLED UP.
INSIDE of MY HEAD but now they're
flowing
Like A RIVER
RUNNING THREW MY BLOOD LIKE LED.
Attempting
2 Poison MY HEART.
SO I STOP and ASK myself,
THE MILLION DOLLAR QUESTION,
WHERE IN THE HELL DO I START?
ONCE CONFUSED…
TO HOW and OPEN MY MIND,
TO ALLOW MY WORDS TO RUN
FROM THE CLUTTERED SPACE, They've
BEEN CONSEALED.
AND HID
FOREVER…
Entirely too too LONG.
My Visions are in there
JUMBLED AND TANGLED UP,

Frozen
And INTERTWINED.
LEAVING ME SUCLUDED, HELPLESS, NUMB AND ONCE
BLIND!
TO this…
MY LIFE
My….
UNSECURED REALITY.
It's now time for me to leave the past behind
And allow myself some NEW opportunities.
The chance to be myself
The chance to be free
The chance to be open
The chance to be me!
You see,
@ 33 YEARS OLD
I'm NOW finally ABLE TO OPEN UP?
Too…
POP MY TOP
Too
SPIT MY FLOW?
There is no more POISION.
RUNNING THREW these VEINS,
HELL NAW, NO SIR,
NO more.
Once was ENSLAVED to MY OWN constructed PRISON.
TORTURED BY MY INNER THOUGHTS,
So Listen,
The LOVED ONES, THE WORLD…
IT'S NO DIFFERENCE – HELL,
when it comes down to it,
the shit
it ALL HURTS.
So I welcome you to
come
NOW
Read MY PAIN,
Now…
sEE my WORDS.
Come hear MY LOVE,
Now
ENDURE MY NERVE.

Chapter 1

The waiting room was filled with a variation of characters. They were all scattered about simply doing their own thing. I allowed my eyes to survey the four soft colored pastel walls. These walls held up what I considered to be inexpensive contemporary art. "Not *too bad, just a bit too bland for my taste," I said softly to myself.*

I walked towards the receptionist. She was positioned directly across from the entrance sitting under a sign so boldly labeled, *check in.* She sat at her desk yawning and looking exhausted from what I assumed had been a long day. "*Well, that would make two of us.*"

By the looks of it she didn't want to be here anymore than I did. I gained my composure and slowly made the approached to her desk. "Yes mam, may I help you?" she said.

I leaned into her and whispered my name, "Eden Night. I have a 5:30 appointment."

The receptionist gave me her tired smile. Showing off her stained yellow and tan teeth, "Oh yes Ms. Night. I just need you to sign a couple of forms."

She placed them on top of the counter in front of me, "Make sure all of your information is correct across the top, initial down the page and sign at the bottom. Then all I need is a signature at the bottom of this page here."

I couldn't help but smell the pungent stench of day old coffee emanating from her breath as she provided me with instructions and a pen. I held my breath trying not to expose my true feelings in regards to her hygiene. I took the pen reluctantly and scribbled my name across the forms.

"Thank you Ms. Night."

"You're welcome."

I stood there trying with everything I had not to breathe in her words as she continued to rattle off more sentences. Except now her voice started fading. My thoughts began ascending rapidly in my head. I remained motionless while this foul breathed woman spat out what I assumed were formalities to this process. I tried to maintain control but I felt my mind drifting. It was too late. I was being pulled away from reality and taken back to when I was deprived of so many things, *"My youth. My childhood. My innocence!"*

The flashbacks started back up and were becoming more and more frequent. They're replaying like a full length featured film inside my head, *"So real and vivid."*

The things I would see when I'd blink my eyes, the dreams that were beginning to consume my mind, the voices in my head and now the nightmares. It was all becoming too much to handle. *"I can't deal."*

I felt myself slowly reverting back to that lost little girl who had no control. I was sliding back to that same little girl who was often scared and who felt all alone.

The longer the receptionist rattled on the louder the thoughts rang. My anxiety was heightening with every passing minute and I felt my breathing escalating. *"I need her to shut up!"*

I need to walk away before I lose control and become paralyzed from these emotions. "*You cannot spaz out right here Victoria…not here! Just breathe Vickie…deep breaths and get – it – together!*"

The receptionist began motioning me towards the empty seats away from her desk. "*And just in time, had I stood there any longer*"

I turned quickly from her in search of fresh air. I immediately noticed the tropical themed fish tank off in the far corner across the room. Nobody was sitting there so I begin my retreat. It was almost like I didn't have a choice. It was drawing me in and I allowed myself to be taken by the various colors illuminated by the single florescent light. The colors beaming from the tank reminded me of the 55-gallon aquarium we had when we lived in Paddle Brook North Townhomes. "*It was beautiful. I would sneak down stairs at night and just sit and stare at it. Get lost in the colors watching the fish swim.*"

This one was a bit smaller but shared many of the same similarities. I closed my eyes and I saw myself…

I was back in our townhome sitting on the couch directly across from our fish tank. There I was on the couch but I wasn't alone. I was with him sitting on his lap. Daydreaming and crying silently as I starred helplessly at our fish tank wishing I was swimming with the fishes instead of sitting with him.

I pulled myself away from the vision. "*It was just a flash. No worries Vickie you're fine.*"

I looked around the room to see if anybody noticed the change in my demeanor. I took a couple of breaths and tried refocusing my attention. Looking back at the fish tank in the office I tried to remember the good things. Like how I've always been easily captivated by nature and everything science. *Did you know that the earth is made up of 71% water with 96.5% of all Earth's water contained to the ocean?* "*Awe the ocean.*"

It is such a large body of mystery. Exposing so many great wonders and withholding far more. "*If I had it my way, I'd come back as one of largest animals on Earth, the Blue Whale.*"

They are about the only mammals that we know of which can swim the vast open waters of the ocean. They can explore far more of her beauty than any other known creature in the water. The blue whale is able to share the water with almost anything. They swim around for hours unbothered before coming to the surface to grab a bite to eat or some oxygen. They prefer the deepest and darkest parts of the ocean; diving to about 500 meters deep. Even though they occasionally swim in small groups, you are more likely to find them swimming alone. With the exception of the female who tries to keep her baby close in hopes of building a lifelong relationship, "*Sounds all too familiar. We have so much in common already.*"

But these fish in this moment made everything seem so still and tranquil. Maybe I was becoming paranoid but it felt like every eye in the room was examining me. "*Are these people trying to read my mind? Are my thoughts...that clear?*"

I wouldn't be surprised as loud as they were blaring inside of my head. Hell, sometimes they would get so loud that they'd wake me from my sleep, take me from my dreams and even cause me not to breathe. At times they have even been able to drown out the world, "*Leaving me secluded, helpless, numb and blind.*"

Before now, I thought I had perfected the craft of being able to mask my emotions. I'd gotten real good at hiding the scars even when they were visible. "*But here lately, I've been all over the place.*"

Not really certain if I was coming or going. I use to have the ability to instantly silence my thoughts. Once able to create the illusion of being present when I really was miles away. Now I was unraveling becoming exposed. I tried to suppress the emotions I had building up inside of me but it was just more than one person could stand. "*What in the hell is happening to me?!?*"

At the end of the day, I had become good at being what they wanted to see and who they wanted me to be. So good in fact that I didn't even realize the moment I'd lost myself. I kept my eyes planted on the fish tank arguing with myself. "I mean, who was I really?"

"*You're a ticking time bomb?*"

"I wouldn't have ever guessed I'd be here in this position."

"*Mandatory therapy! Again?!?*"

"Who could really help me?"

"*There isn't anyone. Truth be told, you're seriously just fucked up.*"

"Well, at least I know."

"*Yeah, but you no longer have the energy to pretend anymore.*"

"I am worn out!"

"*You are annoyed!*"

"I am pissed off!"

"*You are disgusted!*"

"Naw, I'm fed up!"

"*With everything?*"

"And everybody!"

I made it my business to not make eye contact with anyone in the room. "*You truly are in fear they would actually gather your truths.*"

"Yes."

"*Scared that they would hear the words I didn't particularly care to hear myself.*"

...life would be so much better...

These words just kept replaying and replaying in my head, "I can't worry about this. Not right now!"

I planted my body in the chair quickly trying to release the thoughts that were pounding in rhythm. The room seemed so much bigger when I first arrived but the longer I sat here allowing myself to be pulled back into my past the more it felt like the walls were closing in on me. I found myself gazing back at fish tank. "I wish my life was that simple."

I watched the biggest fish chase down the smaller one while the other fish swayed gingerly back and forth from one end of the tank to the other. These guys had no worries or cares in the world. They were fish just being good ol' fish. And with a blink of an eye I was back in my bedroom…

I was in my bed lying awake in fear. The room was completely dark but I could see her little mouth quivering…she was praying, "Please god… not tonight."

She just wanted to be left alone. She wanted to not be scared and to be able to lie alone in her bed. While other kids were worried about the boogey man hunting their dream, I was actually living with him. I saw the younger me waiting for him, opening and closing my eyes not sure when or if he would come see me tonight. I saw little Eden curled up with the covers to her eyes. She was gripping the covers so tight that her little hands were cramping from the strain. I saw the fear in her eyes and then… I saw her bedroom door opening. Slowly his body appeared in the doorway and then his face came into full view as he made his way to her.

These visions are only fueling my anger, driving my insanity. The voices are ringing louder …*oh yes yes yes. Life would have been better… all you had to do was go in.*

"Damn it!"

I really hope they hurry up and call my name. I'm not sure how much longer I can continue suppressing these feelings. The voices just wouldn't cease and every time I would blink I'd see his face and my heart would start to race. "Where is my control?"

"I had none."

The visions and the dreams continued to manifest at will and once again I was taken back. This time I found myself sitting in her car…

I was parked in a parking spot just two spaces down from where she lived. I sat starring relentlessly at her door. Sitting there, I allowed her words to motivate me. Too fuel me and ignite my urges. She had just rang my phone threatening to call the police on me. Saying some ol' dumb shit like if I didn't bring her car back to her "immediately if not sooner" then she will have me arrested for theft. *"Theft! Excuse me?"*

I began arguing with myself, "She has pulled some stunts in my day but this by far takes the cake."

"She is fucking crazy!"

"What good is the damn car to her anyways?"

"She is on too many medications."

"Right!"

"Her husband is having surgeries every time you turn around so he can't drive either."

"Exactly!"

"So again, what is the point?!"

"I don't know."

I use to think that because she was my mom that the necessities were guaranteed, but not if my stepfather had anything to do with it. *"Did I really think I was going to be able to borrow their car without hassle?"*

"Who was I kidding?"

Her husband always had something to say about something. As for her well, she is just unpredictable.

"They like pointing the finger at each other."

"Hoping we get confused, get lost in the shuffle and not notice."

"Well, I was onto them both."

"Truth be told she is the ringleader and he is her puppet."

"Or is he the ringleader and she is his puppet?"

"He is intelligent and manipulative."

"And she is straight crazy and deranged."

"See this is what she does. First, she feeds you everything you want to hear. Pretends to be on your side then, she reels you in all close and tight so that your back is against the wall and then BAM! She'll just drop the floor from out under you to leave you drowning up shit's creek without a paddle, raft or a flare."

"I must have been tripping to believe this was going to be work."

"You should have just listened to your gut."

"Well why not Eden?" Momma said.

"I just don't think it's a good ideal mom."

"Oh, come on Eden. You can use the money to get back on your feet. Plus, he can't drive no way baby. He refuses to take time off work and I can't get up early like that every day with all of these medications they got me on."

"I don't know ma." I remained hesitant.

"The car would just be sitting here anyways baby."

"She eventually wore you down and now look!"

"I can't believe I fell for her shit, yet again!"

"I told myself…"

"Self, after the last time you encountered her crazy ass you said you weren't EVER going to take anything else from her again."

I mimicked her voice, *"Sale your car Eden, she says. Save some money Eden, she says."*

"Yeah it all sounds good."

"Until, she is fucking you over and leaving you out in the cold. Hell, if I didn't have any sense I'd been dead from hypothermia by now."

Whenever it came to dealing with momma, you can and should always expect a few minor stipulations and even more hidden ones in the return. "*Again, what was I thinking?*"

In this case… run all of their errands without any contribution to the gas, pick up and drop off her husband to work daily and submit to any other daily request she had upon demand. Bad enough I would wake up extra early in the morning to go pick him up from his apartment, drop him off to work and then go back home to get myself and my kid ready for the day. After all of that and I still had to get my son off to school and me to work. "*On time…by the way.*"

After a day of dealing with obnoxious customers, pretentious managers and a multitude of personalities, I would then have to zip back across town in rush hour traffic only to arrive to an impatient, evil, scared and broken down little man. "*Her husband…my stepfather.*"

Once I retrieved him, we would then run whatever errands she had requested of him throughout the day. I choose to drop him off first before heading back across town to take her all the items we had collected off her list. Finally, I'd get to go home and try to decompress from the long depressing day.

"There really was not enough time in a day. Being that I am a mother I still had to prepare dinner, take showers, homework and have me some bubba time."

"*Trying to juggle so many things at once* it's so challenging but I have no other choice but to deal with it."

"*You already sold your car. So…*"

"I had better shut my mouth, bite my tongue and hurry up and get my shit together."

There was no turning back. What was done was done. It was only a matter of time before this situation went left. But I would have never guessed that it would have happen as soon as it did and so drastically.

My mother could do a lot of things but what I couldn't allow was her to jeopardize my lively hood and what little I did have going for myself and my child. The disrespect and dehumanizing slander is nothing new. My baby however is off limits. *"Period, and no I don't care who you are he is the exception."*

The sun had just disappeared behind the clouds. The hum of the idling engine became over powered by my conversation… *"Just do it!"*

I demanded to myself but immediately I tried rejecting the commands. Shaking my head I screamed, *"NO NO NO! I just can't… I can't K-I-L-L…"*

The words stammered out past my lips before I could stop them from spilling completely from my tongue. I became still in my skin and tried to be silent but I continued whimpering and debating with myself, *"How did I get here?"*

My mind in total disarray! The voices escalating and spinning at a rapid pace *"Just get out of the car and go do it!"*

"But… but…" I whimpered back.

Before I could finish the thought it felt as if the entire world had stopped. It was like I came out of my body and was looking directly at myself. I saw me sitting there with this blank emotionless expression. Tears running rampantly down my face and my body shook violently out of control. I witnessed her pain and it was real. Her struggle was indeed definite. I finally saw the little girl inside of the broken woman. I sat there stunned soaking in the words that I witnessed coming out from my own mouth, *"You know what you have to do!"*

I tried talking myself out of it but the more I tried the more sense it made. I was weak in that moment just simply defeated. I sat confronting myself, going back and forth with my thoughts. At some point everything disappeared from my view and I only saw myself and I saw her. I was strong in my convictions and was locked into what I wanted to do. I just knew she would be in there sitting on her couch just beyond the door. *"Waiting for me."*

"She'd be calling me every name in the book"

"Probably talking to him."

"Reminding him how I don't want none of her and how bad she could fuck me up."

"I'd be all kind of bitches and everything else but the very name she gave to me."

"She'd be in there conjuring up every lie she could to make herself look like the victim and me the devil she saw me as."

"He's probably encouraging her."

"I just know if she got the opportunity she would hit me."

"No doubt."

"And that was what I was most afraid of."

I can hear her now throwing her favorite line at me, "I brought you in this world and I will take you out."

A slew of unanswered questions rapidly rushed across my mind as the conversation continued, "Why is she always doing this to me?"

"Why me?"

"What did I do to deserve this?"

"Of all people?"

"My own mother!"

"No Vickie you lost your mother a loooooooooong time ago."

"I don't remember?"

"The day you tried explaining to her that the stranger she left you with was beating you... daily! Remember, that was the day she turned to you and said, 'Just a little while longer baby.'

"That was the day."

"The day you lost her?"

"Whatever bit of hope I had left in my 8-yearold body dissipated with her when she drove away from my sister and me."

This conversation had only engrossed me more. The very woman who, once upon a time I couldn't stand to be apart from was now the very same woman I couldn't stand to be around. "*Sad.*"

"Fuck her!"

"*I can't take this shit anymore!*"

"I'm done!"

"I JUST CAN'T TAKE THIS SHIT ANYMORE!"

The words belted from my mouth so loud I could have broken the windows in her vehicle. I sat stewing while my breathing became more panicked. My anxiety kicked up yet another notch and the debate continued, "*You should be used to it…*"

"Why continue to let her do this to you?"

I tried rationalizing with myself.

"*Just go do it!*"

"No!"

"*You do realize life would be better…now wouldn't it?*"

"No more abuse?"

"*No more name-calling!*"

"The rejection?"

"*The disrespect.*"

"The physical attacks and all the spastic behavior…?"

"*It would be gone.*"

I sat in silence allowing my words to marinate. I released a sigh of relief. Confident in my decision I turned off the car.

I knew what I had to do.

Chapter 2

Nichelle and I weren't close at all. We grew up in the same house, went to the same schools but lived very dissimilar lives. She was the golden child and could do no wrong especially, in our father's eyes. I on the other hand was a walking target for all their bullshit. Being that I was all quiet and reserved, unbothered by most unnoticed by many. Nichelle would steal my bottles from me and even get caught drinking them in her favorite hiding spot. She even tried taking my clothes but she was too big to wear them. Yeah I was younger, shorter, thicker, darker, uglier maybe. But I was smarter even more intuitive than she was. My older sister worked me over for a long time. She continued trying that is until I got too old for her antics and decided to work her ass back. It took us both some time to figure it out but after years of her torment and a few ass whippings later, we eventually got the hint.

Nichelle grew up pampered and praised by everybody in our family. She was the only child for 23 whole months before I came along. In that time, she grew to be a very selfish individual. Caring and looking out for herself mostly. With them glorifying her in the way they did only enchained her selfishness. These actions did nothing for her but leave her vulnerable to succumb to those who never had her best interest at heart. The environment in which she grew up made it rather plausible for her to follow up behind others. *"And from what I've witnessed she does that very well"*

With me rarely ever being acknowledged, I had to learn quickly how to stand alone on my own two feet. I had no choice but to become self-sufficient and independent. Unlike my mother who didn't have much but she did at least have her siblings. The oldest was responsible for teaching the next. That one was then responsible for teaching the next and so on and so on. All the way down the line of 13. Momma took the time to teach Nichelle all of what she knew about being a woman, which *unfortunately was basic.* However, it was expected for her to pass that knowledge down to me. But, Nichelle passed down nothing. She explained nothing and provided nothing to me. I stood alone; leading myself as a result of not having anyone else to follow after. *"I was born to lead!"*

My mother tried her best with us coming from where she came from. Her home was just as dysfunctional if not more. My father was too far gone in the fast lane for her to keep up. She just wanted a good life for her and her girls but instead she ran into the big bad wolf. *"And she has been running ever since"*

A smirk rose in the corner of my mouth as I let the memory fade. Suddenly I was back inside of the waiting room. I thought about how Nichelle is always inadvertently inserting herself into somebody else's bullshit. One time she ran all the way up to the mall selling wolf tickets to a show she wasn't staring in. Granted it was in defense of my cousin but she let her baby's daddy's drama get her locked up. My cousin didn't even get a chance to go head to head with him for Nichelle jumping in to the rescues. Of course, I ran up there after my sister. She was already being carted away by the time I came in with reinforcement. His scary ass started crying from more police so I had to get out of dodge before I ended up in handcuffs too. Another time, an argument broke out over at the same cousin's house and again, Nichelle jumped in writing checks and got her ass cashed in the process. "*You'd think she would learn from some of her mishaps but NOOOOOO not Nichelle.*"

My mother has always sheltered her regardless of what she did. For whatever reason, I too have always felt the need to protect her as well. There is always somebody there to catch her when she falls. "*I hate to see that day nobodies around and she hits the pavement.*"

The irony is she saved us both that night.

I don't know what I was thinking that night. All I remember was that I couldn't wait any more. I had made my mind up. I honestly thought that I would be doing what's best for everybody." *Hell I might even be doing her ass a favor. There's no telling how she's internalized this situation. Remaining married to him and all. I know she had to be affected but could momma have been so naïve? So broken herself?*"

Just as I was getting ready to get out the car to head to her door my eyes caught the light flashing from my cell phone. I saw my niece's face looking up at me from the passenger's seat but it was my sister's name that came across the screen, both breaking my concentration. "Now what does Nichelle want?"

"*If it aint one thing it's another. And that is one of the reasons why I assigned my niece's photo to her contact. I'm less tempted to ignore the call.*"

I worry about her and my nephew too. "*Of course I'm going to pick up the phone... I always do.*"

"Hello?"

"Heeeeey little Vickie. What are you doing?"

"Sitting in front of your mother's…"

"Wait, what's the matter? Why are you over her house?" She said.

"Wouldn't life just be so much better… without her here Nikki?"

"What do you mean Vickie?"

"I'm tired…I'm tired of her! I can't do this shit no more."

"I just can't Nichelle!"

"Meet me at the gas station Eden."

"Naw, I have to go."

"Where are you going?"

"Imma go on inside to take care of her."

"Little Vickie, wait… what about Darrius?"

"Don't do that sister…I don't have time for this."

I hung up the phone and got out the car only to run right into her. *"Where in the hell did she come from?"*

Nichelle had been making her way to me the whole time we were on the phone together. She made me get into her car. We drove around the city for hours. Mostly in silence but her sneaking up on me that night rewrote my entire future, "Oh God!"

I shivered at the thought.

I was so consumed in my little corner fighting my thoughts that I hadn't realized my name was being called. These damn flashes were so vivid that every other noise in the room was muffled in comparison. "Eden Night."

"Damn, is that my name?"

I swung my head in either direction unsure since I had blanked out from reality. In my haze I noticed the receptionist had left her desk. She was now standing in the doorway blocking the entrance to which separated the waiting room and the back offices. Her body language gave away her annoyance to my withdrawn presence. Her face held a puzzling expression emphasizing the bags under her eyes. She repeated my name, "Eden Night."

Releasing a long sigh just as our eyes met. I honed in on the tall woman propping open the door with her long body. Her dried out blonde hair was pulled back into a lumpy dysfunctional ponytail. Her lipstick was faded I'm sure from her lips pressing against her coffee mug all morning. Her pink and purple poke-a-dotted scrub top accented her now obvious fresh catsup stain splattered down the front of her top.

"Bless her heart."

I truly hope she was just having one of those days and this wasn't a regular occurrence. She stood there with her clipboard in hand scanning the attached forms in preparation for my approach. I'm not sure why I wasn't able to move. In an instance, a blanket of emotions coated my body and my feet became anchors restraining me to the chair. *"Why am I here?"*

Looking in the direction of the door I seriously contemplated heading right for the exit. "I am not ready for this!"

"I don't need to talk to anybody about…"

"Why am I so angry?"

"I know why I'm so angry."

"I hate them all!!!"

"Fuck!"

"Then why keep putting yourself through this? Why keep riding the same fucked up jagged ass roller coaster?"

I stood to grab my items to head for the exit but his face was looking up at me for the lock screen of my Galaxy S5. His smile was infectious showing off the dimples in his chin with that lonely one that fell into his right cheek. I smiled releasing the breath I held expended in my lungs.

"You're doing this for him…"

"Everything you do is for him."

"My bubba."

His picture released my trance. Just in time to hear my name being called yet again. If the people weren't looking at me before they sure in the hell was looking at me now.

"Eden Night!"

She hammered out my name like she was my mother requesting the damn remote. I jumped, grabbed my phone and headed in the direction of the familiar smell of day old coffee. She was halfway to me by the time I finally acknowledge my name. Raising my hand to halt her approach I answered meekly, "Yeeessss, sorry… sorry sorry."

She paused, "Is everything okay, Ms. Night?"

"Giving me her didn't you hear me calling your name face. Replying in a faint whisper I gave her my regular old defaulted response, "Yep, I am fine mam. Everything is fine."

She seemed confused by my response. Considering, I had become deaf and mute in the matter of minutes. She continued filling the air with her breath. She rambled on while she led us down a maze of hallways. "This way Ms. Night", she said.

My mind wondered back to my previous thoughts. *"All you had to do was go in…."*

The receptionist interrupted me coming to an empty room, "Please make yourself comfortable and Dr. Smith will be right in."

She ushered me into the empty room and shut the door behind me. I shuttered from being in the unfamiliar space and went back to observing the area. My nerves crept over my entire body while I stood there looking around trying to absorb the atmosphere. The lay out was not at all what I expected. I saw two chairs positioned diagonally from one another. A long table extended from the right side of a chair that was caddying the corner. The opposite chair sat next to a long window that stretched from the ceiling to the floor. On the table sat a colorful floral arrangement and a box of Kleenex all prepped and ready for use. The sight of the Kleenex made me laugh out loud. "I was no crybaby, I only shed tears from anger and even that was rare."

I had to remember that I'm here for a reason. I've lost control somewhere along the way and I need to get it back. I am well aware that I have problems especially with my need to control everything. *"I trust no one and nothing."*

I'm standing here in this unfamiliar room trying to convince myself to relax. *"One-step at a time Vickie one-step at a time."*

"This wasn't my first time at this rodeo," I confessed out loud.

Looking around the room to confirm I was still alone. Although it's been some time, I still remember my first session like it was yesterday. It felt more like an interrogation while we sat there inside of this dull room….

The bottom half of the walls were made of wood and the top half was made of translucent glass. The florescence lights hitting off this kind of glass along with, the darkness of wood ended up giving off a yellow tent to the entire room. There in the room, was a single table with a microphone dead smack in the middle. I sat there at this empty table cold, scared and helpless. I was already reserved, now severely confused yet vigilant to the situation. *I knew something was off.* But so much was happening at one time I was having a hard time trying to keep up with it all. *"What was this all leading to?"*

No one really took the time to explain much of anything to me. Shit just started unfolding rapidly with no explanation. One minute I'm at school all enthused about learning and the next I'm being drug off to a hospital. *"And yet I wasn't sick…I had questions but no one wanted to answer me."*

My mother looked a little confused as well. *"Do you blame her?"*

I could tell by the look on her face that she was doing all she could to reframe herself from losing it. Nichelle was off in la la land. She was all too happy to just be out of school. Her expression changed once they started poking and probing all over us. The hospital was the last time we saw our mother and that had been over 8 days ago. The social worker was misleading. Telling us she was just taking us out for some ice cream, "Ice cream, would you girls like some ice cream?" She said.

"*Uhmmmmmm no, what I would like is… for you to cut the shit, tell me what's going on and uhmmm go ahead and take me back to my momma.*"

She cradled Nichelle under her arm and pulled me along by the hand. We drove away from the hospital in a shiny black Lincoln with Nichelle steadily crying and hyperventilating.

"*She had to know more than me, otherwise why else would she be crying so hard about getting ice cream.*"

"*I was right!*" After Nichelle ate her ice cream we did not return to our mother. We were carted off to a Guardians home. The Guardians home was a large brick building that was built to house trouble and unwanted children. Everybody wanted to know who the new girls were. There was only one bed available when we arrived to the Guardians home and once we got settled, I went ahead and gave it to Nichelle and took the floor. They provided me with the paper-thin blanket and sunken-in pillow. "*I guess this will have to do.*"

Nikki was in any condition to be sleeping on the floor. I wasn't used to seeing my sister like this, "F*ragile.*"

Her eyes were red and swollen from the downpour of tears. She was refusing to eat and she already lost her voice. She hasn't stopped crying sent we left the hospital and I kind of needed her too. These kids were ruthless up in here. "*If I have to beat up one more person for trying to mess with my sister, I might not ever make it back to the third floor.*

The Guardian's home had five floors. There was the main level where all the offices were located. The lower level or the basement is where we all went to eat breakfast, lunch and dinner. The other three floors had an open layout with bathrooms on either side of the room for us to use as needed. During the day, we were allowed to socialize and mingle on our designated floor. Your behavior dictated which floor you would be assigned to with the really bad kids sleeping on fifth floor, the mildly troubled kids on the fourth floor while newcomers and the well behaved children stayed on the third floor. At night the 3 floors were transferred into sleeping area perfectly designed to arrange thousands of cots for all the restless and unwanted children. We were always being monitored by an adult but that didn't stop bad things from happening. I had to be strong for the both of us. Even though my family ran over me often I took nothing off of a stranger. See I was raised up in bright wood, on the east side in the city of Indianapolis. In my hood, we played no games and everything was about business. This place was no different to me.

Sadly, we had no access to anyone in the outside world. For weeks we sat behind these walls clueless. The second or third day is the day they started pulling me into the dull room for our so-called "sessions". I only saw Nichelle mainly during chow time. Otherwise, I was stuck doing some kind of work detail in results to fighting. Or I would be stuck in the integration room being questioned about being molested. "*Huh…molested?*"

"Is that what they call it?"

I had pretty much shut down externally at this point. I stopped talking, eating and feeling. "*Basically I stopped being human.*"

They forced me to sit across a table from a different person each time they wanted to have a session. All they did was yell out the same questions each time. "Where did he touch you? When did the molesting take place? Are you okay? Tell me what he did to you? Did he instruct you not to talk? Do you need anything?"

"Yes, I would like to collect my sister and go home to my mother."

I began losing track of time, the days blended into nights and nights blended into days. I chose not to answer any questions since nobody chose not to answer any of mine. I had become numb to the bullshit and detached from reality. My body sat tolerant to every question but my spirit was elsewhere. *"Wait was I in shock?"*

What was stopping me from forming the words they so desperately needed to hear?

"How could I answer them?"

I wasn't sure what was going on with us myself. I didn't want to think about this anymore. I really just wanted to be left alone.

Chapter 3

I heard the knock on the door. Snapping me back to where the receptionist left me waiting in the room. Whoever it was didn't wait for my response before entering. "Ms. Night, hello I'm Dr. Smith."

He walked right into the room extending his hand for a proper greeting. My voice was shaky but I reciprocated his introduction "Hello, I'm Eden."

I walked over to shake his hand. "Please sit." He said.

He pointed out my obvious options. I took another quick look around the room and then back to him. I debated silently in my head and took what I thought was the best seat in the room. I opted for the chair aligned with the thin window. It felt the less claustrophobic and if I had to I could be line right for the door. The window stretched from the floor to the ceiling exposing the trees and shrubbery from outdoors. Dr. Smith decided on the chair caddying the corner across from me.

I looked him over trying to get a read on him but I was too distracted. I would have preferred a woman therapist but there were no women available on such a short notice. However, after reviewing the options I went ahead and settled with a Dr. John Smith,

MSW, LCSW. He received a Master's degree in Social work from the University of Missouri. He specializes in addictions, anxiety, bi-polar disorder, depression, and variation of other stressors. He was more than qualified. I would have been fine with anyone as long as they weren't African American, tall, have a low cut beard or any characteristics resembling my molester. Dr. Smith certainly was quite the opposite. He was a little taller than I was. Making him about 5'8. He in his late fifties and wore thin circular rimmed glasses. He had an all-white beard that flowed to his chest. *"Reminding me of the Kernel from the chicken commercials…he's harmless."*

Dr. Smith broke our silence, "Before we get started, I'd like to just throw out a few things. First and foremost the goal, Eden is to provide a positive environment free of all judgment. What you say in here stays in here between you and me. My number one priority is to ensure your comfort with an intense focus on dissecting some of the deeper rooted issues that may be bothering you."

"Uhmmm huh, he sounds for real enough but I know what he is thinking when he looks at me" My expression must have given away my thoughts. I noticed his face tighten just as I was rolling my eyes up into my head.

"That means we both need to be open to creating a natural setting suitable for you to once and for all confront the emotions, behaviors and influences to which have caused us to cross one another's paths."

"I wonder exactly, what he does know about me?"

He continued not bothered, "Ms. Night, do you have any questions before I move on?"

I started fidgeting with my bangs and decided to engage him. Stammering out my question, "Uhm yeah well uhmm actually I do uhmmm…how long am I expected to come here?"

"That all depends on you." He said.

"So how long you are thinking?"

"As long as it takes Ms. Night."

My anxiety instantly revved up and hit the roof, "O-okay so look, Dr. Smith I'm thinking like what…three or four sessions. I talk about why I am here. You tell me I have child hood issues which, I already know. Yes I hate my mother and I'm sure you read the entire file on me. So I'm pretty sure you know the rest."

"Yes I have some back ground on you but only what they've provided. Some words on a piece of paper. I'd like to hear from you."

"Soooo, five maybe six sessions?"

I waited for him to answer but still he was unmoved. "As long as it takes Ms. Night, As long as it takes."

"Okay, but he is not answering the question?"

I tried to look as composed as he was but I'm sure my emotions where readable all through my body. "Ms. Night I understand you have been through a great deal. We don't have to rush through this. You have been through a series of traumatic events and this is going to take some time. How long is not of importance. But you are."

"Okay, you got my attention." I said to myself.

"You are scared. And that's ok. I need you to know that you are safe here."

"Dr. Smith. I appreciate the reassurance but I promise you I'm fine. I had a moment of weakness and I know it will never happen again."

"What will never happen again?"

"Like you said, you've read up on some background."

"Okay, let's forget for a second that you have to be here. But since you are here, what is it that you would like to get from these sessions?"

Although I was hesitant to the treatment I knew exactly what I wanted. *"I wanted a peace of mind, I wanted to lie down in my bed and not be scared to close my eyes. I wanted to sleep at night. I wanted to not be afraid to nap in a dark room. I wanted to be without the fear of someone coming in on me while I slept. I wanted to not have to sleep with the television on at night. I wanted…to find myself."*

I had no time to lose myself in my feelings since his voice was back ringing in my ears, "Sounds like to me you are on the same page?"

"Considering… I suppose now is as good of a time as any." I said to myself.

"I suppose I have allowed my past to consume entirely too much of my life."

"Well okay then."

"Yeah, but…"

"But you do agree it's time?"

"Yeah, but I confront these feeling daily."

"Ever out loud and to anyone else?"

"Yeah."

"Besides yourself?"

"That was a read, but no shade."

"Ok so no."

"Have you ever sought out therapy before Ms. Night?"

"Please", call me Vickie, Ms. Night is just so formal and well Eden, that's my grandmother's name. God rest her soul don't get me wrong, I am grateful and honored to carry her name but for real I'm only 26 so maybe when I'm rocking out in my 70's I'll firmly go with Eden but until then you can call me Vicki written with an IE not a Y"

We shared our first laugh. "Now to answer your question NO! No sir I've never 'sought out' therapy before", giving him my air quotation marks.

"However, when I was younger I was kind of 'MADE' too go", repeating the same actions. "But you see how effective that must have been huh?"

He asked curiously, "Do you recall your age?"

Reluctantly my mind started wondering back to that very first session, I saw the younger me sitting at that long table all timid and helpless.

"I recall everything Dr. Smith and yeah I was eight," I mumbled.

I became distance. I was trying not to relive the dreaded memories all over again. Dr. Smith took notice to my struggle. Attempting to change the mode he quickly asked, "Vickie, why don't you tell me in your own words something about you that I haven't read off of a piece of paper."

I took a deep breath and exhaled… "Well I am single mother; I have a 12 year old son. Who definitely keeps me busy."

I can't help but to smile when I talk about him. He truly is my heart. "He plays all kinds of sports mostly football but he also plays basketball, track and field, wrestles and has even dabbled a little in baseball."

"I knew when I found out I was having a boy that I was going to have to keep him heavily involved in activities or risk losing him to the streets, crime or a better yet…a little girl.

Mostly, it was for him to get that male interaction he so badly needed."

We were so young and with the circumstances…well it wouldn't hurt none. I was all team bubba and my son and I have been in sync from day one. Dia Numero uno!

"Whatever he was involved in mommy was too! I am like his buddy. Where ever he goes I'm going to go. I am the football mom which is a part-time gig in itself. If I wasn't in the stands routing him on I was somewhere around the concession stand or helping out on the sidelines.

I tried to volunteer regularly throughout the seasons for all his sports but football consumed more of my time the any other. His dad stepped in where he could but he has other children now so his time is spread quiet thin. Outside of him and his sports, I work full-time in the insurance industry; settling claims and providing various forms of customer service. I hold an Associate's degree in Deaf culture and with that I acquired a second language."

"American Sign Language?"

"Yep."

"What got you interested in signing?"

"Long story short, I gave birth to my son my junior year of high school. I wasn't really interested in having kids before then."

I stopped speaking and sat in silent for moment. Before he could catch onto my pain I started speaking again. "I wasn't interested in exposing a kid to the hell I've witnessed but my beliefs outweighed my wants and I was instantly was a teenage mother. After his birth, I became more depressed and lost interest in school. My son was suffering from ear infections and I had flunked just about every class my junior year except for maybe keyboarding and if I wanted to graduate on time I would of needed to take all of my junior core requirements and any remaining senior core requirements."

"I was tired to say the lease and wasn't looking forward to attending anyone's college at that point." I said to myself.

"Once upon a time, I was gearing up to go to Spellman. I was aiming for a track scholarship and wanted to become a wildlife zoologist. Once my GPA dropped below a 4.0 I knew Spellman was out of the picture. I guess I was happy to have graduated on time."

"You played sports in school?"

"I did! I was a bad girl back in my days Dr. Smith. I still hold the record in both shot put and discus at my middle school. I could pretty much play anything but I chose basketball and track and field. I use to be so good Dr. Smith that my school brought an entire rowing machine just so I can train off season."

He took note of my excitement as I sat there and reminisced on my past experiences and accomplishments.

"You really found an outlet in your sports."

"I did, that was the most productive way for me to release any tension."

"Not to say it was the only way." I whispered to myself.

During my senior year of high school my English teacher Ms. Simon, required use to fill out college applications and turn them in for a grade. I picked what I thought would be the easiest and shortest since I had no real expectations on even getting accepted. I wasn't sure anymore what I even wanted to do with my life. I somehow was under the impression that it was too late for me. *"What else can I do now beside be a young mom?"*

To my surprise, I had received an acceptance letter from Vincennes University, welcoming me into the American Sign Language program. It didn't surprise me that Ms. Simon sent in the application on my behalf. She was young, fresh out of college and passionate about teaching. She pushed me hard and never gave up on my education even when I wanted to.

Coincidently, just as I was entering the ASL program my son's doctor had discovered my son had developed a profound hearing loss from his battle with ear infections. Happily, I continued my education at Indiana University Purdue University of Indianapolis (IUPUI) concentrating in interpreting English to ASL. The money was lucrative plus I would be able to communicate with my son. *"Nothing like killing two birds with one stone."*

"You know Dr. Smith; I've always had a certain excitement for learning. There is something about the power of our minds that keeps me interested in pushing my brain to new levels.

Math and science are my two strongest subject not to say English isn't I just don't care for it as much I do the others. I wanted to follow my passion and decided to try my hand in forensics but the program proved to be more of a struggle then I expected. My son, who got brains from him momma tested gifted during a standardized test. Shortly after, he started bringing home more homework than me and I was in college. My education had to take a back seat in order to allow him the opportunity to explore his talents. "I didn't mind."

He continues to amaze me daily. Especially, with all things he has went through with his ear infections. I'm sure he wasn't sure if he was coming or going with the fluctuating hearing. He was mainstreamed, got along well at school but at home is where he was most comfortable. "I made sure my son was able to keep up with his peers. We would come home and go over everything he had done in class. We would practice vocabulary in English and in ASL. I also kept tags on everything around the house to help with memorization and spelling."

"Impressive, what a lucky kid?"

"I did what had to do. I threw myself into my work, concentrated on our educations and utilized our talents most beneficial to us. I took a gamble and moved to another state. It didn't work out so I moved back and here I am."

"Where did you just recently move from?"

"Charlotte, North Carolina."

"Do you regret it?"

"Regret what?"

"Moving back to Indianapolis?"

"Yes and No."

I was making a lot of money down there, having fun and doing quite well for myself. I also was spending my money as fast as it was coming in. I spent a lot of it traveling back and forth to here to Indy. Then I had to continue keeping the little guy busy. Not to mention the before and after care programs I had him enrolled in. Since I was working all sorts of weird hours I also had to pay for extended care. I spent a great deal of time away from my son trying to better my life in order to better his. If it wasn't at school I was at work and if it wasn't at work I was at school. Although I've been going hard for him since his birth, this situation wasn't the same. At least back at home he had the family and friends. There in Charlotte he had nobody but me. I was used to being alone but he was not. "If I were a selfish human being I would have stayed in Charlotte. I was more at peace there than I had ever been back home in Indy."

I was growing in my career, growing in my life and finally opening up to the world. "*But my peace wasn't worth his happiness.*"

I worked hard every day tiring myself out in order to stay afloat and provide for my son. "That I don't regret but we barely got back in town before she was back up to her old ways.

"She?"

"My mother…my biggest problem, my most painful conflict, the other half of my heart, my hardest love, my biggest concern… my kryptonite…"

"*My mother!*"

"Does she have anything to do with your being here today?"

I sat back in the chair placing my back firmly against the cushions. I thought real hard about his question. I could hear my mother's voice in my head, *"You blame me for everything!"*

"Yes, she is the primary reason I am sitting in this chair today but she is just a big piece of a largely scattered puzzle."

"I understand. You say she is the primary reason you are here today. Do you care to elaborate on that?"

I took a deep breath expelling the air from my lungs and let the words fall right on off my tongue. The very words I have been avoiding since that night I sat in her car. Since the day I went to the hospital zombie out. I stumbled over my words trying to rephrase them but no matter how I tried to annunciate the outcome was the same... "I tried to kill my mother."

LETTER TO MY UNBORN SON

Dear Bubba,

IT WAS THE DAY WHEN THE SUN ALIGNED WITH THE MOON. MORE DARKNESS and MY HEART SADENS BUT IM IMMUMED…

YOU WILL ARRIVE SOON! YET, I Feel DOOMED. I WANT TO SWOON BUT DAMIT I'M TOO CONSUMED. I've been WAITING FOR YOUR SMILE, YOUR EYES, YOUR LOVE…TO maybe SEAL MY WOUNDS? WHAT IS IT EXCATELY THAT I HAVE TO PROVE? LITTLE BABY CAN YOU TELL ME, WHAT IT IS I AM SUPOSSED TO DO? IM SCARED, WE'RE ALONE AND ITS'S JUST ME AND YOU. the anger I feel to know it is I who will BRING YOU INTO THIS… OPEN WORLD, WHEN sadly IT'S REALLY just A LARGE LOCKED ROOM.

A KID MYSELF at 16 YEARS OLD, LOST AND COMPLETLY CONFUSED. STUCK IN A WORLD ALL ALONE BATTERED, DEPRIVED, BROKEN, AND BRUISED. oh how I DON'T WANT THIS 4 YOU. I LOOK TO THE HEAVENS TO MY SAVIOR. IN FACT THEE ONLY ONE I KNEW. TO COUNT ON AND TRUST IN AND LOOK - TO - ESPECIALLY WHEN IT CAME TO YOU.

FOR STRENGTH, GUIDANCE, PATIENCE…A RIGHTOUS PATH TO LEAD US ALONG THE WAY. CONSTATNTLY, finding myself DROPPING TO MY KNEES IN ORDER TO MEDITATE, clear my mind to lift my spirit AND PRAY. to the heaven, the gods, the sun and the earth. why? because

MY SPRIRT IS WEAK, MY TEARS THEY STING, my PAIN IS DEEP…MY PAST IS DAUNTING! alarming AND IT IS really really TRY – ING.

2 TAKE ME. where?

TO THE COLDEST AND DARKEST DEPTHS OF THESE TRENCHES of my life

and it sad FOR THEM ALL TO JUST STAND BACK ANDALLOW THE SHIT THEY'D WITNESSED. with the DEVIL ON his LIFE LONG PRUSUIT…WHAT A SERIOUSLY MesseD UP MISSION.

MY VISIONS, THEY ARE RELENTLESS.

A CONSTANT REMINDER OF ALL I'VE WITNESSED. BECOMING A MOTHER AND HAVING TO DEAL AND MAKE ALL THE DECISIONS. I HAD TO LEARN HOW TO RAISE YOU FROM A BOY TO A MAN. OH HOW I PRAYED YOU GROW TO BE ALL THAT YOU CAN BE. THIS WORLD, VERY SENSLESS. BUT THANKS TO ALL MY many SESSIONS, I NOW CAN CONFESS. HOW I KNOW EXTERALLY I LOOK FINE BUT INSIDE I'M completely A MESS. USE TO BE HELPLESS AND ANGRY ONCE even RUNNING OUT OF BREATH. BUT IT WAS YOU who CAME ALONG AND GAVE ME BACK MY power and some of my STRENGTH.

I AM SO REMOVED. MY PSHYE…IS SCREWED! MY SITUATION… DANG, WHO KNEW?

THAT 17 YEARS I'D still BE Here screaming…I WILL NOT LOSE!

MY LIFE IS NO SHORT STORY. SO tune in and LISTEN UP CLOSELY. TO WHAT IMMA BOUT TO REVEAL TO YOU. MY SHIT… THESE SORRIES, I HOLD ON TO…still. BECAUSE IN MY ADOLESCE I just COULD NOT DEAL WITH my ordeal. MY ORGINAL THOUGTS ON HOW I NOT JUST WANTED TO BUT ACTUALLY TIRED TO GIVE UP. THE IDEAL of ABORTION ALONG WITH THE SUCIDE ATTEMPTS …AS I WRITE THIS LETTER TO YOU NOW THE THOUGHT ALONE just MAKES ME SICK. BREAK OUR BOND. I CAN'T !

IT's TOO LATE. I'M CO-MITT-ED. TO THIS…US AND OUR LIVES. YEAH I KNOW, THIS IS SOME REAL SHIT. BUBBA THIS IS SERIOUS THE ORDEAL IS REAL AND MOMMAS NOT PLAYING NOR AM I KIDDING!

SO LISTEN.

MY STORY, INDEED THEY'RE ALL TRUE. YOUR MOTHER, THE ONE YOU'VE KNOWN AS YOUR ROCK IS INTERNALY BROKEN, BATTERED, BRUISED, MISUED AND ABUSED. SO NO THIS WON'T BE EASY TO DO BUT FEAR NOT MY SON FOR THE MOMENT YOU COME MY LIFE WILL definitely RENEW. IM BLESSED MY CHILD surrounded BY THE BLOOD THEREFORE; THE DAY THAT YOU'RE DUE, THE ANGLES WILL COME down and THOU's work SHALL BE DONE. No worries. I WILL KNOW EXCATELY WHAT IT IS IM SUSPPOSED TO DO.

JUST KNOW, THERE IS NOTHING IN THIS WORLD THAT I WOULDN'T DO FOR YOU. SMOTHER YOU WITH LOVE, PUT YOU FIRST. GIVE

YOU LIFE. TAKE A BULLET, KILL, AND STEAL... LIVE FOR YOU. I'D EVEN LIE DOWN ON A KNIFE ...GIVE MY LAST BREATH FOR YOU. MY UNBORN SON, YOU ARE MY LOVE, MY WORLD MY LIFE NOW RENEWED.

LOVE YOU TO THE MOON AND BACK
~MOMMMY

Chapter 4

I-465 was a hot mess; traffic poured in from every entrance and flooded all the exits. Cars weaved in and out of all lanes while others played games with their breaks. I sped north in my newly purchased 2001 Chevrolet Malibu. *"Thank you to whoever had the car before me for keeping it in such immaculate condition! I only paid twenty-five hundred for it, all cash, no attachments and no complaints."*

Once I got my wheels back I felt somewhat normal again. I kept up with traffic, zipping through the Castleton area right pass the Allisonville Road exit. His vocals spilled out my speakers reminding me how I am *one in a million.*

I continued westbound until I came up on my exit. I maneuvered my way from the fast lane to the far right lane cutting off whoever was in my way. Michigan Road was backed up to the high heavens as usual. *"Every single car on the freeway was trying to find a place in the sea of traffic."*

I let the music lead me all the way to the elementary school where Darrius was practicing football. I harmonized with Lauren Hill while searching for a place to park. I pulled up just in time to witness the end of practice. This was his third year playing for the Washington

Township Jr. Football League. I finally lightened up to the ideal of him playing football all together. I've never been a true fan of the game; too physical and the risk of injury was pretty much a done deal. *"I'm more of a basketball kind of gal but whatever."*

The thought of my son being hit and potentially getting hurt was just not at all appealing to me. The mere thought of it made me sick to my stomach.

Trying to raise a man proved to be a hell of lot harder than what I expected. You could have all the education in the world and still wouldn't be able to fulfill the necessities a young man needs for his journey in becoming a man. I mean, as a mother you naturally want to protect them at all times and at all cost. I realize that I have to prepare him to build an exterior strong enough to withstand whatever this world has to offer him. As his mom, I can provide him with all the fundamentals and material things but I cannot teach him how to piss as men do. I cannot tell him how he should deal with the rush of hormones when he gets that urge from seeing the girl with the big booty. I can love him and lead him to the water but it I will not be able to make him drink. All we can do as parents is prepare them the best way we know how for what lay ahead. I knew him playing sports would allow him access to the type of environment and influential male leaders he would need to fill that void his dad and I could not. *"If I could, I would hold his hand forever but realistically, I know it's just not possible.* I see the competitive spirit in him. He's athletic, super creative, imaginative and artistic…*just to name a few*. He is also stubborn and a know it all but he still is my baby. I'd like to think he got his fight from me. I see how he challenges himself to be better than what he was the day before. I see how hard he goes just to gain an inch and never giving up along the way. He was born to lead like his momma. Witnessing his struggle and how hard he's fought for his every win. He has given me the extra push I need to continue my fight. He has to learn early that as he gets older it doesn't get any easier and the sooner he realizes that the better off he will be. *"Because nothing in this life is given to you for free; not if it's worth anything."*

I am a very proud mother. He's my little fighter. My little hero!

I felt a smile building across my face while I sat there in awe watching him power through practice. I still remember the day he was born. I wish I can say it was the best experience of my life, but I'd be lying. He and I both were at risk from the time I discovered I was pregnant until the time I gave birth. I had gained over 120 lbs., adopting high blood pressure, was at risk for gestational diabetes and experienced some of the worst pains imaginable. I had the weirdest cravings, couldn't keep any food down and on top of that I was severely depressed. I had to have my labor stopped twice and the second time I dilated to three centimeters. He was crowned at seven mouths and pinched every nerve ranging from my pelvic to my thighs. The only enjoyment I got was from feeling him move about inside of my stomach.

It was a Thursday morning. The day was March 25, 1999. I arrived at the clinic for a routine follow up. I was going every week now since my due date was right around the corner. I stepped on the scale for us to discover that my weight had dropped about 20 pounds since the last appointment. "*Red flag number one.*"

My blood pressure had spiked to an unsafe levels for me and the baby. "*Red flag number two.*"

Being that I was already at a high risk. The clinic staff wasn't trying to wait around for a third sign. Nurse Tony looked at me and asked, "Are you ready to have your baby?"

"Yeah, if you say so."

At 38 weeks, I was miserable. All I did know was that I was ready to NOT be pregnant anymore. If that meant delivering the baby now then that's what it meant. I left the clinic by ambulance to arrive at Wishard Memorial hospital right around 9:oo am that morning. My mom, the baby and I sat right at the nurse's station while the staff prepared a room for me. She quickly returned, "Alright Ms. Night. Let's come this way."

"No, I'm not going anywhere without Darrien."

I refused to move. Darrien and I did everything together and this was no exception.

"But you can wait for him in your room Ms. Night. That way we can at least be getting you all prepped while he makes his way on up here."

"Or I can wait for him right here!"

It really hadn't hit me how serious this situation was. I was in no additional pain outside of what I had already been feeling. I looked at my mom waiting for her to cosign but she was too overwhelmed with nerves. She looked like a deer caught in headlights. *"She's not going to be any help."* I said to myself.

Just as I was about to concede to their requests Darrien, his sister Shareka and their mother Mrs. Collins, were racing full speed ahead down the hallway towards the nurse's station.

Darrien was my boyfriend. He was the only boy in his family and the oldest of four siblings. When I first met Shareka I couldn't believe she was his younger sister. *Baby girl was strapped. She looked my age but she was a few years younger than us.*

They all were pretty girls. I feel in love with them the first day I met them. *The younger two, Brittney and Stephanie stole my heart automatically.*

I instantly became protective and they all became my little sisters. Mrs. Collins was soft spoken and caring. She was always making sure I was comfortable while I was in her presence. She took me into her family and I became one of her girls. *"I can't recall a time I've ever seen her angry. She is such a calming soul that it is hard to even be angry when you are around her.*

Darrien lead the way rushing right up to my chair, "Are you ok baby?"

"Now I am!"

I rolled my eyes at the aggressive nurse, "Okay now we can go into the room."

She wasn't fazed by my attitude, smiled and led the way. Once in the room, a different nurse struggled with placing the IV into my arm. Nichelle had now arrived and was having a fit about the lack of experience displayed by the nurse. "Oh my god! Why can't you just get somebody else to do this? Cleary, you are having a hard time poking at my sister!"

Nichelle paced the floor back and forth beside my bed. "If you haven't gotten it by now, I mean I really don't think you are!"

"It's ok Nichelle. Let's give her some space so she can try one more time." I said.

"How much space does she need? NO! Little Vickie, she needs to call somebody else!"

Nichelle was ready to pounce all over this poor girl.

The nurse tried to reassure everybody that she was going to get it but Nichelle wasn't hearing it. "Mam, stop and go get somebody else now!"

Nichelle didn't wait around for a response. She was off in search of another nurse. The defeated nurse continued poking at my arm and now I was growing irritated with her attempts. By the time she finally agreed to stop sticking my hands Nichelle was already returning to the room with a nurse from oncology. "Let's give her a try." She said sternly.

"They're having a hard time finding a vein for you Ms. Night." The new nurse said while massaging the punctured area.

I didn't have to answer. Nichelle was all over it, "That tack head just kept poking at my sister and didn't know what the hell she was doing."

The nurse had my IV in place and she was removing her gloves before Nichelle could even finish her sentence.

"Now see, how hard was that?" Nichelle said.

"Thank you." Darrien said.

"It's no problem. We are used to dealing with irregular veins. Good luck Ms. Night and congratulations."

The nurse left the room and was replaced by yet another idiot. Nichelle couldn't handle it; she had to leave the room. Darrien did a great job of keeping me distracted while this one repeatedly poked at my lower back in attempts to administer an epidural. *Can you say epic fail?*

He finally got it right but not before transforming it into a bonafide pincushion. *I didn't have any energy to express anything. I was just about over it all at.*

I had completely lost tract of time but knew we had been there a while already. I was tired but had to wait for all of the machines to get hooked up before I could actually try and rest. I wasn't sure what lay ahead but I was soon to find out. After what seemed like an eternity, I was finally able to get as comfortable as the baby would allow for the medicines to take their course. I remember the room being somewhat empty while Darrien sat beside me rubbing my belly and soothing the baby. I finally dozed off. I dreamt about my baby. I dreamt of what he would look like, smell like, and what he would actually feel like when I got to finally hold him in my arms. It was time to welcome this little guy and all his treasures into the world. *Am I ready? After all these months I was ready to meet my son, my angel.*"

I was 16 weeks by the time the sixth pregnancy test came back positive. Phenyx, one of my closest friends at the time gave me my very first test over at her house. It came back negative but we still weren't convinced. A few days later, Darrien and I took another one over at my house. Again, that test came back negative. Still the thought lingered in the back of my mind. *Something was wrong, but what? Maybe it was just my body changing. Maybe I was overdoing it with school, sports and my job. Or maybe it was from me gaining and losing weight all the time. I don't know what was happening to me but I knew something was up.*

Even though the test came back negative, I still wasn't satisfied. I made Nichelle take me to the actual clinic to have yet another test administered. *What the piss?*

For that test to only come back negative too. This game went on for a couple of more months and two more tests. I finally gave up on the ideal and went on with my life. *At this point, I'd rather it be mystery than the test to be positive. I have bigger fish to fry.*

While I was busy pretending, a majority of my classmates from what I witnessed had basic worries. Like peer pressure, puberty, who was more popular, who had the best clothes or the latest shoes…*Shit like that.*

They could have been hiding their ugly truths just like I was. *Who really knows?*

Nobody really knew what another person was truly going through. But out of all my friends Bethanie was the only one who knew everything about me. Bethanie and I had the most in common with one another. Unconsciously we became each other's shelter throughout the rain. She and I weren't concerned with fitting in with the "in crowd". We were more concerned with the alcoholism, low income, and various types of abuse going on at our house. She helped coach me through my bullshit and I helped coach her through hers. *Although our situations were different they were strangely similar.*

I spent a lot of time with Phenyx and even more with Michelle but most of my time was spent between Jenny and Bethanie's house. Phenyx's parents were super strict but they were her parents. Outside of their harsh rules they showed me nothing but kindness and hospitality. My house was off limits. Phenyx and I would always find ways of getting around them and their rules. When we did hang out at her house it was usually when her parents were still at work or away from the house. We'd sit around and gossip about the boys that paid us no attention and the ones that did. We both drove but Phenyx had her own car. A tan Ford Taurus and it had enough bumper stickers to hand one to each hippie still alive. Outside of that her wheels had us rolling. My mother tried to be funny with her car when it came to me driving so Phenyx usually supplied the wheels. There wasn't much for us to do outside of hanging out at the mall or cruise the city but it didn't matter. We wanted to be away from adults and out of the house. Phenyx and I didn't get to hang out as much as we would have liked outside school. Mostly because of our schedules but at school, we were inseparable. We shared lockers and even had a note book with Bethanie we would rotated the between the three of us at least 3 times a day. *There was a lot to gossip about in school and you better believe we kept each other in the loop.*

I tried being optimistic about what I was feeling however, deep down inside I knew something was there. Something was going on with my body. *But what?*

I needed to know. *Why am I so tired?*

One morning I was supposed to be at work but instead opted to call-in just so I could stay home in bed and sleep. *Awhhhh sleep... something I didn't do often.*

I laid there giving Z's up to the gods when my mother pulled me from my slumber. She was knocking on my door like she was the damn police. "Eeeeeden...? Open the door."

She waited a second before repeating her actions. I let her stand there for a minute while I debated to pretend I was still sleep or answer the door? She was too damn loud for me to pretend to be sleep so I answered in my sluggish and bothered voice instead of my angry and aggressive one, "Yea ma."

She knew I wasn't opening the door so she yelled through, "Have this test completed by the time I return home from church."

I was exhausted so I really didn't catch all of what she said but just answered her to get her to go away.

"Okay ma."

All I wanted to do was go back to sleep but now I had to use the bathroom. On the way out of my room I had kicked something lying at my feet.

"What...another pregnancy test?"

The light bulb went off, "Oh this is what momma was talking about."

I wasn't worried. After all, the first five were all negative. I didn't see what made this one any different from the other ones.

"I'm sure whatever she was getting ready to be on... this negative pregnancy test should shut her right up."

I could barely pull the stick away from my va-jayjay before the double lines appeared.

"Pregnant!"

"Aint this a bitch!?!"

"I can't have a baby! I am a straight A student with goals. I have dreams and they don't involve me bringing a baby along."

"How far could you really get with a baby on your hip?"

"Oh my god, I would be trapped…we would be trapped. I just can't! I can't! I can't!"

"You know what you have to do."

"Nooooooooooooooo…"

"You have to get rid of it."

"Oh my god!"

"Eden, if you think you are bringing a baby up into this house and into this world, you got to be crazy!"

"My god, please help me! An abortion!?!"

"Yes!"

"But Wait! Who is the father?"

"Does it matter? We have to get rid of it."

"I don't know."

"We would never get out of here if we don't."

My mother came home banging on my door breaking up the argument I had going with myself.

"What were the results?"

"It was positive mom."

"I knew it Eden!"

Did she?

Momma began screaming, crying and cheering, "Imma be a grandmother."

"I'm not having it!"

I guess my decision made her stop her celebration. "What do you mean you're not keeping it?"

"I can't mom!"

"Eden Victoria Night, YOU ARE NOT HAVING AN ABORTION."

"Here we go!"

We argued back and forth about my decisions and my life. "Mom, we can't even get along! We fight every other day. You're constantly kicking me out and trying to call me in as a runaway. This place is hell. And then there's him…you know what? I am not about to do this with you today. I am not having the baby and that is that."

"We getting out of here." I said to myself.

"Eden if you were adult enough to lie down and open your legs then you will take the consequences that come with that. If you think for one minute I'm going to allow you to kill my grandbaby then you have another thing coming!"

"I don't even want to be here. What does it look like for me to bring a baby up in here? This is crazy…No I am not having it!"

I walked away ending the conversation but still mumbling to myself, "This is crazy, she is crazy, I just wanna die."

"We will see about that Eden." I heard her yelling at the back of my head.

Of course my stepfather was in agreement with me. He was possessive and didn't want me having a baby nor a boyfriend for that matter. *He has always wanted me for himself but not if my God had anything to do with it.*

He really hated Darrien. Even more so after momma walked in on us having sex.

"Wait," Dr. Smith interrupted. "Your mother caught you two having sex."

"Yes. I'm not proud of it but it did happen."

I covered my face to hide my embarrassment. "Well that must have been a scene."

"Oh my god, yes! Surprisingly, she didn't do anything to either one of us. She only told Darrien to get dressed so my stepfather could take him home and I locked myself in my room for the rest of night."

Since the day I found out about this little guy, I've tried avoiding the new truth of my situation. The truth was I lived at home with my molester. I lived at home with a wacked out mother with multiple personalities and I clashed with every single one of them except one. *The one I was just arguing with.*

In any other situation I would have already been kicked out. That is after she hit me...or tried to anyways. She is *always trying to hit me.*

I lived with a selfish and confused sister who tried staying away from here just as much as I tried. Now, I was pregnant at 16. I hadn't even had a chance to fully process that I had been raped. It wasn't like I didn't have other shit going on and now I get to carry around the guilt of killing a human on my conscience. *Too much!*

Darrien wasn't too excited himself about the pregnancy either but he was going to support me in whatever. We were babies ourselves. Neither of us wanted to think about this but the shit was real. For me it didn't matter as much that the baby could have potentially been conceived by rape. I was more worried about the baby having to deal with the same shit I dealt with in life. The physical and sexual abuse was way far worse in my opinion. "Plus, at least the baby would have me.

"I could love it. Right?" I asked myself.

"I told you what you should have done."

Darrien left the decision up to me. He tried to reassure me that everything was going to be ok but I just fell deeper into my black hole. Only hanging on to his notion that *everything's was going to be ok...*

"Is it?"

I cried for 3 whole days straight just from the thought of aborting a life. I decided I couldn't go along with it. I suppressed my feelings, continued blocking the rape like every other horrible event in my life

"It was one of the hardest decisions I've ever had to make in my life."

"I hope I chose right."

I woke back up from my sleep and the room was different. I now had an oxygen mask strapped to my face and a room full of people with worried expressions smeared across their faces. My hospital room had turned into a storage facility for machinery. *They were all over the place!*

I tried removing the mask but my mom interjected, "No No No... Don't take that off. The baby needs it. He isn't doing to good Eden. You need to keep that on so he can get that oxygen."

"Wait, what do you mean he needs it?"

Before I could panic, Darrien ran over to the bed to explain everything to me. My mother didn't know how to be subtle especially when she was rattled.

Apparently, the baby was lying on his umbilical cord. Reducing his airflow and causing him some distress. A steady stream of nurses and interns continued to flow in and out of the room checking my progress and the baby's heartbeat. A group of 5 entered at once to complete an internal exam. *I wasn't in the mood.*

"Wait! If you think all ya are about to take turns going in and out of my box... lies. Rock paper scissor this shit. The winner gets to stay the other can kick rocks."

Everybody in the room seemed to get a kick out of my humor and assumed it was just the pain talking, until I almost came up out of my bed. They moved to the corner as if no one could see them fighting for the spot. The winner proudly stepped up to his position and the other four left the room.

"The baby will be ready in no time", he reminded us after finishing the examination.

His voice was full of enthusiasm as he explained how to get a hold of the nurse if we needed anything. Soon after he left it felt like a rocket was ready to shoot out of my rear. The nurse didn't take me serious until she removed her hand from my box, "Well I'll be. Mom you were just at seven centimeters and now honey you are at ten! Are you ready because the baby is?"

I was laying there damn near strapped to a bed with cords protruding from every part body and she was asking if I was ready? *"What do you think???"*

Within seconds the room had flooded with more nurses and masked assistants than any of us could count. Family members started leaving the room except for my mother, Mrs. Collins and Darrien. The Staff huddled around the foot of my hospital bed and a team gathered in wait of the baby. "Okay mommy let's bring him on out."

The pain was immeasurable. *It had me all fucked up.*

There was no turning back. I had to do what I had to do. I wasn't sure however, if I was going to make it. *The pain was no joke.*

The task seemed impossible. My body was trying to give out. "I don't know if I will be able to do this."

I heard 800 women die daily from childbirth or from child birthing related incidents. I'm praying I don't become part of that statistic.

My blood pressure was already out of control and getting worse. They were becoming concerned about me seizing. I was struggling to push, worrying about my baby not breathing and trying to fight the pain. All the while I had my mother running around the room like a chicken with her head cut off. One of the first things they tell you to do before pushing is to put your chin to your chest and bear down. Well my mother insisted on helping and in doing so, tried to push my chin through my chest. Keeping in rhythm with my contractions she kept moving back and forth from the head of my bed to help me "bear down" to the foot of the bed where she could get right and good into the faces of the nurses. She had been giving attitude since I woke up with the oxygen mask on my face. She was confused to why they weren't getting the baby out fast enough. *I knew she meant well but nervous Nelly had to go!*

My blood pressure was still on the rise, my breathing was far from controlled, and my mother was making matters worse. I couldn't take it no more. "Get the fuck out!" I shouted in between pushes.

"I'm sorry…I'm sorry." She whispered backing out of the room.

"Momma, please you got to go."

I heard her shout out a few more obscenities towards the nurses before blowing me a kiss and opening the door for her dramatic exit. She frantically disappeared from sight and now the rest was up to me. I protested, "I give up! Make them cut me open. I can't do it anymore."

Darrien looked down at me with the most sincerity he has ever displayed, "You have to do this Vickie. The baby needs you to do this."

I really wasn't trying to hear anything other than let's cut her open. "Okay, you can get out too!"

"I'm not going anywhere." He said.

And he didn't budge. I had no time to argue with him about not leaving. I begin bargaining with anyone else who would listen. Fortunately, my words fell on deaf ears.

The nurse with her hands up my box interrupted my antics, "Mom we don't have time for any more debating. If you want your baby here and alive then I'm going to need you to concentrate and push for me. Vickie, push for your baby. He is losing oxygen by the minute and if we don't get him out of there soon…well" She took a quick pause, "Well mom he won't make it."

The shit got real! I stopped arguing, provided the nurse my full attention and gave everything I had. Finally, eighteen hour after arriving I was finally able to push his head out. As I was ready to start pushing again the nurse screamed out stopping my attempts, "Okay okay let's just stop right here."

"Excuse me?"

"Good job mom. Take this time to rest. We are almost there. The hard part is over."

"You did it Vickie. You got his head out." Mrs. Collins wiped my face and kissed my forehead.

"What the hell do you mean stop right here? After all these hours of pushing, the denials to my requests and now you just want me to stop pushing?" I screamed.

The nurse chuckled, "We have to wait for the doctor to get here."

Looking around the room I'm like, out of all these damn people in here and not nare one of them is a doctor?

"What in the piss…" I said to myself

"What kind of operation are ya'll running up in here?!?"

They assured me the doctor was on his way, "We've had him paged and he was just right down the hall."

Before I could click off anymore Dr. Cunningham appeared at the foot of my bed.

He was a man of color looking snazzy in his labor and delivery wardrobe. He was over 6'4 standing taller than everybody in the room. He snapped on his gloves and said, "Is somebody having a baby?"

Uh duh there is a head sticking out of my vagina…What do you think?

"Yeah we are ready. Are you?"

He laughed and got into position. "Ok mom one more good push for me and let's bring baby on out."

Again, I gave everything I had left and pushed as hard as I could. With the grace of God, my baby slid on out the rest of the way. The room was so silent in that moment that I could literally hear him physically entering into the world. I held my breath waiting for his cries but instead heard Dr. Cunningham scream out, "It's a boy!"

The entire room broke into cheer as the baby was lifted above the doctor's head and into my path of vision. But instead of passing him to me he was quickly passed him off to the team waiting off to the side. "You did it baby." Darrian said.

"Wait, why can't I hold him? Something's the matter. Darrian what's the matter with him?"

"They are just cleaning him up baby don't worry."

"No something is the matter...What is the matter? Why isn't he crying? Why hasn't he called out for me?

Chapter 5

Although I was trying to fade out, I couldn't concentrate on what was happening to me for worrying about the baby. I was more concerned with why he wasn't crying. I felt my body weakening but I had to hang on in order to find out what was going on with him. I refused to give into the exhaustion. *I would fight as long as I had to.*

Just then, the faintest of little whimpers sprang out from his lungs. *It was like music to my ears.* He finally called out to me. Tears instantly fell from my eyes. Knowing in that moment I was now a mom, his mom. He made his entrance into this ring at 2:29 pm on a Friday afternoon. It was the 26th day of March in the year of 1999. Weighing in at 6lbs 13.6 ounces we welcomed Darrius Tyrone Collins!

My eyes were definitely at war with my eyelids. Fighting hard to keep them open but they were winning the battle. "I'm going to close them for just a bit."

I opened my eyes back up just in time to see him being carted off. "Wait…wait…wait, where are they taking him?" I said.

Darrien was quick on his feet, "They had to take him to a different room since it was getting a bit crowded in here."

He grabbed my hand to assure me, "They are going to take good care him Vickie don't worry."

I couldn't if I wanted to. I literally had no more energy left to do too much of anything. I finally conceded to the defeat and allowed my eyes to close all the way. I faded off into a deep sleep. *Not enough room my ass!*

There had to be more to it than just space.

Three days after giving birth I woke up. I was still in the same hospital bed. The room smelt of labor and delivery and my throat was dry as hell. It took a second but my eyes finally adjusted to the lights glaring from the television screen. The LA Lakers had just finished beating the Knicks 91-99. Darrien was asleep on the couch across from the bed. He was in the same exact clothes he had on the day we first arrived at the hospital. I could have sworn I saw Darrien holding the baby on his chest but I was I wrong. "Where is my baby?"

I sat there for a second reading the stats from tonight's game and arguing with the broadcasters. Kobe Bryant played 39 minutes had five rebounds, three assists, five steals, one block and scored 29 points. He played the most minutes out of everybody on the team outside of Shaquille, who played the same amount of time as him. Shaq got nine rebounds… only 4 more than Kobe, no assists, no steals and only had two blocks.

"He only scored 21 points… and they call him the better player?"

Lies, Kobe is one of the coldest ball players since Michael Jordan. They don't call him the black mamba for nothing. The man has idolized MJ since day one and since when has mimicking one of the greatest of all times been a bad thing to do?

"And they want to be mad at Kobe, for what? There is nothing wrong with wanting to be better than the best; otherwise what are you in it for?"

I think the people are mistaking his confidence and ambitions as cocky and selfish. He damn near does everything MJ does and the world praises him and the ground he walks on but wanna look down on this man...this ball player all because he balls out?

"Who don't want to be like Mike?"

Not Kobe he wants to be better than Mike.

"Look at this... Kobe shot 55 percent while Shaquille shot 51 percent. With him playing center and being listed at what... 7 feet 1 inch tall. Weighing in at about 325lbs. Dude better be a powerhouse. Who wouldn't be able to dunk the ball with the rim practically being at eye level?"

Shaq's success has steamed mostly off his ability to dunk the ball. Don't get me wrong he balls too but all he has to do is make it down the court, stay inside the paint, find the rim and put that thang in. What's so hard about that?

"And dunking the ball makes you MVP? Not in my book especially, when you got the black mamba running all over the damn court. "I'm curious to who they will name the MVP this year? MJ was named Most Value Player the previous year and I think Kobe should get it this year."

Since entering the league in 84, Michael Jordan has been dominating the NBA. *I really don't have to go down the list of his accomplishments. Do I?*

"Michael just recently announced his retirement on the 13ᵗʰ of January."

For what, the second time now.

"I'm sure Mr. Bryant will use this window as an opportunity. Although, Shaq is playing some of the best ball of his career, I don't think he has anything on my boy Kobe."

Shaquille might be bringing down backboards but how much longer can 325 withstand the physicality and endurance it takes to get back and forth across that court? Time will tell…

"Awwh, the politics of the game."

Kobe was just that good and he would only get better with time. I could really see him joining the over 60 points in a game club aside Wilt Chamberlain. *Who made the list like 32 times.* Maybe my excitement was from being able to watch one of the greatest players play the game I love. *I didn't get to watch much of Mike and all his glory throughout his career.* What I knew and remember about him was what I'd seen in clips or me ear hustling around the fellas. I didn't so much watch basketball back then as much as I played it. Kobe came in the league right as I began my basketball career in middle school. He instantly caught my attention becoming my favorite baller in the NBA. *It also didn't hurt that he was sexy as hell.* He made art on the court. It was Kobe who made me a Lakers fan. *Well of course Phil Jackson, one of thee best coaches of all times, in my opinion but Kobe was the main motivator.* There are so many great players in the league and it is forever evolving. It is so hard to narrow down one favorite when they all play so well. *You have the LeBron James's, the Stephan Curry's, the Kevin Durant's, the Russell Westbrook's and the Georges; George Hill and Paul George. At the end of the day I'm just a fan of the game.*

Darrien jumped up from the couch and came over to the bed. I must have been talking louder than I thought, "Did I wake you?"

"I thought I heard somebody talking."

"Yeah I was loud."

"I had the highlights on from the game."

Before I could ask about the baby, he was already filling me in on what I missed over the last three days.

"He is doing just fine. He just had to stay in the nursery under observation for a while. No one was allowed to hold him for the first 16 hours. He has a few more days in the special care nursery before they will allow him down in the room with us fulltime."

I was a tad confused but Darrien gave me the complete rundown. Apparently, after the baby left the room I had a seizure. They struggled with my blood pressure and with keeping my fever reduced. We both barely survived the ordeal but by the grace of God we both made it. I am a few days late but I am ready to see my baby. I tried to get up from the bed but noticed I was still plugged into to everything. I rang the bell calling the nurse. "I need to get this damn catheter removed if I was going to go anywhere."

I was being confining to the bed and me away from my child. The nurse advised against removing the catheter stating I needed to stay in the bed for at least one more day. Even though I was still weak, I reputed her advisement and requested my son. Darrien whispered in my ear reminding me of my condition. Darrius was napping so I decided not to fuss and stayed in bed.

The next day my tubing was removed and I was there outside of the nursery window looking for my baby. He was so small, so frail and so yellow… "W*ait, yellow?*"

He was laid out under the lights on top of the Winnie the Pooh blanket we bought from home. He was wearing only his diaper exposing his little man chest and tiny appendages.

Darrien was right; yesterday I wouldn't have been able to handle all of this. Clearly he was fighting for his strength and dreadfully he wasn't Darrien's baby. *I was devastated.* Darrius was lighter than my mother. *Yeah our genes were strong but my baby looked mixed.*

"*Please tell me that he doesn't have his eyes!*" I was screaming to myself.

"I just need to see if he has his eyes… Darrien How am I going to be able to look at him if he has this man's eyes?"

I broke down inside and died just a little. "I have to see his eyes."

Darrian held me up and held me close. We stood there for a while until I could bring myself to walk away from the window. I was scared to look at him fearing what who would be looking back at me. I wasn't ready to let anyone see my emotions about him yet including Darrien. No matter what it was no longer about me but all about Darrius, my bubba. I was a mother rather I was ready to be or not.

Darrien and I slowly strolled down to the cafeteria. We barely had 2 pennies to rub between the two of us but Darrien was able to scrape up a few dollars. We split a slice of pizza and shared a coke. Darrien was quiet but remained supportive. He had his own feelings to digest. He wasn't the daddy biologically but he had every intention on being there for Darrius. Darrien and the Collins wanted Darrius just as much as I did. I don't know where I would be without the Collins. We sat over our food and talked about the baby and our plans. "You must have been having some pretty serious dreams." He said

"Why you say that?"

"While you were sleeping you kept talking, fighting, screaming and crying in your sleep."

"Oh no, what did he overhear?"

"Do you remember what you were dreaming about?"

"I remember."

I actually dream about it every night. *My rape is just another film in my collection of nightmares.*

"I had no ideal I was so vocal during my dreams."

I was supposed to be going with the manager to another store to pick up gift cards. Sadly, that is not what happened at all…

After driving for a good hour, we pulled up to an apartment. She told me we were going to make a quick stop before heading to the other store. After entering the apartment I quickly realized we were at her boyfriend's spot. His roommate was there sitting on the couch with the television blaring. I was distracted by the movie on the television I hadn't notice when she left the apartment. Three hours later, she returned and found me locked in the bathroom. We drove in silence all the way back to my house. I finally got home at 4 am in the morning and my mother said I was as white as a ghost. I had just been set up by some grown, sneaky, perverted; sick ass white people.

I couldn't look Darrien in the face, ashamed of what he may have overheard. Regardless, Darrien refused to leave my side. He stuck with me and cared for the baby thirteen of the fourteen days we were retained to the hospital. Day thirteen I demanded he go home and clean up, get some rest and come back and pick us up tomorrow. This would be the first time I would be alone with Darrius. I was no longer scared of being a mother I was more scared of turning into my mother. I was scared of failing him. *How was I going to be able to shield him when I couldn't shield myself?*

I held my son in my arms and watched him sleep. "I'm so grateful you look like my uncle."

I couldn't imagine if he looked like my rapist.

"God knew what he was doing."

Darrius was having a hard time latching on and didn't want to take my breast milk. I was told it was due to the high levels of Pitocin and other medications running through my system. Not only would he not latch to my nipple but he would pull from a bottle either. I rocked him, begged and pleaded with him. The staff had warned me that if I couldn't get him to eat more than he was then they were going to be forced to put him on a feeding tube. I don't cry often. As a matter of fact I rarely cry at all. My daddy installed the fear of god in me before he cut out of our lives. When it came to crying, "Shedding tears were a sign of weakness." My father would say.

He would like to test my strength by seeing how many times he could hit me before I'd break. It wouldn't take long. He always started out hitting hard and it wouldn't get any softer from there. Today I cried freely and directly to my son. I prayed that he would stand strong with me. I shared with him my strengths and confessed all my weakness. I vowed that we would be a team and grow in life together.

"Please little baby tell what it is I'm supposed to do. We are all alone, I'm truly scared and it's just me and you."

He just sat there in my arms all precious and innocent. God must have heard my pleas because at that very moment he began to eat.

"I don't know how to love but you don't either so maybe we can learn how to do this together. I promise I won't let us fail. I promise to protect you and keep you from all the hell I've endured and more. I'm not perfect by far but you have already changed my life. I look forward to our tomorrow. I know this is going to be hard for the both of us but we are in this together! You might not understand this yet but I need you just as much if not more than you need me."

Chapter 6

It looked like practice was still in play when I arrived to the field. I pulled into the parking spot and turned off the engine. Darrien and I had exchanged a few words before he took off on his candy red and black 1300 Suzuki Busa stretch motorcycle. He wore his leather jacket to go with the red and black snake skinned seat on his bike. I heard T.I blaring from his speakers talking about how *she could have whatever she liked*, as he made a right hand turn onto Westfield Blvd. I sat there with the radio on low while I waited for practice to wrap up. My thoughts shifted back to the previous session I had with the Dr. Smith. He really had me reconsidering my life and how I dealt with things. I couldn't believe how receptive I was to his therapy. He allowed me to ramble on and on about my feelings only jumping in when he felt the need to elaborate. He also knew how to get me together when I would get stubborn with my thoughts and behavior. Most importantly, he knew how to bring me back to the present before I'd get lost in my past. I was beginning to realize how dark my black was and how deep it went.

"One day at a time Vickie. One day at a time."

I shook away the thoughts and sang along to the soft flows of Jill Scott. I was ready to get home and take off my clothes, slip down into a nice hot bath and turn on me some Raheem DeVaughn. *If you don't know about Raheem then you aint been served up honey! Oh lawd, that man can sing. His swag is poetic I would dim my lights. Sit in the living room with my laptop a glass of wine, and a blunt. Turn his albums on shuffle /repeat and create some of my best work.*

I was disturbed by three of the biggest sixth graders demanding access to my car. The doors flung open and the car quickly filled with their boyish stench. A collective sound of voices yelled at me all at once, "Hi Momma!" Darrius said.

He leaned in from the passenger's seat to connect a kiss on my cheek.

"Hi Darrius's mom!" The two James screamed in unison.

"Hey bubba and hello boys, how was school?"

"It was ok." They all screamed together, almost like it was scripted. I just shook my head laughing. I knew they weren't going to volunteer much more than that. James Johnson blurted out about a dance off that took place in the cafeteria. They all became rowdy spouting out different versions of the story. Darrius and James Johnson went as far as imitating some of the dance moves. James Davidson didn't dance but he didn't hesitate to bring back the beat. Darrius and James Johnson also were in band together but they all have played for the same league. They've even all been on the same team for a few seasons now.

My house seemed to be filled with Darrius's friends. *All the time!*

I kind of made it my business to have it that way. I'm real picky about where Darrius goes to spend the night. *Let's just say I had a little issue with trust. Plus how else was I going to know what he was up to? I'd rather have a few extra in the house if it meant less of a chance for him get lost to these streets. I know what I was doing out there and I couldn't imagine in the world we live today.*

I got a kick out of listening to them interact with each other. I am a girl and it was quite interesting to be able to get an insight into a man's world. Don't get me wrong, I've hung around boys my entire life but this was different. *This was my son.*

"Do you boys need a ride home?"

"Yes'mam."

"Then come on, get in and let's get going."

The boys grabbed their belongings and jumped in the car. They began rattling off about football practice, girls and everyday drama from around school. James Davidson lived rather close to the school so his conversations were generally short and sweet.

"Thanks mom", James screamed on his way out of the car. He did his special handshake with Darrius before running off in the direction of his apartment.

1 down and 2 to go...

"Are you boys' hungry?"

That was pretty much a rhetorical question. I knew they were hungry. They were growing energetic and athletic boys. Darrius can eat a house and well James, he eats like he has a tape worn. James Johnson's mother really wasn't able to be present. I'm sure as much as she would have liked. For what I gathered she was extremely sick. This left James to fend for himself a lot of the time. She does the best she can for him but he is very active for her. That is one of the reasons I don't mind helping out. She is on a lot of medications but I will say this, she is at every single one of his games; screaming and cheering for her baby like the rest of us. James lived in the same neighborhood as us so it made it rather easy to keep an eye out on him for her.

The boys had their food smashed well before I could get James to his front door. He jumped out the car and ran up to his house.

"I'll get at you later Darrius. Thanks mom." He said.

"You are welcome baby, we will see you later."

"Aight James." Darrius said.

James shut the door and headed to his house. "Ok bubba, when we get in house…"

"…Let the dog out, and get ready for my shower…yeah I know mom I know mom." He quickly interrupted.

We pulled up into our driveway and Darrius jumped out the car.

"Do you have any homework?"

"Nooooo!" He screamed running up to the house.

"Do you have any papers to give to me?"

And there was no respond. I looked up and Darrius was out of sight but Diesel was in the yard. I wasn't sure if he was happy to see me or if was because he needed to relieve his bladder.

"Dieeeeeseeelllllllll.", I called out to him.

This foo could barely finish releasing his bladder before he was running over to greet him mommy.

Since the fence was blocking his path he sat in waited for me to enter the gate with his tail beating the ground.

Diesel is a three-year-old full-blooded German Shepherd. His breed by nature is to be watchful, curious, confident, courageous and alert. They are obedient and loyal. Their intelligence is remarkable with them having one of the highest learning abilities. He's a survivor. He was only five weeks old when I found him wandering the streets in Broad Ripple. He was barely even old enough to be away from him mommy let alone be out on the streets by himself. *Especially, in this Indianapolis winter weather?*

It was entirely too cold outside for him to have made it. The plan was to get him all cleaned up to find him a home. We didn't look that hard. Darrius had grown fawn of him and he had me at day one. I had no intentions on having another dog but at the end of the day we became attached to each other. I can tell Diesel is grateful from the way he displays his love towards us. I love him just as much as I love my son; my 5ft 1 in, 135lb 12 year old Defensive Tackle. Diesel weighs in at a whopping 80lbs and stands a little over 26 inches. *Diesel definitely is nothing to toy with.* He is very protective over us but when it comes down to it he is a big ol' softy. The poor thing, struggles with separation anxiety. Every time I come home he acts like I've been gone for years. Sometimes I feel bad for Darrius because all he wants is Diesel to follow behind him but Diesel doesn't move without his momma's permission. I see him slowing letting his guard down but Shepherds are preferably loyal to one instead of many.

Diesel followed me into the house and we heard Michael Jackson's lyrics ringing from the bathroom walls. Darrius had already made it into the shower by the time we finally came into the house. He was in there singing like he was the one on tour. I stood there to listen for a minute before going into my room. I put my things down and released my feet from the confinement of my shackles. I sat on my bed rubbing my feet and reflecting on my long day.

"Let me go check this boy's book bag before I get too comfortable."

Darrius dropped his book bag in the middle of his floor. His clothes from today were sprawled about in his closet with some actually making it inside of the hamper. Darrius's room was pretty basic. *If you consider basic having a 32 inch flat screen television, Xbox, a queen size bed with batman décor all over the walls; except for the one wall that's covered by the 1964 Chevy Corvette fathead basic… well.*

What can I say he's my only baby! Yeah he is spoiled but he is nowhere near rotten. *We utilize morals and install values around here. He has to earn his keep.*

All I ask is that he makes good grades. He needs to complete his chores around the house without being reminded and give everything he tries 110%. If you give no effort towards nothing then you will get nothing. Most importantly, be a kid as long as he can.

I shuffled through his book bag to only find a couple of announcements from the PTO asking for volunteers and money. Darrius was still singing Michael Jackson when he came through the door of his room. He ran over and gave me a kisses and wet hugs. "Bubba, you got start drying off."

We harmonized a couple of lines together and after she was more than a beauty queen… it was time to get to business. "Ok bubba, let's read and get ready for bed."

He pressed the guide button on the remote to check what he would watch when we were done. A look of disappointment swept over his face when he realized he'd only have fifteen minutes of TV time after we'd finish reading. I met his expression and remind him the faster we get it done the faster he can get to his television. I made him this way turning him into a movie fanatic. Television was another one of my escapes. Darrius has been going to the movies with me since his birth. He snapped off the television and quickly snatched up a book to read. We laughed at his seriousness and then jump right into it. Twenty minutes later, reading time was over and Darrius wrapped his arms around me for more hugs and kisses.

"Goodnight mommy."

"Goodnight my bubba."

"Mom I love you!"

"I love you too baby!"

Darrius crawled under his covers and turned on his television. I turned off his lights, cracked his door and watched him struggle with his sleepiness. "Finally, it was time for my bath."

I let the water run while I changed out of my clothes, pulled out some pj's and checked my phone.

"One missed text message from baby daddy, one from Nathan and one from Jerome."

I quickly shot Darrien a text message letting him know we made it home. "The other two, I will deal with when I get out of the bathtub."

I couldn't wait to get into this water. "I need to release and clear my mind. No thanks to this damn insomnia."

I haven't been sleeping well since we returned back from the Carolinas. My nightmares were in full effect and my visions were more intense than ever. I threw the phone onto the bed and went to poke my head in on Darrius. My baby was knocked out. Diesel was at the end of his bed sprawled out all over the floor. I turned his television off and made a beeline straight for the bathroom. Raheem's playlist was set to shuffle and I let his R&B neo-centric sounds guide me into the water. "I can't imagine what would have happen had Nichelle not called and interrupted me."

I drifted off into a light unconsciousness. *Would I have actually killed her?*

The cold water stung me awake. I wrapped the towel around my body and again checked in on my babies for the last time. Diesel had found him a new spot on the floor and Darrius was now all over his bed. I stole a couple of kisses and instructed Diesel to stay with D before leaving them alone. When I returned to my room my phone was flashing a missed call from Jerome. "Where is the emergency?"

He is only curious to know about my whereabouts and he doesn't get to get them pleasures anymore."

"Right, I have no intentions on calling him back tonight or no time soon for that matter. Now that Nathan on the other hand, he could get it! If only I weren't in my feelings. I would invite him right over."

I responded to his text message.

Nathan: Hey big sexy, you want some company?

Me: Hey boo, sorry I was in the tub. Can we rain check?

Me: Not really in a good mood tonight.

Nathan: You going to tell me you were in the tub and then ask for a rain check? lol ☺

Nathan: You ok?

Me: Ha ha ha, more for the imagination. ☺

Me: Yeah, I'm good though, nothing a good night's rest won't cure.

Nathan: Aight then, I'll just get with you tomorrow?

Me: That's fine…until then.

Nathan: Goodnight.

Me: Night night.

I put my phone down and started leathering my body with lotion. "Maybe I should have let him come over."

He surely knows how to get my mind off of things."

"Honestly, I just wanted to lie down in my bed and try not to have nightmares tonight. This not sleeping thing has got me all messed up. Ooo maybe I can score some Mary to help me relax a bit. Ahhh, maybe I'll consider it but until then I'll do a few reps, some crunches and few squats to exert some of this energy."

I laid there with my television on mute allowing only the colors from the discovery channel to light up my room.

"Don't look at the clock, don't look at the clock. Go to bed, go to sleep and don't look at the clock."

I fought my exhaustion as long as I could but at some point I gave up and the nightmares took over.

Chapter 7

Every session started exposing a different emotion and revealing far more than I had expected. This was causing me to dig deeper and feel what I have been avoiding for a really long time now. People are so quick to tell me how strong I am. How my mother doesn't worry about me because I can handle whatever comes my way. "But honestly how strong am I really?"

If that were true I wouldn't be sitting through these mandatory sessions reliving all of this bullshit. *Now would I? I am human not a robot. I am only as strong as my mind and right now…well that's saying a lot.*

Truth is, I needed help a long time ago and unfortunately, my life has come to a cross roads. I need to deal with my past in order to look ahead to my future. Otherwise, it will consume my life. *And they win.*

I cannot continue to allow him to keep molesting me and them to keep controlling me. *Expend my world.*

My therapist did say it would get worse before it got better and time will only tell. I've always known these things I had gone through weren't necessarily my fault but that didn't stop me from feeling the way I did. Everybody has their role in the bullshit but the problem is I could never define what my role was. My perception on life was clouded by pain, evil and deception. *Could I have prevented any of this from occurring? The physical abuse, the sexual misuse, the emotional cruelty…I don't know.*

The one thing I did know was that I allowed myself to detach from the world a long time ago. *And I'm struggling to get back.*

"How have you been coping since our last session?" Dr. Smith Asked.

"Well, I haven't been sleeping much if that's what you're asking."

"Why do you think that is?"

"Oh I know why it is, I am afraid of having to relive them nightmares. They just keep replaying in my head like someone's pressed repeat and broke the damn button."

"Is that so?"

"Yeah, they feel so real. I wake up in cold sweats feeling sick to stomach. Sometimes it feels like I can't breathe. I think the nightmares are getting worse."

"You're confronting…dealing with your fears."

"Oh ok, is that what this is?"

"How much sleep are you getting a night?"

"On average I'd say 2 to 3 hours a night."

"Okay what about your daytime episodes?

"They're not so bad since I've been coming here. I still have my days where I blank out and get lost in my thoughts."

"I'm sure the not sleeping is not helping much."

"That might have a little bit to do with it." I said with a laugh.

"Okay look. Let's do this. Get a notebook and a pen. Carry it with you but most importantly have it available for when you wake up out of your nightmares. The next time it happens, I want you to immediately write down what you remember. Express your emotions good, bad, happy or sad. Whatever you are feeling in that moment is what I'd like you to write down."

"Do I have to share them?"

"Only if you want. But the goal here is to pull some of the thoughts from your mind. Release some of that buildup."

"Okay, transferring them from one place to another?"

"Yes, and it's going to be hard at first but confronting those feelings will only allow you to do what you need in order to progress."

"I got you."

"I don't have to tell you how important sleep is to your well-being. You are overwhelmed. Your mind has been on overdrive probably since birth. In order to begin your healing we are going to have to confront some of these dreams sooner or later. You've been fighting for your sanity, with your mind and against everything for a long time."

"I'm drained."

"Yes and if you continue to ignore the signs I fear this is going to result in something far worse than mandatory therapy."

"Is this my rock bottom?"

"It can be."

I sat silent for a second and took in his words. "Yeah, I'm sure I am overdue but I don't think I can deal with this all by myself though."

"You don't have to. We are in this together remember?"

I sat in silence after shaking my head to acknowledge his words. *"I can't be losing it like I did before with my mother. My stomach still turns every time I think about how that situation could have turned out. Fuck! I have a whole other person to take care of. I've lost years of sleep trying not to relive, think, or dream of this shit. Now I've just got to welcome it? I've never shared these details of my life with anyone before. This is going to be a challenge."* I said to myself.

"My earlier abuse is easier to talk about."

"Why do you think that is?"

"My father didn't care where we were or who was around. If he felt like beating my ass then that is what he did."

"Is there a certain memory that hunts you more than any other?"

"Yeah."

"Do you mind sharing?"

"No."

"The floor is yours."

"It looks like I was in preschool. I remember my teacher being concerned about some of the behaviors I was displaying."

"What kind of behaviors?"

"It was hard for me to sit still. Not like bouncing off the walls but I had this rock I would do. I was always anxious and nervous acting. Flinching and ducking at everything. I would pull at my hair so bad to the point I was pulling it out."

Dr. Smith jotted down some notes and asked me to continue. "I remember the teacher calling home after witnessing one of my episodes during nap time. It was so bad that I flipped off my cot waking everybody up from their sleep."

"Can you remember what it was that actually woke you?"

"Yeah, I was running from my father."

"Tell me more."

"Unfortunately it was my father who answered her call. He came all the way up to my preschool I guess to teach me a lesson." The faces on my teachers when they saw my father storm in the building with his black leather belt in hand. I already knew what was up when I saw him and not my mother. He grabbed me up before the teachers would speak and beat the hell out of me in front of everybody."

"Did anybody try and stop him?"

"Yeah but it took them a minute. I don't think anybody expected him to do what he did."

"I'm sure."

"I suppose I'm lucky we were at school."

"Why do you say that?"

"Because had we been at home... who knows? But it wasn't until I got older did I really start thinking about why he used to beat on me the way he did. Was it the drugs? Was it because he hated my mother? Was it because I was his darkest child or was it because he felt like I wasn't his."

"Is there a chance?"

"What that my father might not be my father? I never thought about it. Not until after he passed away but it wouldn't matter to me. He was mean!"

"Your father was brutal."

"Ha, that's putting it lightly. My mother says he used to be a really cool guy and that he was very intelligent. Then he got hooked on drugs. He became abusive, hostile and unpredictable."

"I see."

"He was never nice, always pouring his frustrations out onto my mother and me. He might not have put his hands on my sister but he didn't do her any good either. He hated my mother and me both equally and didn't care about expressing it in front of my sister. He was that one that was always stealing from us and pawning the stuff off for drug money."

"*We couldn't keep shit!*" I thought to myself.

"Momma eventually got tired of his shit. She said, once the drug lords started threatening me and my sister's life is when she decided she had to go and for good. My father was never a stable man, smart but not stable. Hell he had thirteen kids by at least nine different women, avoided child support for every single one of them and was still able to collect money from the government.

"Thirteen?"

"That we know of. Outside of the twins, my sister and I are the only ones who have the same mother."

"Are the youngest?"

"I am."

"Have you ever met any of your other siblings?"

"Only one, but once we got away from my father I wasn't interested in looking back. My mom did try to keep us engaged with that side of the family and because of that I made the best of what it was. Don't get me wrong, I had a blast making memories with them but as I got older it was harder to be around my father."

"I could imagine."

"My father and I could be in the same room and not say more than two words to each other. I knew he didn't like me and it resonated so heavily that everyone else knew it too. I mainly stayed tucked up under my grandmother when I was over there. She didn't play with my father when it came to me. I adored her. As a matter of fact, after her passing I disassociated myself from them for a really long time."

"How old were you when she passed?"

"Let's see, I was in the seventh grade. She had gotten sick and was put in the hospital. We went to go visit her and while we were there her and I sat and talked while my mom and sister went to the cafeteria."

"You too were close?"

"Yeah, she tried to get me to take her home. Never mind that I was too young to drive and she was too weak to walk. So she ordered I get her dressed and onto a bus in order to get her home. I pleaded with my grandma to stay in the bed but she insisted. Luckily, my mother came back into the room before grandma could get all the way out of the bed. After getting her and her attitude settled I kissed my granny for what would be the last time."

Dr. Smith handed me some Kleenex as I let a tear slide down my face. "Her death hit you hard?" He asked.

"It did! I couldn't even go to her funeral. I was too mad at myself for not helping her escape."

"Sounds more like to me that she just wanted to be at home."

"That's all she wanted and I couldn't help her."

"You don't believe you did? Isn't home exactly where she went?"

"Touché sir."

He nodded his head in acceptance. "If nothing more, her passing forced me to understand death." *A peace I so envied!*

After so long, I hated being with my stepfather. He was so sneaky and conniving that I don't think anyone suspected him of doing anything wrong. My mother entrusted him with me when I was just one year old. Lucky for Nichelle, she was always welcomed at any one of our family member's houses. Mommy was always at work, Nichelle was gone and I was usually left with him. Finding a babysitter for me seemed a bit more challenging for my mom. Maybe because they didn't like me as much or maybe it was because I cried all the time like I was being murdered. Either way my options were slim. My mother made a deal with the devil and for that we all paid the ultimate price. Of course he started out being my mother's tall and dark knight, riding in on his white horse and flinging around all his shinny things. He was all for rescuing the damsel in distress from the big bad abusive drug-welding maniac of a baby daddy. He provided a clean and comfortable home with all the goodies she could have ever wanted. Dating him allowed her more opportunities she so longed for. However, *only he, God and I knew what really went down when the lights were turned out or when we were home alone.* As soon as I said that my mind began fading back and what I saw was his apartment…

His bookshelf held his record player and collection. Pictures were scattered about the shelves in no particular order. His apartment was clean and smelled of a mixture of incents and pot. The couch was full of yellows and reds that jumped out from behind the brown which created a burnt orange plaited pattern. Marvin Gay played in the back ground while I watched my mother hand me off to the monster. As soon as she left he walked us down the short hall, pass the bathroom towards the room he kept closed off.

I blurted out, "That was our room, his playroom!"

When I reopened my eyes the tears were already pouring down my face. My breathing became erratic and I pushed out, "I can smell him."

"Vickie!"

"He's touching me, I can feel him!"

"Let try and take a minute. Vickie, look at me."

I found his face and together we did a few breathing exercises. When I was ready we went back to tackling the vision.

"Are you ok?"

"Yeah."

"What do you remember?"

"I remember him playing his records. I remember songs by Al green and Marvin Gay. I can remember how lost in the moment he would get when we were in that room together. But as I got older his actions became bolder. I was able to recognize more. He used every opportunity he could to tap into his urges. Portraying to be the perfect stepfather and doing everything to be perceived as such. Sadly, he really was a wolf in sheep clothing."

"He had everybody fooled huh?"

"Hell yeah! After that last run-in with my father, my mother gave him an ultimatum. She told him to marry her or get the hell on! He said he would if she could take care of us so all he would need to do is take care of the house and her."

"What kind of deal is that?"

"One a naïve person obviously couldn't see through because momma agreed and they got married."

"It had to sound good to her."

"I agree."

"That was probably her first red flag."

"Yeah well she missed it."

"Let's back up a bit."

"Okay."

"The last time you all had a run-in with your father?"

"What about it?"

"I'm a bit curious. You care to share?"

I started laughing at the memory. Out of all of the things my father did, this incident was the most comical. All the neighborhood kids were over to the house for yet another one of our infamous sleepovers. Now that we were away from our father, momma didn't mind us having company outside of family. Momma ran out to the store leaving specific instruction with us to not let anyone in her house while she was gone. Five minutes after her leaving, there was a knock at the door. Hard headed ass Nichelle opened it with no hesitation. "Where's ya'll mammy?" He asked.

My father was standing there at the door with a cigarette dangled from his lips. "She's at the store." Nichelle answered.

Nichelle not only let him in but also was telling him all our business. He helped himself to some hotdogs and made himself comfortable while he waited for our mother to return. Momma was pissed when she walked through that door and saw him sitting on her couch with his feet propped up on the table. "What the fuck are you doing here? Oh hell na. You need to GET OUT!" Momma said.

Momma looked over at us, "How in the hell did he get in here?"

I was quick to respond, "Nichelle let him in."

"What I tell you girl…?"

My father interjected, "What did you tell my daughter?"

"Look you need to go and you need to go now?"

"I'm not leaving until you tell me what you told my daughter?"

From there, shit just got real ugly real fast. They started fighting and kids began scattering everywhere trying not to get hit. For the first time, I saw my mother stand up for herself and was actually keeping up with my father. He wasn't use to her responding and didn't know how to handle her blows. Momma yelled out, "What I tell ya'll to do if ya'll daddy ever found us?"

Right on queue we all said, "Call the police!"

He was shocked, "You taught my kids to call the law on me?"

"Momma went flying from the living room and into the kitchen. All the kids went for the door to go call the police. We were moving so fast that kids started spilling down the steps. I was smart and jumped on fat Karen's back and rode her until we reached the bottom. From there we all ran to Karen's house all the way at the end of the row. We all tried telling the story at once but we were interrupted by gunshots. Three shots rang out and by the time we made it back outside to see what was going on my father was speeding away on two wheels. Tires were squealing, break lights were glaring and my mother was hanging out the window trying to unjam her gun."

"She was the one doing the shooting."

"Yep, she was trying to kill that dude.

"Did you all have any more problems from him after that?"

"Naw, nothing from him after that. Plus, we moved in with the stepdad like a week later."

"Oh ok."

"Who would have known we were leaving one drama infested situation just to enter another?"

Sweet Dreams

I thought I was dreaming one night
That is…
Until he woke me from my sleep.
At first I thought …naw noway
you must wake up
because there is just no way in hell that this
would be happening.
What was actually occurring… right now?
Of course, I just had to be dreaming.
But Wait,
Why would I be?
Allowing my subconscious to focus on such Dreaming about he????
A sheep in wolves clothing?
Doing nothing but pretending
Bending,
Breaking rules,
Lying, actually not caring?
Imagine…
Waking to his head there in between your legs.
How you would feel????????
When all you could do was stop breathing, calm up and try and lay still.
Try and pretend you're dead!
Having to get use to the unrealistic games
You've now learned to play inside of your little head.
In order to take you away from the demon
that choose to sneak into your bed.
Yell and scream
Plead and beg
Punch and kick
But YOU only cry
Instead…
Why can't I move?
At least go run and hide? Paralyzed by my luck
Ready to Just give up.
Because I'm stuck from the weight of his body
And that's what actually woke you up.
These undefined sensations, My mind confused and now it's racing
I'm stuck in this rut. Now struggling to adjust
My eyes to the movement in all this darkness

It's consuming. I'm losing!
His face becoming all too clear and that's when I realized
All of this shit was real.
What in thee hell?
The man lying on top of me, It is him- my
stepfather the figure that I'm seeing.
Our eyes met and he started to sweat.
I'm sure he wasn't banking on this moment I'm almost certain of it.
But yet, there was no time for me to react.
He slid his mouth across my face then pressed his lips against my neck..
He was careful not to leave his mark. Soft and
gentle; the skills of a genuine pervert.
Don't worry baby girl he said. Don't be scared
There is nothing here for you to fear. You don't have to be afraid
It's just me, Yeah that's right. Shhhhh, your daddy's right here.
He made sure to leave wet kisses so his words would drip and spill
Into my ear and then he would then say "my
sweet girl it's all going to be ok.
Go on ahead and go back to sleep because soon it will be a new day,"
This… tonight our special little SESSION.
Nobody has to know about any of my other late night missions
So this can be our little secret to stay between you and me.
Now close your eyes my sweet little girl and Go on back to sleep
I'm done for now so you can relax, Take a breath.
I promise for tonight I'll let you be.
For tomorrows is a new day and I will return.
But for now good night and…
Sweet dreams

Chapter 8

He had been manipulating my young self beyond my understanding for a long time now. I had gotten use to the feelings but I never got use to him touching me. I never got use to him coming into my bed and interrupting my sleep. He did things no grown man should ever do with a child. Unwanted things that I knew weren't supposed to be happening but didn't know how to stop it from continuing. It had been going on for so long that I had been rendered powerless. I was so busy trying to hide from my pain that I couldn't see past it. I often struggled with my inner thoughts since I wasn't sure that anybody cared. *Why would they? I mean my father use to beat me senseless and nobody could do a thing.*

So, why would this situation be any different? I remember looking over and seeing Nichelle lying asleep in the bed just across the room from me. I would pray she would wake up and possibly set me free. But then what?

Maybe, just maybe this was all a dream. Why else would he come into my room, crawl into my bed and get on top of me? Isn't that what my mother was for, his wife, the woman that's supposed to fulfill his needs? *I was merely confused, brokenhearted and just not understanding. This man who is supposed to be my protector, my dad is now what a molester?*

There were nights when he thought we were all asleep but that wasn't the case at all. I was fully aware that he was out and about lurking. His visits becoming more frequent. His behaviors were evolving. Some nights he'd even stay longer attempting to violate my entire body.

How bold he was to leave my mother lying alone in just the other room sleeping. *She was exhausted.*

He knew she wasn't going to get up. She couldn't hear an elephant in the room if it were stomping through the house. The rush he must have felt knowing we were just across the hall vulnerable, innocent, and oblivious to his manipulations. I never knew what time he was coming but I knew he was coming. Some nights I'd be jolted from my sleep; unaware that he would be in my bed lingering just beneath my sheets. Maybe if I screamed loud enough he would have to stop and leave. But anytime I would try he'd stop me and whisper, "Shhh, quite now baby girl we don't want to wake your sister."

His mouth would rub up against my ear. His hands were places they shouldn't have been. And I well I was stuck falling numb to his actions. *Frozen by the fear!*

I learned to just lay there, with my eyes closed tight trying hard with everything I had to remove myself from the fight. *Inadvertently my mind decided to take flight.*

Floating away to the place I'd created way back before my stepfather came into the picture. There I would retreat in order be free. Allowing myself the chance to run from the insanity and hide away from all the pain. There I was free of the worries and away from all the shame. In my place there were no beatings and it sure as hell wasn't any time for his late night meetings. In my place I was no longer the scared little girl longing to be me. There I was strong, confident, and invincible. Everything was magical and most importantly I was powerful. There in my place I would stay until he was all finished up with me and I no longer had to see him there lingering.

Back to their room and off to sleep peacefully while I had to lay awake struggling with my horror. His words remaining stinging my ears, "Shhhhh baby girl it's all going to be ok. Go on back to sleep now because soon it will be a new day."

Is this what I get to look forward to now? What I should expect my life to be? "*Perpetrating as a royal family and our king is really a creep. This horrid new start was nothing more than the beginning of my nightmares.*"

I sat still in my chair looking down at my lap. Dr. Smith remained quiet allowing me to process all that was said over the last hour. I stood and went to look out the window. I started feeling sick to my stomach. *The thought of those nights really took a lot out of me. It took everything I had not to cry. I hated feeling defeated and every time I seen his face it sent chills down my spine.* I looked over at Dr. Smith. He nodded his head at me silently asking if I was ok. I shook my head in acknowledgment of his concern. "You know Dr. Smith I used to ask myself all the time why he used to do these things to me."

"Because he is a pedophile Vickie and that is what pedophiles do."

"I realize this now but my younger self just couldn't make sense of it. I mean how he could touch me and go back and sleep with my mother."

I remember waking Nichelle one night because I thought someone was hurting her but she knew better. She pulled me into her bed, told me it would be ok and held me until I went back to sleep. *Does he have this kind of relationship with Nichelle too? She hasn't said anything to me but I haven't said anything to her either and he definitely was touching me.*

I thought for a really long time that what he was doing was normal. I placed my face into my hands. Ashamed of what I just revealed to him. I wasn't sure how to look at my therapist. I kept my face there in my hands until I felt the disgust leave my body.

"Where are your thoughts?" Dr. Smith asked gently.

"I just don't understand how nobody knew? Nobody?!?"

I stopped to take a moment. My emotions were hitting me hard at that very moment. "I know this is hard for you, reliving there memories But I have to say Vickie, I am incredibly proud of you. The fact that you're still sitting here today speaks volume. He no longer has the control. You hold all the power. Not him. Acknowledging these emotions is what's going to help you with your healing."

"I understand. I just always wondered why me? What was I sent her for? Do you believe that everything happens for a reason and that everybody has a purpose?"

"I do."

"So is this why I was sent here. To be beaten, battered and sexually abused?"

"I can't answer that for you Vickie. But what I will say is that you weren't meant to be weak and in time your purpose will be revealed to you."

"Maybe I was a terrible person in another life."

"You think this is Karma coming back to haunt you."

"That or I have some serious bad luck."

I use to lie in bed and try to think back on all of my actions. What w*as it that I did to bring on so much of this dysfunction?* First it was my father with his physical and verbal abuse. Now I was being sexually abused by the only man I ever trusted. "I idolized him. He was my hero. I walked around proudly claiming to be his daughter. *He was my dad.*

He was supposed to keep us safe. Promising us the world but instead he ended up rocking it and turning it upside down. Took us from the hood, showered my mother with gifts and all sorts of opportunities she couldn't ignore or resist. *He knew what he was doing.*

"Abuse became my new normal."

"There is nothing normal about what he was doing. He manipulated your mother to gain access to you, her kids.

"That's just so fucked up. I know my mommy didn't ask for this. She deserved better."

"Sometimes we are tested in life. It is up to us to stand clear of the smoke and rise above. You taking this step to even come here to my office, is you standing making an attempt to stand clear of your smoke."

"Thank you for helping me."

"This is all you Vickie. You are the one opening these doors. It is you who is confronting what has to come through that doorway. Just keep concentrating on where you are today and where you want to go tomorrow. It is time to release your baggage so you can rise above. Do you remember how hesitant you were the first time you started coming to see me?"

"I do."

"Look at the strides you've made from then to now."

I listened to him attentively. Dr. Smith laid down some encouraging words that settled in my mind and most importantly on my heart. *He was right!*

I have to let go of my past if I were ever going to move forward. I connected with my Doctor's mind. He challenged my thoughts, which stirred my emotions and kept me from falling deeper into an already murky depression. I realized at this moment, I was safe in his room. I realized I was ready to see the rest of these movies play through and accept whatever else was needed to allow me to regain my sanity. *Regain my life. I am a grown woman and I'm still afraid of lying alone in a dark room…still afraid of sleeping with the television off… still having anxiety attacks around sex and still will cringe at the sight of a penis.*

"Vickie, be proud of you. It's time to rise above."

We both sat quite. "I think this may be a good spot for us to end for today."

"Yeah, I agree."

He stood and walked towards the door. We shook hands. "Next week?"

"I'll be right here." He said.

I left Dr. Smith's office with mixed emotions. I was somewhat drained but liberated by the breakthrough I had. "I understand now, In order for me to move forward I have to remove some of the baggage I'd been carrying around." *I hate this!*

I definitely could use some laughs right about now. I knew exactly who I could call. I was always guaranteed an ab workout whenever I would talk to Kalvin. He and I met several years back when we first started our careers in the insurance industry. We connected instantly and now we couldn't get rid of each other. Him and I would do almost everything together except Kalvin bats for the other team and is only willing to referee for mines. We can argue sometimes being that we are a little stubborn, both intelligent and strong headed. Hell when I'm right I am right but let Kalvin tell it everything is a matter of opinion. He is witty and not only is he good with his words but quick with them too. However, 12 years later I'm still watching his back and he is still watching mines. I dialed Kalvin's number and his voice lit up my ears, "How you doing? Miss Girl, spill the T."

"Heeeey boo you busy?"

"Just leaving this job. Hustling on this highway."

"Where you rushing off to? You got a date?"

"Girl just with my bathroom."

"You are stupid."

"I need to drop these kids off. Do you hear me?"

I couldn't do nothing but laugh. "You are so silly!"

"Girl one of my students stopped me on the way out the door trying to hold conversation. My stomach got to bubbling. I was trying to tell him I had to go but baby before I could..."

We both broke out in laughter. I was used to finishing his sentences and was well aware where this conversation was headed.

"Honety these cheeks just could hold on...that poot came tumbling out."

I couldn't stop laughing and he didn't break character while he finished giving me his dramatic ending to his day. I gave him a quick rundown of my session. He didn't care to hear about the depressive stuff so on cue he changed the subject. By the time I pulled up to the house I was in stiches from laughing with his goofy ass. *Mission accomplished.*

I came into the house and dropped everything in my room. I decided to get a few miles in on the treadmill before jumping in the shower. After I was warmed up, I cranked the speed to about 5.0 and went for it. I allowed my thoughts to take me back to the day when the shit really hit the fan...

My cousin, Sasha had been over to the house for a couple of days. It was a surprise to see her since she barley comes around anymore. Not since she lost her daddy, my favorite uncle. Since his passing, she really hasn't been the same. She was older and little more ruff around the edges. She didn't have the best upbringing either but she was family.

Us three were left alone this particular evening. Nikki and I sat in the bathroom with her while she took a bath. At first we started out talking about random childhood stories, what happens when we show up to family gatherings and just catching up on each other's lives. *I'm not even sure how the question came up but it did.*

"Do ya know the difference between good touch and bad touch?"

I was puzzled by her question, "Good touch bad touch?"

"Yes, Good touch bad touch."

"I think so", Nichelle said

I didn't speak but merely shook my head.

Sasha rose up from the water and began explaining the difference between good touch and bad touch. When she was finished she asked, "Now, has anyone ever touched ya in a way that makes you feel uncomfortable?"

I starred at my cousin like a deer caught in headlights and just nodding my head. I heard my sister whisper, "Yes."

Nichelle and I looked at each other in surprise of one another's response. Then finally I said it out loud, "Dad comes into our room and visits me almost every night."

Sasha's eyes bucked out of her head and Nichelle's body tensed up. Her eyes filled with tears. My sister pulled me close and held me tight. "I didn't know little Vickie, I didn't know." She said.

Her too! So he was messing with her too? That son of bitch!

I didn't cry. I just looked at up at my older sister and told her, "We were going to be alright"

Who would have guessed that a simple question would have populated such a response...? **But nobody has ever asked before that day.**

Chapter 9

Like before, I was broken from my thoughts by my phone ringing. Jerome was calling me again. "He's going to want to know why I haven't reached out to him since I've been back in town."

I decide to stop my run and answer. I was a little over my 2 mile goal and I had been avoiding him for long enough. I had met Jerome when I was fresh out of high school. Darrien and I had finally stopped the game play and broke it off for good. I moved out from the Collins's and was ready to be completely out on my own. Jerome was five years older than me and was working for the same pharmaceutical company as I was. He drove around all day on this large machine moving narcotics from one area of the warehouse to the other. I tried to stay busy in my section and away from all the work drama. Jerome would come over to my section twice a day to pick up my trash and then I would see him again on the docks when it was time for the deliveries. We officially met the day I had returned from a 2 week vacation. I was on the dock minding my own business dancing to the sounds of Michael Jackson's Thriller blaring from the overhead speakers. I thought I was by myself but apparently, he was watching me from a distance. He rolled up on me in his machine right as the song was ending.

He complimented me on my moves and I blushed in embarrassment. I played it cool by badgering him for stalking me and he played right along. *Giving me some freshness I wasn't ready for.* Jerome stood about 6'2 and the machine he drove gave him another 4 to 5 inches. I tried not to pay attention to any of the guys at the workplace. I had no interest in mixing business and pleasure. I would listen to the other girls sit around and gawk about the fine specimens roaming the warehouse but I kept my comments to a minimum. These girls would flirt with whoever paid attention and then go back and fuss over them. I called myself staying clear of the nonsense but that day on the dock, I looked up only to stare directly into his green and hazel eyes. *Where did those come from?*

For the first time I took notice to his deep black lashes which only accented his sexy eyes. He kept a shaved head, and his skin toned was a nice smooth caramel. He was military so he always kept his facial hair low and clean. He was much sexier than I had originally given him credit for. His muscles couldn't help but bulge out of his shirt. He was easily 200 lbs. of solid muscle. I wouldn't dare tell any of the women that I had a slight crush on Jerome but they noticed are frequent chats and the jig was up. *After that day the haters increased and I had to shut a few down. Females are a trip and I for one don't have time to be arguing over no man.*

Jerome was no stranger to my situation. We had dated off and on for over six years. I hadn't talked to him really since the day before I left for North Carolina. The last conversation we had I let him know that I was leaving. I was in search of better opportunities, peace of mind, and a new beginning. I gave him the choice to get serious about what we had or else. What I didn't tell him was that I was leaving the very next day. Jerome had been calling and texting for some time trying to come see me but I knew tonight wouldn't be a good night. Darrien was on his way to drop off D and I didn't have time to be getting in the middle of those two. They have never really been able to get along. Darrien had it in his mind that I cheated on him with Jerome before we had actually broken up. Darrien was never ok with how anything transpired in Jerome's and my relationship. The last time these two had a run-in it almost got ugly. D was about five and Darrien was stopping by to pick up clothes for his weekend. They just so happen to pull up at the same time. Darrien beat Jerome to the door and even though Jerome was right behind him, Darrien decided to shut the door right in Jerome's face. *I'm not about to say my baby daddy a punk but…He was really trying to play with fire.*

Jerome caught the door before he could shut it all the way and came on in bringing his attitude right along with him. Of course he had to display his dominance which didn't make the situation any better. He pulled me close, kissed me all deep and grabbed my entire ass directly in front of Darrien. Now baby daddy felt a certain kind of way. Words were exchanged but luckily no blows were thrown. However, the tension remained between the two of them and it has never thinned.

I finally agreed to meet with Jerome but it would just have to be for another day. We definitely had some unresolved business to resolve and I felt like I owed him that much. Moments later the doorbell rang and I could hear Darrius and Darrien talking about football practice from the other side of the door. Darrius was excited about his new position and Darrien was feeding him pointers. I opened the door in time to witness Darrius hugging Darrien. Off to his room he ran with Diesel at his heels. We discussed our schedules for the rest of the week and just like that Darrien was off. He and I have progressed such a long way from when we first met. I mean we can have some serious arguments but at the end of the day he is my best friend. *We love to hate each other and that's that.*

Diesel ran back to the door when he heard it reopen to make sure the exit was smooth. Once I locked back up the house he quickly darted back to Darrius's room. I made my way to the ruckus coming from upstairs. My boys were there in D's room wrestling. My baby brought so much joy to my life. He was everything I needed! I interrupted by throwing myself down in between them. We talked while he laid out his clothes for the next day.

I couldn't help but to think back on the earlier therapy sessions. I couldn't allow Darius to notice my current distractions. I thought I would never see the day where I could talk freely about what had happened to me as a little girl. I suppose I was wishing for instant relief but clearly this was a work in progress. I was more scared to go to bed tonight than had been any other night. I know how vivid my dreams could get and I'd really had enough for one day. I kissed Darrius before crawling into bed for the night. I tried watching some television and felt my eyes getting heavy. I'm not sure what time it when I last looked at the clock but I knew it was pass 2:00 am. No sooner than I closed my eyes there she was…

The lost little girl standing at the end of the bed he shared with her mother. The dresser was behind her with the television on. He stood at the top of the bed between his computer table and nightstand. The clock was sitting next to the lamp on her mother's nightstand. *3:13pm it read. "Mommy wasn't due home until after 6:00 so that meant another three plus hours alone with him."*

He had on the blue sweatpants and a white V-neck t-shirt. "Wanna play a game?" He asked little Eden.

"What kind of game?"

He pulled his pants down just enough to let his penis fall out. He started walking towards her but she backed away until her back was again their dresser. *"I don't know how to play this game."*

He moved closer to her massaging his manhood in his hand. "All you got to do is put it in your hands and do the same thing I'm doing… see?"

"Is that all I have to do?"

"Here, why don't you try it?"

"Okay."

Eden constantly kept her eyes on the clock. 3:20. *"Ok now can I go?"*

"I was thinking that maybe you can put it in your mouth too."

"Put that in my mouth?" She asked.

"Uhm huh."

"I don't think I want to!" She protested.

I saw her becoming frightened. I saw her confused. I saw her objections and I saw his amuse. She didn't want to play his game anymore but he continued pressing. "Let's just try it. Look doesn't it look fun?"

What was so fun about him putting his penis in my face? I saw her backing away from his advances. "I don't want to play your game! I don't want to put that in my mouth!"

"Come on baby girl it's just like when you lick your ice cream."

I watched him beg her as she stood there shaken. "Okay okay, we don't have to put it there. But you have other places we can put it. Why don't we see if you like it there instead?"

She watched his perverted grin rise across his face.

I woke up screaming in a cold sweat. I wiped my brow and placed my hands over my eyes. His face was still right there in view. I could feel his hands, and I became sick to my stomach. I rushed to the bathroom to throw some cold water on my face. "Rise above Vickie Rise above." I went back to my room and started watching what was on the TV I had finally gotten myself back to sleep to only end up right back in his room. It was like I pressed pause on the DVD player, went to the bathroom and came back to press play.

"What are you trying to do to me?" She asked.

"It's just a game!"

"But isn't that stuff adults do? Should you even be playing this game with me?"

His expression changed startled by my response. He slid his penis back into his blue sweatpants and tried to talk around it. The little girl was not hearing any of it. She stormed out of the room and left him standing there in defeat.

He had been prepping me for that moment for a long time but my angles wouldn't hear of it. *Not that day.* I suppose he could have taken it but he didn't crave that kind of power. He wasn't a rapist he was a pedophile. I woke up again in another cold sweat. This time I felt empowered. I felt like I could tackle anything. I looked over at the clock, "Damit! Only 5:00 am."

I fell back onto my pillows irritated for not getting more sleep. "You should have taken the prescription."

I was too scared of getting stuck in a nightmare. I needed to able to wake myself up if I needed to. I wanted to close my eyes but I wasn't sure which vision would cloud my mind. The television was playing an infomercial about some kind of strong towel that could soak up the ocean all in 1 wipe. It could be yours for 3 easy payments of 19.99 plus shipping and handling. I surfed through the channels until my alarm went off. "Well, now it's time to get up."

Chapter 10

After my cousin told my mom what we had told her everything and I do mean everything had changed. We had gone from living in our suburban apartment to being placed in a guardian's and from there a foster parent. There was something wrong with my mother but I couldn't put my finger on it. She just wasn't the same woman I was born to. Nichelle and I had no idea what lay ahead for us since Momma hadn't told us much after picking us up from the Guardian's home. All we knew was that dad was in jail, mommy couldn't take us home and now we were being introduced to Ms. Mary. "Girls, she is going to watch over you for a few while mommy can get your room back together."

"Who is she?" Nichelle asked.

"Why can't we just go over to G-mommy's house?" I asked.

"Your godmother is on the other side of town and I would rather have ya'll closer to me so I can come visit you girls after work and in between."

Ms. Mary was an older southern woman of color. She was one of those church ladies always smiling, laughing and being blessed. She had never been married and was single with three kids, 2 girls and

1 boy. All three of them were over the ages of twenty. They all were sympathetic and welcoming; promising my mother they would look after us for the summer. "There is no need to worry baby, Jesus has sent you straight to me chile. He knows you need the help and I am here for you and your churen." She said.

She looked over to us from her chair, "We'z here are gonna take good carez of ya while ya momma work on gettin ya back to ya own beds"

My mother was so appreciative and thankful. "Chile, they'z in good hands here with us. Now don't you worry ya here?"

"Yes mam. Thank you! Thank you!"

"Why are we even here? And why can't we just go home?" I said to myself.

Nichelle and I tried our best to get settled in there at their home. They all started off being nice, warm and caring to us. Her girls would take us along with them to go shopping and run all sorts of errands. This was around the same time Mariah Carry was singing about her vision of love. *Apparently, that was all that he'd given to her.*

We all would sing along to the songs on the radio, which was something refreshing. My stepfather would get upset whenever we'd try to sing along to the music. "What is the point of having the radio on if you're going to sing over it?" He would say.

The summer was just in start and I was actually looking forward to being back in contact with some of my old friends from school. I lived closer to them now than I had before since moving in with Ms. Mary. I hadn't seen any of them since I was snatched out of math class and whisked away from all I knew. *I wonder if they missed me as much as I missed them?*

Lisa and I left on bad terms since the smack down I had to give her on the playground right before I left. She tried me and she got told…the hard way. Unfortunately, we never had a chance to talk after that. *With all that just occurred in my life, I needed all of my friends.*

I didn't have many since we moved around a lot. We were always running from my father rarely able to settle down in one place long enough. Lisa, Jillian and JT were the closest I had. I was grateful we were at least able to stay on the same side of town this time. Jillian lived closer to the school but I knew she hung out over in this area. I just knew I would be able to play with them especially since I found out JT lived in the same apartments as Ms. Mary but she had other plans for us.

Nichelle and I shared a twin size day bed that was big enough for one of us. It was obvious the room in which we slept used to be the youngest daughter's room. It was full of pinks, whites and purples. There was a small television which sat on a dresser where our clothes were housed. Sadly, we weren't allowed to turn it on and we would soon find out that television was the least of our worries. "How bad could this really be? After all, we would be going home at the end of the summer. Plus we would be outside anyways…right?"

It sure as hell wasn't the Guardian's home and Nichelle did seem to be holding up alright."

"We are going to be fine."…so I thought.

My excitement slowly faded when I noticed her girl's attitudes starting to fluctuate. Nichelle and I were always good to ride but could never get anything to bring back home. "If you can't buy it, don't touch it"…*is what they used to say to us.*

Momma must have only been giving her enough money to sustain our room and board because we got no extras. Her children had all moved out but you couldn't tell. They were always there visiting after work, after bible study, during family dinners and definitely every Sunday after church. The girls would never spend the night but from time to time her son would come and crash out on the couch. I saw the way he looked at my sister. He wouldn't have been as lucky as my stepfather. *I couldn't bare anybody else touching us.*

Ms. Mary had us attending church on Sundays, bible study on Wednesdays, she had some club meeting on Tuesdays and choir practice on Thursday. I didn't mind going to church. I went to church with my godmother all the time. My godmother introduced us to religion and spirituality early in our childhood. *Gratefully, since I found myself looking to heavens often for strength.* Momma tried to see us as often as she could but god only knows what she is going through over in her world. I noticed momma not coming around as much. At the same time we were being confined to the house. I still wasn't talking as much and now the hope I so desperately tried to hold on too was quickly fading. Ms. Mary required us to answer yes'mam and no'mam to everything and everyone especially in her present. *Don't you get caught being disrespectful. Mrs. Mary didn't tolerate an ounce of disrespect.* I had to at least make myself say that much since a head nod would get me placed in the corner.

When we were at the house, Nichelle and I pretty much kept to ourselves. Our love for books got us through most of the dark and rainy days. The lights weren't allowed on in the daytime so we would sit in our "rented room" with the curtains open reading our book. Even then, Nichelle and I didn't talk much. I don't think it had anything to do with her disliking me like before I think we were just stunned by all the madness. *We needed each other and we* didn't have say it to have an understanding in knowing that I was there for her and she was there for me. I don't know how she was really feeling inside but I did see her retreating into herself as well. I would sit on the floor in the corner closest to the window while Nikki usually took the bed. We would read for hours in silence with nothing but the sounds of pages turning. We both had chores we were responsible for daily and you better believe we did them quietly, quickly and without argument. Otherwise we would anger the beast and neither one of us wanted to deal with that. Especially me, since I'd become the designated punching bag. When we first arrived we were only responsible for the upkeep of our rented room. Slowly the bathrooms were added then the kitchen, living room and eventually the entire house.

The atmosphere was definitely changing around her place. I'm not sure what their plan was for us but after a few weeks of "comfort" and showing my mother we was being taken care of… shit just took a 360 degree turn for the worse. Things were strict before but this was turning into something different. I tried telling myself, *"It wasn't the guardian's home. I at least had a mattress to sleep on, food to eat, my sister by my side and most importantly, no more late night sessions."*

"I wonder what is stopping us from going home?"

"I supposed the most important thing is that we were safe and able to still to be together." I tried telling myself. "Momma did say we would be going home soon. So just hang in there."

"Yeah ok but for what, more abuse?"

"We do just keep being passed around like some ol' rag dolls."

"I mean what the fuck!"

Her calming demeanor changed into a mid-western evil witch. She became verbally abusive with both Nichelle and I. At some point the corner wasn't enough and the whippings turned into routine beating. *Towards me and only me, yet again!*

This situation had caused me to withdrawal even more. Nichelle would beg me to answer the woman but why bother talking to anyone? It surly didn't matter, I already couldn't do anything right. If she didn't like what Nichelle was doing, I'd get a beating. If her day went bad then I would get a beating. It didn't matter I was still going to get in beating either way. Back into my head I went. It was about the safest place I could be.

I needed help and there was nobody. Every night before bed I would have to go outside to this large tree right in front of the apartment. There I would stand searching for the right switch to hand this woman just so she could use it to beat me in return. *"How do you correctly pick a switch?"*

I'd pick her weapon based on my energy level for that day. There were some days that were worse than others but in the end of the day a switch would be going across my skin. If I could endure the thicker ones I would. The smaller ones always left marks. They stung more too but the beatings were swifter. Oh no, she wasn't scared of leaving marks…she was more afraid of leaving too many marks and in the wrong places "You better be still or it will be you who can't go outside."

At least until the marks went away.

Even though the girls had attitudes, we would use them to at least get out of the house. But even they had gotten so bad that we started hating going anywhere with them. They were just as bad as their momma. They liked to pick on my sister and shovel shit to their mother. They definitely got a kick out of missing with Nichelle but I wasn't sure what their intentions where when they fed lies to their mother. *This family was sick.*

We could expect a full workup when they all would be at the house together. They wouldn't let Nichelle eat dinner until her teeth were brushed to their perfection. She would be in the bathroom sometimes for hours brushing going at it. Hoping that this time would be the last time. Not if they weren't tired. By the time they did decide to let her eat her food it was stone cold. She didn't get to reheat it or anything. They didn't like wasting food so sometime they would force me to eat it and send her to bed hungry. "After all, there are children who don't have anything to eat." They reminded us. If I couldn't finish both of our plates I became ungrateful, unappreciative, disobedient, and of course, disrespectful. If I could I would try and sneak some food to the room so she could have something to eat. I understood the risk but I was sure to get a beating so it didn't matter. I know Nichelle felt the same sympathy for me that I felt for her when I had to go through my episodes with their mother.

My faith was slowly slipping away along with my soul...

Ms. Mary claimed to not be feeling well and decided she was going to stay home from choir practice. She really must have not been feeling good since she never missed the opportunity to sing in front of the reverend. On this particular day we trotted along with her daughters and sat quietly as we always did. Nichelle and I sat on the first row of the center pew while her daughters were up in the choir stands practicing for this upcoming revival. A church elder walked by and stopped to tell us how well-mannered we were being. *The irony... First of all, it was choir practice. So most if not everybody in the church was participating in the practice and up in choir stands. Nichelle and I were just about the only ones sitting down in the congregation area and I still offered the elder a seat.*

She declined and thanked me for the kind gesture. She went along about her business and sat down at the end of row that we were sitting on. On the next break, the daughter called her mother to inform her of this god awful thing I had just done. I saw her leave from the middle of practice but after she returned to drag me to the phone, it didn't take long for me to figure out that it wasn't for a bathroom break. She told her mother that I had refused my seat to the elder. *Now how she know when she was up in the choir section but whatever.*

Ms. Mary chastised me for what seemed like an hours and her daughter stood there and watched the entire time. Mrs. Mary guaranteed I'd be sorry for displaying such disrespect in her church. "You think just because I am not there that you can act up in any kind of way?"

"No mam."

"Ooooo you just wait."

I handed the phone back to the daughter and went back to my seat. I could have tried to explain the truth to her but then I would have been a liar making it worse on me. Mrs. Mary was furious. I thought it was best to say as less as possible. *I already knew tonight was going to be a bad one.* This was the first time in a long time I had been scared to return home to a beating. I had become pretty good at escaping and numbing my body to her licks but I knew this was going to be the exception.

Ms. Mary wouldn't even let me into the house when we arrived home from church. She stood in the doorway and pointed to the tree. "Make sure you grab three of them this time. And I want cha to braid'em. Ya little heifer, you'z gonna learn today!"

She slammed the door and left me outside to my task. At that moment I had an entire outer body experience. My spirit floated from my body and I stood above the little girl trying to stand tall, trying to be hard, strong and tuff. But she was none of things. She was empty! My spirit cried for her while she picked the leaves from the branches. Eden was preparing herself mentally for her this beating. Like any other night, a beating she did absolutely nothing to deserve. Yeah, I cried for the little girl because she was too broken to cry for herself.

THE LITTLE GIRL INSIDE OF ME

WHEN I LOOK IN THE MIRROR…
I'M NOT QUITE SURE WHO I SEE!
IS IT THE frightened SCARED LITTLE GIRL LONGING TO BE FREE?
HIDING BEHIND THE EYES THAT MAKES ME ME.
LINGERING AND WAITING FOR HER CHANCE TO BE.
I LOOK IN THE MIRROR
BUT WHO DO I SEE
SCARED TO STARE AT MY SOUL
AFRAID OF THE UNKNOWN
WHO IS IT ME?
Or is it She?
THE LITTLE GIRL LOOKING BACK AT ME?
A LOST LONELY FIGURE WITH SUCH A CONFUSED GLARE
STRICKEN BY GRIEF that ALL I SEE IS her and her DEFEAT.
STRAINED from THE OBVIOUS… her PAIN…
I TRY AND LOOK DEEPER BUT heart is stained
And MY SOUL I CAN'T FIND.
DO I REACH FOR THIS Shadowy figure THAT'S
LURKING JUST THERE from BEHIND?
I CONTINUE TO STARE,
AS MY FACE WRINKLES AND ANGER FILLS THE AIR.
DON'T RUN LITTLE GIRL… come back because I TOO AM SCARED.
IF NO ONE ELSE DOESN'T, I promise you I truly do CARE!
MY PERSONALITIES GROW, MY BLOOD A CONTINUOUS FLOW,
MY MIND IMPROVING, OFTEN STUCK BUT ALWAYS MOVING.
MY SPIRIT'S NUMB and yet.
MOTHER FUCKAS BE DUMB.
UNAWARE OF THE DAILY CHANGE THAT
UNLEASHES ALL of MY SHAME.
HIDING MY SANE …ITY,
LOYAL TO THE NEG A TIVITY…
and NOW DEAD TO MY REALITY? MAM YOUR VULNERABILITY!
But HONESTLY,
SOME ONE SHOULD be QUESTIONing MY PISSTIVITY.
Hell, I HAVE MY REASONS,
SHIT.
COPING WITH THESE DEMONS, SCREAMING,
CRYING, LIVING AND DYING,
TOUGH AND RESERVED, BUT LOST AND FULL OF NERVE

E. Victoria

I keep DEALING WITH THE HARSHNESS OF THE
BULLSHIT SURROUNDING ME,
SMH THIS NASTY MOTHERFUCKER AND
HIS STANKIN fucking INFIDELITY,
THE BASTARD, PUNK ass COWARD… THIS WEAK ASS CREEP.
STILL WONDERING HOW SHE STANDS THERE AND HIDES BEHIND
weak ass ME
AMAZED THAT SHE…
IS STILL AROUND TO SEE.
THAT AT THE END OF THE DAY IT'S JUST ME BEING ME
EDEN VICTORIA
THE BROKEN DOWN WOMAN MASKED FROM THEE
WORLD, MYSELF, THE PEOPLE THAT AND ALL that SHE SEES.
I HADN'T REALIZED UNTIL FINALLY…
LOOKING REALLY REALLY DEEP THAT
THE LITTLE GIRL WHO IS ANGRY AND HINDING.
TRYING TO LIE LAY
DORMANT INSIDE
Is ME.

Chapter 11

I braided the three switches together taking my time dreading the wrath I was about to endure from this horrible woman. I prayed hard and asked my angels to surround me. I needed it in order to be able to walk back into that house instead of running and leaving my sister behind. I started to question myself, *"What would come of Nichelle if I just took off and never looked back?"*

"I can't leave her in there by herself."

"Then what…go back in there and just hand her this branch to beat you with it?"

"I guess so."

I took my braided branch and met Ms. Mary upstairs in her bedroom. Her bed sat against the far wall to the right of the room. Her nightstand sat next to the head of her bed and under her window. Her favorite chair was caddying the left corner on the other side of the window. She kept a rug in the middle of the floor closest to her bed. She kept her house shoes there whenever she didn't have them on. By the time I made it back into the house everybody was gone and Nichelle had already gotten into the bed. *"How long was I out there?"*

She stood there with her arms folded resting on top of her stomach. Her jury curl hung right below her jaw line and she wore a scowl that reminded me of momma from the movie The Goonies. She extended her hand silently requesting the branch. I handed it to her and she wasted no time striking me.

I'd gotten used to the beatings but this was the first time I was beaten with a handmade branch. I tried to keep still and as quiet as possible. I knew better not to make her mad while she was in the middle of a beating. I couldn't help it and I screamed out as the branch broke across my eye.

"What did you do that for?"

"I'm sorry!"

"You're going to make her mad."

She was out of breath but still managed to get her point across. "Oh, so you wanna talk back?"

"No mam, no. I'm sorry. I'm …I'm. It's just my eye."

I laid there across her rug with my hand cupping my face. "Pull yourself on together and go get me another switch. I'll teach you to back talk." She said.

She sent me limping right back out to my tree to replace the switch she just broke on my face. *"See what you did."*

"I couldn't help it."

"How is she going to say I interrupted her with back talk?"

"I don't know. But how did I make her break that switch?"

"I mean did I tell her to make sure she hit me across the eye?"

"When is this going to end?"

"Be careful."

"But I can't see."

"I'll teach you about talking back…she said. Fuck her!"

I grabbed a skinny switch and went back towards the apartment that hid a whole different kind of monster. *Apparently, they are everywhere!*

Nichelle was waiting up for me when I finally made it to the room. She pulled back the covers offering me my spot next to her in the twin size day bed. I just shook my head, rejecting her offer. My body hurt so bad that I couldn't handle anything touching or rubbing up against me. "It would only irritate my wounds."

Nichelle cried for me as I stood there in the middle of our rented room. She jumped out of bed to hug me but I pleaded, "Please Nichelle, not right now."

She didn't argue just laid back in the bed facing the wall. Nichelle ended up crying herself to sleep. I stood there all night just thinking about my life. "There can't be a God?"

"Yes there is!"

"Then where is he?"

"He is right here."

"Then why can't he hear me? Why doesn't he save me? Why?"

You might not think so but he hasn't left your side once. How else could you withstand this?

Dr. Smith sat there and listened as I spilled my guts. "Vickie, you have to be exhausted."

"And confused…a little bit of all the above Dr. Smith."

"What about your mother?"

"I have a hard time with her. I use to hate her soooo much. I wasn't outside her apartment because of anything that occurred in my past. I was outside her door for the things she continues to do."

"It's just the things from your past only intensifies your anxiety driving the anger you feel for her in any particular moment."

"Exactly! I like to call it the buildup effect. You know, you let the shit build up and then you end up blowing up. It's so hard to show respect to her when I can barely look at her as my mother. I know she gave birth to me but I stopped looking at her that very day she drove away from us that day…"

I became real quite struggling to articulate my words out loud.

"Please Vickie continue."

"I remember like it was yesterday. I relive it every time she does something to me."

I looked the doctor directly in the eyes, "I thought about it right before I was about to go into her apartment."

"My sister cried all the way to the door after momma drove away. I was hesitant but I felt that was the perfect opportunity to present her with my ideal. "Nikki let's runaway!"

"But where would we go?"

"Anywhere but here…"

"Could we go home?"

"Nikki momma doesn't want us. She would have taken us with her especially after I told her about the beatings. You heard what she said."

"But I want mommy."

"But she doesn't want us."

Nichelle fixed her face and opened the door. *I knew she wasn't going to go for it.* She looked at me all apologetic in her expression and walked back into the house of terror.

"I was done right there."

"What did your mother say?" Dr. Smith asked.

"I don't know what all she said. When I realized she was giving me an excuse. I blanked out. The last thing I do remember her saying was to just hang in there a little while longer."

"How did that make you feel?"

"Alone…Pissed…I died that day. I was like fuck them both! Momma didn't care about us and Nichelle was a damn scary cat. My mother should not have ever let us gone back into that house."

"I believe your mother was so lost in herself that she couldn't process what you said."

"She did look so empty and not herself."

"Can you imagine her position?"

"Never, but I definitely have a better understanding now."

I just wanted so badly to get out of there. It didn't have to be home but I couldn't keep taking what she was dishing out. The atmosphere in that house had become so harsh. I'd seen a side of Ms. Mary in those months that no one should have ever have to even witness. The countless beatings and what felt like a lifetime of terror later our mother did come to pick us up to go home. Nikki and I were so happy to be getting out of there. We were all ready to live together again.

"All?" Dr. Smith asked.

"Yes, Nichelle, me, my mother and him.

"Your stepfather"

"Imagine my surprise. One big ol' happy dysfunctional fucked up family all over again! I can't explain the emptiness I felt living back under the same roof as him again. I guess you have to be careful for what you ask for."

I was a walking magnet for abuse or at least that is what it felt like. Living in Ms. Mary's house, being in a guardian's home, the fights, the sexual abuse, my sister and my mother's rejection had turned me into one hellish individual.

"You detached."

"I definitely matured. I sure wasn't the same scared innocent little girl I once was going into this situation. I had become angry, resentful, agitated, guarded, and temperamental. Not caring to display a once of respect for anyone especially my mother."

"So nobody stood a chance?"

"Pretty much. I prayed for the day when I would be back at home with my mom but I never prayed to come back home to him! Nor did I ask to come back to a woman who looked like my mom but she wasn't."

"What did you observe?"

"She was weak, always finding excuses to why this and why that. She was detached from us. She was protective in all the wrong ways. She was a shell. She was mean. She was aggressive. She was hateful."

She was broken down.

"Did that feel good?"

"Yeah it did actually."

"Good."

"You know, by this time I wasn't sure how life was going to play out. Nichelle and I quickly grew apart. My relationship with my mother became strained and now she wanted to beat on me too. Not Nichelle but me. Again! Only this go round I was quick to react."

"Did your mom and stepfather go through any form of therapy?"

"They said they did but their actions didn't reflect. I heard that he even served some time in jail."

"Do you think he did?"

"I didn't care if he did or didn't. I was more concerned with my mom being a beast. The fact I was living with a creep and my sister… she was a mess."

"You said you mother was always making excuses… like what?"

"Like when we asked her why she got back with him or why is he was living with us? She said it's because we told her that's what we wanted."

"Is it?"

"Is …what?

"Is that what you wanted?"

"Hell naw, but even so, she's the adult. Why is that my decision? But to be clear I don't remember saying no dumb shit like that. I probably didn't want to see anything happen to him like I don't want to see anything happen to my mother or my sister. I'm not the monster."

At this stage I hated life, I hated my mother, I hated him and I hated Nichelle, I hated myself. I've always felt different, as if I didn't belong to the family I was born to. I used to find myself daydreaming of all the things that could have been. What my life would have been like if I had a woman in my life that adored me, cherished me… protected me unconditionally. I'd like to pretend my grandmother would have been that woman. The woman I'm named after god rest her soul. I unfortunately never had the opportunity to meet her but from what I hear she was a real firecracker. She was definitely a woman of her word. *A real no-nonsense kind of gal.*

Eden was born in the 1930's during a time when the great depression swept the country, racism was the norm, prohibition was on the rise and gas was 17 cents to the gallon. My great grandmother was a half white and half Native American. She earned her money by picking cotton before migrating from Kentucky to Indiana. She came over during a time when Keystone Ave was a dirt road. My great grandmother fell in love with a full blooded Native American and together they started our legacy here in the city. Being Bi-racial, my grandmother had to learn how to deal with adversity. Especially, growing up as woman of color on the streets of Indianapolis where 77% of the population was white and 21% black. Grandma Eden was a gorgeous woman. She was strong, courageous, outgoing and intelligent. She was the only one out of 15 children to graduate from high school. She could of have chosen anyone to court her but she chose my granddaddy Martin Carter, an ol' cat daddy from around the block.

"Now he is something else, they nick name him Moon Dog."

"Why is that?" Dr. Smith asked.

"They said it's because he was always caught coming home when the sun came up. My grandfather was known to step out on my granny but she didn't hesitate to step off in his ass either. One day, grandpa finally mustarded up the courage to come home after being missing in action for more than a few days. Granny already warned him not to come home but he figured he would wait it out and come on home when he felt it was safe."

"Well?"

"Let me tell you, my granny was waiting for him right at the front door with a pyramid of can goods by her side. She had a pan of hot grease on the stove staying hot just in case she needed back up."

"Oh my! She was ready."

"As soon as he tried entering the house…Wait it really takes my mother to tell this story but she says my grandmother yelled out, 'Didn't I tell you not to bring your no good- do daddy –ass back to THIS motherfucking house?' And as soon as my granddaddy was in view she started hurling them canned goods at him. My grandparents both enjoyed a drink more than they enjoyed the other so it wasn't nothing for neither of them to get loose. Granddad came in the door trying to hide behind his mother."

"He brought his mother with him?"

"Yeah, that's what everybody says. I guess he thought that would help him get out of trouble with my grandma but that changed nothing. My grandma lit up anything that came through that door."

Back in those days marriage really meant until death do us part. Together they had 13 children. Every single one of them having to figure out the fundamentals of life the best way they knew how to. They were low income, both parents' alcoholics with little to no food in the house. They had to share everything starting with their 2 bedroom house that my granddaddy paid for with a dollar bill. Eden was a strong woman and like any other she had her flaws as well. She was a fighter and lived her life to the fullest before passing away from an aneurysm.

"How old was your grandmother when she passed?"

"44."

"My, she was young."

"I know I'd like to think her strength lives through me. My mother likes to say that I would have been her favorite and that's what I hang on too."

I like to think she was one of my angels.

As much as I dislike my mother I can sympathize greatly with her experiences. She didn't have the best upbringing either. I get the kind of environment she was raised in and it was definitely no picnic. In her house the oldest was responsible for trickling down knowledge to the next and with there being so many of them, information got lost. It was literally every person for their selves. "They grew up in the hood, surviving on the streets, sharing food, stealing to live and lying to eat?"

"When did was your mother born?"

"In the late 50's."

"Okay."

"My mother says that my granddad was evil and abusive and that when my granny was ready she too she was liable to knock a head off and clearly she didn't care what she used to do it either."

"Do you think she could have adapted these ways from your grandmother?"

"Behavior is learned but I don't think my mother got her behaviors from her. I know that we all have choices and I feel my mother made the choice to take her aggression out on me. Her hitting me with her fist and hitting me with her words showed her lack of respect for me not just as her daughter but also as a human being. She didn't get this way until this shit with my stepfather came about. I remember my mother being the coolest mother and my cousins would say she was the coolest aunt. Despite all the bull crap that was going on with my father she still tried to make sure we had fun. We might not have had the best clothes or the lived in the best neighborhoods or drove the finest cars but we always made the best of what we had. Mommy had this pinto that would magically fit more of us in it than it was built for. Momma would take us all around the city to various parks, the city pools and whatever else we could get into. Momma was a big ol' kid at heart."

A smile ran across my face, remembering some of the good times we all used to have. "I know my mother loved me but there were times where she made me feel like she didn't. I think because the abuse began so early for me with little to no intervention I became guarded long time before either one of us noticed."

"That's definitely a possibility."

"I saw how my mother tried with us. Witnessed what she went through and saw how she went without so that we can have. I saw her struggles with dealing with her past, with my abusive father and now my stepfather. I am not saying one situation is better than the other but at least we conquered the weather together, no matter how big the storm."

"I can't be 100% sure of course without a proper assessment but it sounds like your mother may have had a psychological break. The combination of her past, the different experiences, the situation with her husband and finally her kids; well that's enough to drive anybody to the brinks. You think?"

"Yeah that makes perfect sense."

"What is your perspective on Nature verses Nurture?"

"In my opinion they equally play a part in any one's development. Who we are raised by and in the conditions of which we are raised in critically plays a role with who we are as people. We unconsciously adapt the behaviors and values of those around us. Mix in some genetics and this is how we evolve into the individuals that we are. The many attributes of one's character or lack thereof empowers us to make the choices we do. With every choice good or bad lies a consequence. So break the cycle or…"

"Continue allowing the same continuous never ending circle of recklessness, right?

"Right and sadly only the strong will survive."

"So stay strong Vickie."

I'm trying.

It's been a lifetime since I even looked for any affection from my mother. When I used to see how my friends interacted with their families growing up, I couldn't help but envy their relationships. I use to think that maybe this dysfunction was isolated to just my family? I had even begun wondering if love was even real. The display of emotions, the behaviors and the way they interacted with each other was different from what I knew. Sitting on daddy's lap, the kissing on the mouth, the long embraces were all of the same things I exchanged with my daddy but the outcome was different. I wondered if their dads would wait until everybody went to sleep to creep quietly into their room or if he would crawl under their sheets and affect their dreams. Or better yet, when no one was watching, fumble around the buttons and zippers of their pants in order to sneak his fingers past their panties too? I never had an issue with their daddy's but I didn't want to risk them being near my dad. I was too scared that he might try and play the same games with them that he played with me. *I didn't want them to know our secrets.*

Tears began to flow down my face. I couldn't believe I was releasing these thoughts verbally for the first time in my life. My voice started trembling and my breathing became uncontrolled. "I can still smell his breath tickling my nose hairs. His saliva burning my skin, please Dr. Smith…"

"Vickie I need you to breath and just calm down, you are having a panic attack."

My heart was pounding out of my chest. I was shaking and getting dizzy. Dr. Smith continued trying to help me regain control.

"I-can't-breathe…,"

I tried to open my eyes but the task seemed impossible. Each blink brought me back to my bedroom where I could see his face and feel him touching on me. All I could see was his seduction pouring from his eyes.

"Get him away from me!" I screamed out

"Who?"

"Him! It's him!"

"Vickie…open your eyes. You are here in the office with Dr. Smith and I need you to breathe deep slow breaths. There is nobody else in here but you and me."

I sat there rocking in fear of what I would see when I did open my eyes. Dr. Smith stayed by my side until I regained control.

The tears slowly dried up and I explained to him, "When we all moved back together, he didn't touch me anymore but he might as well had. He would look at me in this way that would make my skin crawl."

"Like he was undressing you with his eyes?"

"Yes but worse if that is possible."

"You were still worried that he was going to come into your room?"

"There were all kinds of thoughts I had bruising my mind. These were the fears I had while being forced to live with them."

I hated crying. Showing emotion was a form of weakness and weak I was not. The less I felt the more immune I became. I couldn't let people know what was going on with me so I dispensed all my energy into trying to overcome the abuse. I created alter egos to help deal with everything I endured and continued to be exposed to. Particularly, now that I was being forced to live back in the same household as the very man that molested me for eight years; the same man who said he was better but wasn't. The way he looked at me only let me know if he could he would do it all over again. My new environment in combination with my passed pushed the scared little girl to the side and exposed all of the other personalities I'd created in order to deal. I became the popular jock while at school. The laidback no nonsense nonchalant gansta while in the hood and the angry secluded aggressor while at home. *A change was in order.*

Chapter 12

My life had taken another 180-degree turn when we moved into the townhome. Here we were supposed to be starting over fresh and trying to be a real family. *Bullshit!* I guess we were supposed to just forget that he molested us, went to jail while we lived in a guardian's home, abused while in foster care and now what, a party because we are all back together? Does anyone else not see the psychological train wreck we just jumped aboard? *Unbelievable!*

Paddle Brook North Townhomes was a family orientated complex. All the kids in the surrounding neighborhood would some way or another find their way to ours to hangout. We knew all the short cuts and backway routes of the neighborhood. We made it a point to explore every inch of the area in which we lived. We stayed riding bikes, playing kickball or playing some kind of game. My generation didn't too much care about video games. We had plenty of things to do outdoors to keep us busy and when we didn't we created something to do.

This was the first time Nichelle and I had been able to play outside without worrying about a stray bullet or a crack head interfering with our youth. We lived in one of the spacious 2 bedroom townhomes with a 1½ bath. My parents took the smaller of the two rooms since Nichelle and I had to share one yet again share a room. It had a jointed bathroom to the master which was off the walk-in closet and another door which led to the main hallway. "I spent many of nights hiding in that walk-in closet." I expressed to Dr. Smith.

"Hid from what?"

"My family. I'd usually go in there to talk on the phone when I was supposed to be sleeping. And the bathroom was the only place I could find any form of solitude. I would go in there, lock the doors and lose myself in my imagination. I discovered a lot of talents hiding away in that bathroom."

"Like what?"

"Well, I learned how to do hair, where I found my voice and I started writing."

"Is that right?"

"Yes, after the girls saw what I could do to my own hair they were lining up for all kind of hair styles. Of course I wasn't doing hair at my house. Too much to deal with! I didn't want to have to explain the all the locks on the doors."

"All the locks on the doors?" He asked.

"Yeah, unfortunately because of what happened we had installed locks on every door leading in and out to our room. Nichelle always made sure our doors were locked. She would check the locks at least four or five times before she'd actually satisfied her anxiety."

"You know Vickie everybody handles abuse in their own way."

"I did take notice to how some of her childhood behaviors carried over into her adult life. Like how she will click her car alarm a good 30 times before she is comfortable enough to trust that it is locked."

My sister has always been somewhat of an evil person in my eyes but instead of this situation drawing us closer it did the complete opposite.

Nichelle and I would get into it over the pettiest things. We'd fight over stupid stuff like the volume being too loud or who was invading the other's space. I mean we seemed to argue about everything when all I wanted was to be near my sister. Being that we were close in age that shouldn't have been a problem. However, according to her I was annoying and got on her nerves. I could tell even more so when we were around her friends. What she didn't realize was that I wasn't trying to be annoying. I just didn't want to be left home alone with him.

"Did you ever tell her that?"

"We didn't talk like that. If we weren't arguing we weren't really talking at all. Even in school. It was very rare that she and I actually held a conversation."

"Maybe she treated you this way because that is how she saw others treated you and she followed suit."

"I never considered that perspective."

Nichelle did have her sisterly moments but it all stopped when momma got rid of my father. She protected me from our father's lashes when should could. Unfortunately she wasn't always successful in her attempts.

Sadly, she became just like the rest of them in my eyes. She loved to call me names like fat ass, ugly, dirty or whatever flew out of her mouth. She didn't seem to care if we were alone or in front of other people. She had the tendency to say what she felt and didn't care how it came out. We have been side by side our entire lives but she couldn't touch on the terror I had experienced.

"Are you jealous of your sister?"

"Ha! I love it when people ask me that but no not at all. It doesn't bother me that she didn't get mistreated, for that I'm grateful but what did bother me was her lack maturity. She was supposed to be my older sister and yet she acted younger than me. I never fully understood her anger towards me. At first I tried to incorporate it to our past but looking back Nichelle has always been a bitch."

"So you never did anything to her?"

"Yeah I did, I am her little sister. But it was small stuff like wearing her clothes or going on her side of the room but nothing like she would do to me. And I don't even think that started happening until we moved into Paddle Brook. Nichelle was a bully. Trying to control me and always putting others before me."

"Can you give me an example?"

"I can give you plenty."

Every Monday and Friday our school would take us to the big pool to go swim and splash around. Momma instructed us to bring home our swimming suits every weekend to be washed. Of course I followed her instructions and brought my suit home while Nichelle left hers there at the school. Momma didn't get the chance to finish the laundry so she told Nichelle to make sure I received at least one of the three she had there at school. I get to the locker room in search of Nichelle to grab the swimsuit but she had already decided to give the extra suits to two of her friends instead. I pleaded with her. Reminding her of what momma said about sharing her suit with me but she didn't care what I had to say. She and her friends left me standing in the locker and since I had not swimming suit I was forced to sit behind the gates while everyone else played in the pool.

"Of course she had an excuse ready for our mother when we got home and she escaped punishment."

"Really?"

"Yep, my sister didn't care. She very rarely got in trouble. I would try and tell momma stuff before our agreements escalated but momma wouldn't hear of it. Huh, she be like, stop tattling Eden, go back outside and play Eden, go to bed Eden. Don't let me try pressing the issue because then I would really end up in trouble. So now my mother was on the same shit as everybody else. It was clear now she was showing obvious favoritism between us. So jealous no, pissed yes."

"I see."

"That is why my friends were so important to me."

By the time we moved into the Paddle Brook North I was entering the third grade at yet another new school. Right away I connected with Jennifer and Phenyx. We were all in the same classroom and I was placed in between the two of them. They befriended me and took me into their circle. As quite as it was kept I didn't fit in with these girls but I was intrigued by their energy, their personalities and the kindness they gave off.

"Elementary was a tough time for me."

"How so?"

"I was short, overly developed, overweight and ashamed of my secrets. To them I was a quiet, shy and reserved but really I was being observant, cautious, alert and unnerved. I was the new girl with just a little hint of mystery. I was Eden the girl with hidden secrets and another new beginning."

"How many elementary schools had you been through?

"Four. And the girls I encountered at my new school placed no judgments on me and accepted me as I was."

I had purposely put on weight hoping to become less attractive to my stepfather not realizing I was opening myself up to schoolyard bulling. I quickly gained the reputation of the one not too be fucked with. After I broke little Johnny's arm for trying to put me on front street, the boys feared me and the girls just didn't want to be on my bad side. In turn, everybody wanted to be my friend or at least they pretended to.

"Julian, JT and Lisa were all I had known before then and they were gone. I wasn't sure if I was ever going to see them again. We were stupid close. I mean we did everything together including sharing schoolyard crushes. That is how Lisa and I ended up getting into it before I was snatched away."

"What did you all fight about?"

"Some little boy I'm sure." I laughed at the memory.

"Together we all used to dominate the playground. We would routinely jump from the monkey bars like we were doing something spectacular. It didn't help our egos none that everybody swarmed us like they were watching a cirque du soleil performance."

"Fun times?

"Oh man, we caused all kinds of havoc on the bus, the playground and in the classroom. Fun is an understatement."

"They were your friends."

"And my clutch. I leaned on them more than they knew and my new friends were just as reliable."

I soon developed a laundry list of new friends. I left Nichelle and hers alone and found some of my own shit to get into. I was super competitive and somewhat of tomboy by nature. My rough ways allowed me to get along easily with the boys. I preferred to play with them than to gossiping with the girls. I was no longer into boys like that and since JT was the only boy I'd had eyes for and my stepfather took away any other longing for that kind of passion. JT was the first boy I kissed and the last for a long time. Plus I had nothing to gossip about. Nobody wanted to hear about how I was scared to sleep in my own bed or about any of the psychotic sick shit that was going on at my house. I chose to avoid those kinds of conversations. I was scared somebody might actually want to spend the night at my house. I was good at diverting the attention away from me and my family.

At first, I would teeter totter back in forth between Jennifer's and Michelle's. Both of their families welcomed me into their homes with open arms. I'd experienced a love with them I'd forgotten existed. Jennifer was sort of shy, reserved beautiful and smart. She had this golden hair to match her golden skin with a smile that would announce her present. Jenny lived with both her parents down the street from me in these tri-level townhomes. The main level had a kitchen, a rather spacious dining room, a jointed living room, and a bathroom. There was a set of steps leading up to Jenny's bedroom, another full size bathroom and her parent's room. The lower level was less formal. It had a bar, a place for the dogs and the biggest television I've ever seen. Jenny was the only child and was pretty much free to do her own thing. Her mom was gentle and more reserved displaying a sweet subtleness about her but had no problems keeping Jenny and I both in line. *Mrs. Black didn't play that!*

I adored her family and they reciprocated the love. They included me in just about everything they did and referred to me as Jenny's younger sister. Mr. Black was the more outgoing parent. He was quick to take us on some kind of adventurous excursion. We went on limo rides, shopping sprees, and Kings Island trips. Basically whatever we wanted to do. Mrs. Black didn't attend every outing but she always made sure we had everything we needed. Whatever we did her parents made sure we had the best experience two girls could have asked for. *I would have sold my soul to have been the only child, maybe my life would be different, who knows?*

Chapter 13

The Blacks were the best substitute parents anybody could have ever wanted. That is until I met Michelle Garcia. I first met Michelle at recess while she was running in circles around the biggest tree on the playground. She was this long legged, tall Mexican girl. She wore glasses with her long brown hair pulled back into a made shift ponytail. I didn't realize until I got closer to the action that this was no game. The big girl chasing behind Michelle was the school bully. She was threatening to beat her ass but lucky for Michelle could catch up to her. I got tired of watching this fiasco unfold before me and intercepted the dumb shit. I had heard rumors about this bully and in no way was about to just stand by and let this happen. *Never been a fan of bullying.* By the time I was done with chick, she was trying to be both of our friends. Michelle had no more worries out of the bully after that and her and I been friends ever since.

Michelle's family was the complete opposite of Jennifer's but like the Blacks, the Garcia's adopted me like I was their third child. Her family is huge and back then they occupied several different houses on the same street as hers. Michelle lived in this 3-story house with her older brother, mother, father and dog Macho. I learned to appreciate the family values and culture observing their traditions. Mrs. Garcia always made everybody do everything together with the exception of Michelle's older brother Carlos. He was way older than us and too ahead of our time to be worried about what Michelle and I were doing. He was the older brother I never had. Mrs. Garcia was the one that got me interested in cooking. She would drag Michelle and me into the kitchen to assist in making all sorts of Mexican cuisine and pastries. Michelle didn't too much care but I was curious about the difference foods and spices in her kitchen. Michelle would rather dress up in her colorful long flowing Mexican skirts and dance along to one of the best musicals ever made. *Westside story duh.*

"Victoria, I wish you could see the expression you have painted across your face." Dr. Smith said with an unfamiliar grin.

"That's probably because I love these people more than anyone could ever know. I don't think any of them understand fully how grateful I am to them for opening up their hearts and homes to me. It was these families that help mold and install values that I'd lacked so badly back at home. They truly are my family. Each one of these people I speak of Dr. Smith are still in some way part of my life even until this day."

"I'm glad you had them Victoria. Maybe one day when you are in a better place you can share with them your feelings."

"One day Dr. Smith. Maybe."

"Just a thought."

"I got you Dr. Smith but you know what?"

"What's that?

"I'm just sitting her thinking about how sad it was that the only time I had any since of normalcy was when I was away from my home."

"Another positive…could you imagine if you didn't have those places to escape to?"

"No I couldn't. At that age we were uncovering so much about ourselves, our bodies and trying to belong. It would have been an even bigger disaster."

While everyone else was busy finding themselves I was more concerned about not having to be near my stepfather. My appearance never concerned me like it did the other girls. My clothes never played a factor in my daily routine and my hair was always done so I had nothing else to care about. It wasn't until the summer of 6ᵗʰ grade when Jennifer and I went away on this seven day overnight summer camp that I had even remotely begin to care about how anyone else other than my stepfather perceived me.

"Interesting…"

"See, I never had a problem being the cool chick. I never cared if a boy liked me or even wanted to be with me. I know I wasn't the prettiest chick, or the chick with the best body. I knew I was just the chick that everybody wanted to be cool with. I had experienced a lot of different kinds of sadness but nothing like this. I actually cared that none of the boys thought I was pretty like the other girls."

"You were getting older and more aware of yourself."

"I became encouraged by my summer camp experience. I started thinking about how I could be more attractive to others but just not him. By the time the school year came back around I was a completely different person."

Literally, my mind, body and my spirit had evolved.

Meanwhile back at home, I became less and less concerned about hiding my feelings toward how I truly felt about my family. If I wasn't arguing with Nichelle I was trying to avoid my parents at all cost. Momma always seemed to be angry with me and I could never do anything right in her eyes. "I was willing to do whatever she wanted if it meant I didn't have to be in the house any longer than what was required of me. Being on punishment for me was larger than the actual concept itself."

"Living with them was punishment enough huh?"

"See you get it, Dr. Smith." I let out a chuckle and he gave a slight smile. I continued with our session, "At my house nobody talked to each other unless we were fighting or arguing. As I got older, I became more guarded trying to mask the many problems that haunted me. I have never been one to speak on anyone else's experience and yeah everyone has a story but for me it couldn't get worse than being under the same roof as all of them. At home I was Eden; clean the bathrooms Eden, mop the floors Eden, do the dishes Eden, and wash the walls Eden. Oh and make good grades Eden. My stepfather was still looking at me like I was hot dinner roll on a cold winters day and he was a homeless man who hasn't eaten in 3 years."

"What did you do when you caught him looking at you this way?"

"At first, I used to run away to my room, closet, or bathroom. Lock the doors and hide away until I felt it was safe enough to come out. After that summer of 6th grade I started looking back at him like if looks could kill, motherfucka you be dead."

"How did he respond to that?"

"He started turning away from me. Usually he would go off to their room like he was the one scared or something."

"You were gaining confidence."

"I guess so because I sure wasn't scared of his ass anymore. But even though I started acknowledging his bullshit it didn't deter him from acting out. It did slow him down though"

"It wasn't going to stop him. He's sick."

"Don't I know? My house was insane"

I complied with their every rule. If it meant I was free to leave the house. It didn't always work out like I planned but it was my best option. Sometimes I could do everything that was asked of me and it still wouldn't be enough. I kept the kitchen, the floors, the walls, windows, our room and the bathrooms all cleaned and yet they still called me trifling. Reminding me constantly of how nasty I was.

"More name calling?" Dr. Smith asked.

"Yeah, but it didn't bother me, I was thinking that maybe it would keep him the hell away from me since I was so "nasty" in all."

"But it did bother you."

"Okay, so it did!"

After I came back from the summer with my waist slimmer, breasts fuller and my thighs thicker and more muscular I thought I was ready to conquer it all. My new body gained me a few more haters which I wasn't worried about but it was the attention from the boys that I wasn't expecting. To have to come to school, my sanctuary, my place of escape and deal with some of the same bullshit I had to deal with at home was unbearable! I became even more guarded than before, except now my anger was more visible and my temper was super short. I tried to cut down some of the groping at school by wearing multiple layers of clothing.

"I'm talking like many many many layers of clothing."

"How many layers are you talking?"

"Like, two and three bras at a time. Baggy pants with boxer shorts, on top of my panties and two to three shirts."

"I see?"

"I called myself trying to hide as much as my femininity as possible behind a masculine faucet I'd created."

"Did it work?"

"For the most part but they would see more than I would have liked when I had to dress for gym or whatever uniform I was wearing for the season. I was short with the thighs for days, a little waste and well-proportioned attributes that fit well with my athletic built. My attitude was night and day and would change drastically when I was away from home. I played into what people thought of me and became one of the most popular girls in school."

"How was it that they saw you?"

"I was described as cute, mellow and hip. I was the girl with the big personality. I was athletic. I was the one whose name was being heard over the announcements for setting a new record, placing first in my event, or putting up numbers on the board. I was the one who didn't take anything off of no body. I was that person that got expelled 8th grade year for beating a boy with a chair. Because of my attitude nobody could see my intelligence and that I was in honors classes. That in my spare time I was busy volunteering for my community. *I was the one who went above and beyond for others. I was that girl who wasn't comfortable in her skin never being able to find the beauty in myself.*

"I just wasn't your normal teenager. I didn't care too much of about nothing. I was super depressed, guarded, and my stepfather had done enough to my emotional state to have me shy away from anything sexual. I figured if I passed out a hug or two or a kiss here or there that it would slow the boys down."

"Did it?"

"Of course it didn't. They had no control over their hormones." I laughed out loud at my statement.

"What's so funny about that?"

"These boys thought because they were all big that I was just going to be ok with them touching and groping all at my body. Like,

I was going to have no type of reaction what so ever to them touch on me. No no no…negative. Unfortunately, my reactions weren't always so subtle and I didn't care. They got what they got! See these boys didn't know my story no more than I knew theirs. They didn't know how much their touching me made my skin feel like it was being eaten away by acid."

So yeah it became an issue for me.

"The more attention I received the more aggressive I'd become in my reactions. Retaliating against anyone who felt it was ok to put their hands on me in any other way than appropriate."

Dr. Smith allowed me to rant with very little interruption. "I hated feeling like I belonged to them. Like I was just something they could do whatever to when they wanted. I was constantly fighting off boys trying to defend my respect and my body."

"Good for you!"

"The principal wasn't as enthused with my self-defense tactics as you are Dr. Smith. He often tried suspending me because of the brutality of my actions. Of course me being who I am, I challenged him at every turn and I usually ended up with an in house suspension instead. He was quick to remind me however that our school doesn't tolerate violence."

But clearly it tolerated sexual assault?

"You should be proud of yourself for sticking up for what you believed in. No one has the right to touch you without your permission. It's your body, your rules!"

I wish I had known that a long time ago.

Chapter 14

I saw the smile still on my face in the reflection from the window of the car. Yeah I could stop traffic with these legs but body also brought unwanted attention and not just around school. Back in my momma's days they would have called me a brick house. I was the dark-skinned version of her younger self. Momma carried the title of Ms. Brick house of 1978, if that tells you anything. *Yeah she was every bit of 36 - 24 - 36 and not only was momma stopping traffic but she was causing accidents.* I was more like my mother than I even wanted to admit. Momma was a natural born hustler, quick on her feet and new nothing but the streets. She was born right around the time of the civil rights movement, the assassination of Marin Luther King Jr. and the voting rights act of 1965. Life by choice had its own barriers but then to include growing up on the mean streets of Bright wood only made more obstacles for her. Momma and her siblings ran the entire neighborhood causing havoc all around the east side of Indianapolis. Every single one of them resembles each other making it difficult to know who was who. The girls were just as adventurous as the boys and all of them in their own way lived up to the name they were born to. Everybody wanted to hang out with the Carters and nobody wanted any heat with them either. *We can thank my grandparents for that.* My mother was the worse one out of all the girls. Constantly getting into trouble and fighting everybody on the block/school/bus/wherever she went. My aunties often found themselves in sticky situations because my mother had gained a few enemies over the years. *Bitches were jealous…*In no way was my mother ever ok with her sisters having to put up hands because of her. Once she caught wind of any ordeal she'd be on the hunt and it would be no good for her prey. Now, Momma was a beast in the ring and no one was excluded from her list of opponents. She ran 10 miles a day, not including the miles she put in getting back and forth to school daily, she could bench an entire human and swim laps like she was an Olympic champion. *Straight killing it!* This one time, momma had heard from this snitch that these girls had been plotting to get her jumped. Momma was not about to allow that to go down. She got into full beast mode and went on the hunt looking for these girls. She didn't care which one she found first. One was enough. Momma told the snitch, "Let's go find these chicks! All I need you to do is because a distraction and I will handle the rest from there."

She was fully aware of the snitch being part of the plan to have her jumped the entire time. Apparently, the snitch was to lure my mother to a location where these other girls would be waiting for her. They were going to bum rush her. They were trying to tarnish her rep for being the baddest on the block. Momma quickly altered their plans when she finally caught up to one of the girls and she beat the hell out her. Before the snitch could go and report back to the rest of the crew, momma turned and knocked the chick out with a one-time and that was all she wrote. The snitch flew all the way back into a nearby phone booth. Momma then met her in the booth, detached the whole handle of the phone from the machine itself and committed to beating the life outta of the girl. *Neither one of them girls could have foreseen that coming.* Momma was so consumed in beating up the girl that she didn't notice the crowed she'd drawn or how the police had rolled up on the scene. It took both officers to drag her off of the poor girl. *What is that they say…don't kill the messenger.* Of course, she was placed into hand cuffs for resisting arrest and assault to a police officer. Her hands were placed behind her back and she was lifted into the air for better control. Now, from what everybody tells me, she did a double somersault, broke the handcuffs and was outta of sight all before the police could ever radio for back up.

I wouldn't have believed it myself except I was in the grocery store one day and this lady walked up to me. She asked, "Are you related to the Carters?"

Knowing what I know about my family I was a bit hesitant to be truthful, "Yeah." I responded hesitantly.

We stood right there while she recapped the same exact story about my mother being a bonafide beast and cracking this lady and half beating her to death. She went on and on about my family mainly my mother. By the end of the folk lore I figured out that the very lady standing in front of me was the snitch in the story who got hit with the one time.

"You look just like her, wait which one are you?"

"I'm Eden…"

"Okay, you must be…"

"Yes, I'm actually her youngest daughter."

The snitches eyes bucked out of her head and I had no more words.

"You do look just like her." She tried to recover.

"Yep, that's what they say."

"Oh how is she doing any way?"

Girl I am not about to keep siting here talking to you when it was my momma who almost killed you…awkward.

I quickly cut the conversation short to get away from the woman. *Did that really just happen?*

I suppose the apple don't fall far from the tree. I wasn't scared of anybody and feared nothing. Unlike in my mother's days, the girls recognized my crazy and didn't want no parts of what they had witnessed me put down. The few that did try were motivated by jealousy. I couldn't help that they men wanted me. They should have just taken my word when I said I didn't want them. I called myself being in love with this boy named Robert Walker. You couldn't tell me nothing when it came to Robert. In my mind, he was the guy I was going to marry and we were going to be in love forever. I met Robert over the phone threw his cousin. He and I were close friends attending the same school, some of the same classes and even hung around some of the same people. That day, we all ended up on the phone with each other when I called Kenneth to tell him all about our annual Kings Island trip. Kenneth ended up dropping off the line and Robert and I never noticed. We connected instantly and ended up talking for hours and for every day thereafter. He was a year older than me and attended public school. We had a lot of the same interests, goals and aspirations. We spent countless hours on the phone together talking about everything. He was the first boy that I could really open up to and we never even knew what the other officially looked like.

"See Dr. Smith, we didn't have the capability to send selfies back in those days, we just went off imagination and opinion. Our relationship wasn't motivated by sex which made me much more comfortable with him."

"Oh I see."

"I'd even risk getting in trouble just to talk to him past my phone time. I'd sneak in our walk-in closet after hours with my extended phone cord so no one could hear me talking. Every now and then I'd get caught by my stepfather but I was no longer scared of him. I let him think he won and when he was gone I would pull out my extra phone and resume our conversation."

"No regards?"

"None, especially when it came to Robert. He was the first boy I thought was actually interested in finding out about who I was. I told him everything about me except the obvious. I didn't want him viewing me in any other way than how he already saw me. I suppose this is why it hurt so badly when we broke up."

"Tell me about it?"

"Robert had found out I was cheating on him with a boy who went to my school. This guy, George was a mere pond in my war against my stepfather. It didn't hurt that George was constantly spoiling me gifts but I wasn't into to him like I was Robert. I just didn't know how to explain my situation to Robert and because of that it came to bite me in the ass. He eventually forgave me it was too late, he used my indiscretion against me and it all backfired"

"What happened?"

"I started hearing rumors of him cheating on me with this girl who didn't even go to his school. She had lived in the same apartments as his father so that is how they met".

"Naturally?"

"I should have known. The chick ended up calling me through a mutual friend who called themselves liking me so he got a kick out of the whole thing but I wasn't paying him no attention. She and I called Robert on three-way and it was pretty much over from there.

I can still remember his voice when he discovered she was on the phone too."

> Him: Hello,
> Me: Hey Robert,
> Him: Hey baby,
> Me: What you doing?
> Him: Cleaning up, you know so I can get ready to come meet you at the skating rink.
> Me: That's what's up baby. Hum I do have one question for you and then you can get back to cleaning up.
> Him: What's up?
> Me: Do you love me?
> Him: Of course I love you?
> Me: No for real baby, do you love me?
> Him: You ok Eden?
> Me: Yeah I just needed to hear you say it.
> Him: You know I love you Baby…with all my heart.
> Her: Oh you love her…do you?
> Him: Wait who is that?
> Me: You don't recognize your other girlfriend's voice
> Her: Hello
> Me: Hello

"She tired going off on him but he had already disconnected the call."

"Did you ever speak to him again?"

"Yeah, he called me right back. We pretty much ended it after that and agreed we would stay friends. I only say him one other time after that."

I sat there in my favorite seat laughing out loud at the memory and feeling a bit of pain in my heart for Robert. Dr. Smith couldn't help but to chuckle along with me. "At least you can laugh about it now." Dr. Smith stated.

"Yeah I could laugh then."

"Robert seemed like an important person in your life."

"He was. Robert was the first person to connect with my spirit and when I couldn't. I truly cared about him. The way he treated me allowed me to feel good about myself. Robert was something real but George was around to stir up shit between me and my stepfather."

"Stir up what exactly?"

"Him knowing I was talking to boys and bringing home presents drove him crazy. If anybody called the house asking for me he'd pick up the phone and scream I wasn't there and hand up. He was so jealous he couldn't see straight. As soon as I noticed, I started giving out our number to whoever asked, accepting every letter, flower and teddy bear in hopes that he would find it being nosey. This didn't give me a good reputation around school but I really didn't care. I knew what I was doing and if it meant torturing my stepfather I was down."

"Another game to play?" Dr. Smith said sarcastically.

"Ha! I guess you can say that."

It's not like he didn't know my intentions. I flat out asked him, why he looked at me the way he did."

"Did he answer the question?"

"Not really, he tried to act confused like he didn't know what I was talking about. I would get frustrated and walk away. He was just trying to get under my skin and I didn't want to give him the satisfaction."

"Did he stop looking at you after you confronted him?"

"Nope, he kept looking but I swore to myself if he ever touched me again I'd kill him."

"I can understand why you would express those feelings."

"Ugh, he was such a jealous man."

"His sickness only motivated my dysfunctional behavior. George stopping over by the house unexpectedly didn't help matters none."

"What happened?"

"It was still a little light outside when I opened the door to flowers, a beautiful tennis bracelet and a few other gifts. My step father was watching like a hawk from the steps. He was so pissed I could feel his breath on the back of my neck where I was standing. I accepted every single one and gave him the tightest hug. Because he was wanted to keep watching I decided to give him a show. I threw in one of the wettest kisses I could give George before sending him on his way.

As soon as I closed the door, this bastard was all over me like white on rice. Trying to hem me up, spitting and yelling in my face. I got loose from his grip and ran upstairs. I tried shutting the bathroom door behind me but he was too close on my heals. He backed me up against the wall continuing to yell and scream about George coming to the house. Everything was happening so fast and then next thing I knew his hand connected with the side of my face."

"He smacked you?"

"Yes! And hard too."

"What did you do?"

"I hit him in the balls. Took off running down stairs where Nichelle was still sitting confused by the commotion. I picked up the phone and tried to call my mother at her second job. I heard her voice right as he was snatching the cord from the wall."

"He was out of control!"

"Yeah he was. I must have pissed him off because he tried going at me again, He threw me on the couch and that's when Nichelle finally got off the floor and jumped on his back. I saw her legs flaring from side to side while I gave him what I could from being pinned underneath his weight. He couldn't take both of us at the same time which created some space and opportunity. With the cordless phone in hand I disrupted the madness by yelling at the top of my lungs. I told that mother fucka if he didn't take us to my momma and take us to our momma now that I was going to call the police. Nichelle jumped from his back to join me in my protest."

"How did he react?"

"He was stunned for a minute. He threw his head down in defeat and took us to our mother. Nichelle and I sat inside of the sub shop and watched from the window while she threw her finger around in the air and smacked him across his face. He left, momma finished her shift and we went on home."

"Did she ever discuss the situation with ya?"

"Nope, she never asked me anything, reassured us of anything, went home and off to bed."

"And that was that huh!"

"Yep, just like that!"

Life is full of problems like a long road full of speed bumps; you make it over one just to get to the other.

- E. Victoria Nichols

Chapter 15

Nichelle and our conflicts were becoming more intolerable which only created more problems for her with me and me for my mom. Nichelle was always favored in our family but after the shit hit the fan my mother became even more protective and coddling Nichelle even more than before. I can only remember one time my mother actually put her hands on Nichelle. *I am not sure what possessed my sister to do some ol' dumb shit of this nature but I'm not surprised.* I was in the house minding my own business when she asked me to come out side. I didn't want to but I followed along curious to what she wanted. I entered into the laundry facility where Kim was waiting. I sat and tried to be social with these girls zoning in while the conversation played on. I am not sure who brought her up but the conversation did in fact shift to a girl named Mary Anne.

Now Mary Anne was this old tired white girl who thought she was hard and couldn't be touched for whatever reason. She was in my grade, medium built and about the same height as my sister. She walked on her tiptoes creating a natural bounce in her step. She had this chili bowl style haircut that used to flare in the wind whenever she walked. Well, Mary Anne and I would get into verbal altercations all the time. For the most part, I didn't pay the girl any attention but every now and then she would try and push my buttons. Now, back in my day everybody knew better to talk about somebodies else's mother unless you wanted an automatic ass whipping.

She must not have got the memo because she in fact did talk about my mother after a long bus ride of her talking shit and *I tried to beat the life out that old tired ass white girl with the little boy chili bowl haircut!*

Now, I told you all of that to tell you this. Soon as I get downright good and nasty talking mad crazy about this old tired white girl with the chili bowl hair cut with my sister and Kim did this heffa come jumping out the closet like we were best friends and she and my sister were family and I had just stabbed her in the back or something?

"I'm sorry what the fuck just happened?"

I beat Mary Anne's ass again for GP and I went right into the house to tell my momma how conniving my sister was. Usually Nichelle was able to finagle her way out of most situations, especially when it came to my mother but momma was from the old school and you just didn't do no shit like that to your family let alone your sister. Momma called Nichelle from upstairs and introduced her face to the inside of her hand.

"Now, did it make me feel good that my sister got her head knocked off?" Dr. Smith asked.

"Hell yeah, she really needed her ass beat! Nichelle wasn't thinking about me when she went along with a plan to set up her own sister so why should I think about her not being able to hear for two days."

Depending on the perspective, most would say Nichelle had the advantage over me. She had the looks, my mother's heart and she was liked by more. I on the other hand had stamina, the brains, the strength and tenacity to outlast most.

The winter of 96, Nichelle was up to her regular shenanigans. She had been trying all day to get on my nerves. I was ready to go to bed and now she wanted to disturb my sleep. Instead of going back and forth with her I went directly to momma hoping to prevent a fight. Momma listened to what I had to say and called for Nichelle. I went on back to bed thinking she was going to tell her to cut her stuff down and leave me alone. Lies! Momma called me back into the room only to click off on me about bothering Nichelle. *Again! I'm sorry what the fuck just happened? I go into her room to tell on her and I'm getting in trouble? But isn't that how it always goes?* Nichelle could convince my mother of anything and she would believe her. I didn't care to hide my frustration and Momma didn't appreciate me showing it in my body language. She jumped from the bed and told me, "If you don't change your attitude..."

But I was already at a point of no return, I didn't care what kind of energy I was giving off I was tired, pissed and just wanted to go to bed. Apparently, momma cared because before I knew it she was sticking me in my chest with her fist. She also mistook my discomfort and pain for disrespect and stuck me again. I tried to contain my rage by balling my hands into fist but that too was the misinterpreted and frankly the wrong thing to do. She stuck me again in my chest and this time my body reacted before my mind could. I didn't mean to but I knocked her back onto her ass. As soon as I saw her legs and arms flaring I knew it was time to go.

"Get out! Get the Fuck out! Bitch.... who...bitch...think...bitch... Get out my house!"

Oh yeah, she was shitty.

My stepfather made direct eye contact with me while reaching for the phone. I knew where this was going. I knew I needed to get out of there. So many things were running through my head all at once.

I went into survivor mode and went for the necessities. Momma still hadn't gotten up from the one time she got touched with but I knew it wouldn't be long and my time was limited before she'd be on my ass. I wasn't expecting to run into Nichelle in the hall blocking my exit but there she was wearing one of my outfits. Of course she had something to say like she always has something to say and I lost it. I started beating her head into the wall. I didn't have time to draw this shit out. I had to go before momma got up. I drug her into the room and went in on her. I was so busy wearing Nichelle out that it took a minute to realize momma was throwing body blows to my back. At this point, I didn't care who I was connecting with. It was me against them. "Let her go… get off of her…move back move back…"

I didn't recognize the voices but soon snapped out of it when their badges flooded my line of sight. Momma was being drug into the hallway out of sight. Nichelle jumped up after they pulled me from off top her. While they were hemming me up Nichelle was getting held down by a female office. I was quickly arrested for assault and battery and since Nichelle got up swinging she too was then arrested for assault.

"Hey hey hey! What about her?" Pointing to my mother "We shouldn't be the only ones getting locked up for assault. She stuck me in my chest not once but three times." I protest in my defense.

"Well she is your mother and you can't go around putting your hands on your mother", the officer responded with authority.

"Fuck you and her…" I said to myself.

Nichelle and I ended up riding in the back of the same patty wagon. "Let's see how Nichelle handles this situation. Nichelle couldn't bust a grape if she were wearing a 5-inch stiletto heal but what she could do was write a check her scary self just couldn't cash it. *Even if the institution waived the fee and didn't require a signature.*

The officers separated us placing me in a holding cell by myself. Nichelle was placed right next to me within eyesight. Roughly an hour later I saw my mother trot up to the officer's station in the holding area. My sister was taken from her holding cell and released into my mother's custody. Neither of them looked my way when they passed by me to go through the doubled doors to the outside exit. The officers came and got me too but it wasn't to go home. It was to process my fingerprints, take my picture and spray me down with bug spray like I was trash. My adrenaline was still pumping making me numb to the pain I'm sure I would feel later. I wasn't sure what I look liked. *"Did it look like I just got jumped by my mother and sister?* "It doesn't matter I don't want to go back there anyway!"

All of the beds were full so I had to sleep in the holding cell where there was no bed but there was a nice hard metal bench that sat next to a piss stained steal toilet bowl. At 6:30am the next morning I heard a familiar voice and it instantly snapped me from my sleep. There my stepfather stood signing me out for my release. He said all of 5 words during the entire drive. "I'm taking you to school."

"Like this?"

He stayed silent and looked straight ahead. I sat still in the passenger seat anticipating my arrival to school. *"Okay, just another chance for them to try and humiliate me." I said to myself.*

I went straight to the bathroom to check on my damages. I was starting to feel the aftermath of the blows. I starred in the mirror examining my damages.

"Did I really hit her?"

"Yes you did."

"I must have been handling they ass."

"Yeah both of my hands are swollen, bruised and sore."

"My back and my chest hurt with some bruising to my body.

"Okay, I'm missing a few braids. I can hide that and this knot behind a ponytail.

"A few scratches on my neck but… no bruises to the face."

There wasn't much I could do to hide the drama so I played it off responding, "You should see the other people."

I was fully aware of the damage I could cause when I got into a fight. It didn't take much for me to black out and lose total control. I try and give disclaimers but most people are hardheaded. *Once you take me there I am not responsible for my actions or the outcome of the thunder I will apply to yo ass.* Momma always used to tell us, "Don't fight each other but fight for each other."

The older we got the more difficult that became. Nichelle was already in the habit of not listening to my mother and getting away with what she wanted. *I have been defending myself against my sister for a long time without having to cause her any destruction.* That is until the summer of my sophomore year in high school.

Nichelle had been trying to pick a fight with me all day. As usual, I was hiding in the town house talking on the phone to this time talking to Jennifer when she came hopping her happy ass along starting trouble. She just kept messing with me and hanging up the phone on Jenny.

After Nichelle hung up on Jenny for the fifth time the wrestling began. Momma came down stairs and finally got tired of us wrestling in her house. She told us to take it outside and get this fight out of the way once and for all. I ran outside to avoid the confrontation but Nichelle came out behind taunting me, "Come on little sister and show me what you got."

She was steadily pushing me in my chest. "Did she really want this? She knows what I am capable of." I thought to myself.

I didn't understand why she was trying to take me there. I tried to avoid her as long as I could but after about the fifth shove she struck a nerve and I went ballistic, "Show me what you got little sister!"

And I did.

I ran at my sister like a linebacker trying to hit a sled. I gave my sister exactly what she asked for. We went flying into the bushes only to be stopped by the neighbor's fence. I wrapped my hand around her tired ponytail and I just started sticking her in the face. One blow after the other. I hit her for every time she had ever hit me, for every time she called me out of my name and for every time she had humiliated me. I drilled her ass right into the ground. Only backing away from her because I was scared of what I might do if I continued. Nichelle got up dazed, shook it off and ran right into my fist. That jarred her a bit but she came right back only to get closed lined and then she was back on the ground. I placed my foot into her chest and begged her not to get up. She was shitty! She wasn't use to her little sister throwing the hammers on her.

We both were brown belts in Tae Kwan Do in training for our black belts. I could tell if given the opportunity she would tap into her skills and try something on me. And that is what she did!

"Let me up little Vickie!" she screamed.

I backed away from her allowing her the chance to regain her balance. This fight had become the truth. That day outside, Nichelle and I tried to kill each other. She ended up getting a death grip to my rib cage and I in return placed a death grip to her throat. Our stepfather had to use a belt to finally get us separated. We made it back into the house and momma started yelling at me, "Why you have to beat her like that. Eden. Just look at her face!"

Nichelle looked like she just stepped out the ring with the female heavy weight. My hands were badly swollen and sore as hell but

Nichelle had a bruised cheek bone, black eyes, busted lip, my finger prints in the middle of her neck and she had countless bruises to the body. If her friends didn't know about me before they did after that fight. I was constantly being harassed by them over this fight. "So you are little sister," her friends would say.

"Why you do her like that?"

"She asked for it… literally."

I was so used to lying about everything that it kind of stunned me that she told them that it was me who gave her the war wounds and the truth behind them. *What can I say, Nichelle was overdue!*

Jordan was the only one of Nichelle's friends that I could really get down with. She was a really care free soul that saw the good in everybody. She had to be talented to see my good but in any case she did and never once treated Nichelle or me any different. We were equals in her eyes and that is probably why I could get down with Jordan. Although she was Nichelle's friend, she would invite me over and include me in their plans. Eventually, Jordan started coming to the house asking, "Can Nikki and Vickie come out?" I was so use to hiding behind Nichelle and being in her shadow that Jordan coming along into our lives exposed me to an entirely new light. I was ready to stop being "Nichelle's little sister" and start being me? But *who was that?*

Jordan literally lived right outside our door. We could walk out ours and be at hers. I stopped spending as much time over Michelle's and became the third wheel to the Nichelle and Jordan show. We all shared many adventures exploring the surrounding neighborhood and growing up together. We would ride bikes on the sunny days and have pow wows in the laundry rooms on the rainy ones. Everybody from the neighborhoods would come together to play all sorts of games in our complex from hide and go seek, kickball, dodge ball even football with the boys. We did carwashes, rollerbladed, swam I mean if you can name it we probably did it. It wasn't nothing for us to get up and be gone all day. As long as we were back inside the complex by the time the streetlights came on we were good. Even then we were ok to stay out on our court and play a little longer. There was so many of us we could always find something to do before turning in for the night. Our generation had no problem with participating in the sport of being outdoors; a sport which has become extinct with the generation of the millennials. Our adventures only expanded once Jordan and her family moved out of Paddle Brook North. They didn't go far but it was yet another escape away for the drama in my home. The further away from my hell the better... so I thought.

Chapter 16

There I was sitting on the couch over Jordan's talking on the phone when in walks a couple of her cousins. I ignored their presence specifically because one of them had a thing for me. Never mind that I was entirely too young for him but he didn't seem to care. Every time we saw him it was something. It became so obvious that Jordan's mom had pulled him to the side to call him out on his ignorance. Dude was super aggressive and didn't like taking no for an answer. I had already had a previous run in with him a couple nights before when he slammed me on top of a car in an attempt to kiss me. Me not paying him any attention only fueled his ego and he wanted to make himself visible to me. He snatched up my pager and ran off to hide it somewhere in her apartment. When I paged my pager I heard it vibrating in the bathroom rumbling around in the drawer. Next thing I know, he standing behind the bathroom door and watching him lock the door and lean his weight back against it. *Is this really happening?*

"Get over here!" He yelled.

I realized he was done playing and was ready to use this as his opportunity to make his move he had be desperately trying to make for some time now. I start yelling for Jordan and Nichelle, "Get me out of here."

They tried to enter but he was not letting up off the door. "No! No! No! No! No! No! No!…get off me!

The shit happened so fast!

I tried to fight him off but I was no match for his weight or his size. He hit my head against the linen closet door and I drifted down to the floor. When I woke, my bra was under my chin and my shirt was ripped open up the front. My panties were stretched over to the side and my boxers were half torn off clinging to the elastic on the waistband. I had the biggest headache and it gradually intensified with the screaming coming from the other side of the door.

"Is he still here?"

I stumbled out of the hallway and my vision came into full focus just in time to witness Jordan run right into his fist. The impact in combination with her braces e split her month wide open. He caught me out the corner of his eye. He came charging at me knocking us over into the kitchen. He was back on top of me trying to put his fingers where they didn't belong. He had my hands pinned over my head. I tried biting and kicking him but it wasn't until Nichelle jumped on his back that he let me go. Jordan was still stunned from the blow she took to the mouth. He flung Nichelle across the room before retreating back towards me. This time I was ready. So I thought. Dude sent me flying through the furnace door. At the same time Nichelle picked up a chair and broke it over his back. It didn't stop him but is slowed him down. Jordan finally snapped from her shock grabbed a knife from the kitchen. Is this Ninja on something? Dude was handling all three of us at the same damn time. Might I add with no problem!

The knife must have put the situation into perspective for him. Jordan held the knife up while he inched his way out of the apartment. We couldn't get the door closed fast enough before he was trying to force his way back in. "Really?" Nichelle screamed.

He ended up taking the door off the hinges but didn't get a chance to come back in to do any further damage. One of the neighbors must have called the boys because he took off to the sounds of the approaching sirens.

Dr. Smith took a minute to interject, "Victoria, my goodness."

"What can I say Doc?"

"You should write a book."

"You wouldn't be the first one to recommend that. After all of that, I needed some much needed space. That is when I started spending all my extra time at Bethanie's."

"Bethanie is your childhood friend?"

"You got it Dr. Smith. The best person god could have placed in my life."

I met her early on in third grade when I first arrived to the township. We didn't become besties until the end of middle school and then when I moved to North Carolina, she became my person. Bethanie had just as much going on in her life as I did and still our entire friendship she has kept me balanced. *I love her for that.* She is the one I run to; the one that I call on, the one that knows my struggles, my strengths and my weakness and the one who still accepts me for me, flaws and all. She is my rock! I've leaned on her for many years and she doesn't even realize that she was the one holding me up all this time. She opened her door for me when all the others shut. Bethanie shared her twin size bed with me when I was too scared to sleep in mines. The amount of dysfunction we both were exposed to was real and we did it together. We watched each other grow, have babies together, be homeless together, play together, hustle together and cry together.

"At her house we were able to be girls you know? Jump around and sing songs, do each other's hair and share secretes."

"She knew the venerable you."

"She did."

I've never really been able to get along well with other females in the same tempo as I could males. I like to think I can get along with anybody but most females can be catty, competitive in the wrong categories, superficial, and they like to bitch all the time. Me, I'm more laid back, mellow, non-confrontational and I don't like to bitch at all. Bethanie is the same way except she has more patience than I do.

I would normally spend the weekends at her house but then I found myself over there after practice and then after school until I was eventually moved in. Staying over Bethanie's allowed me easier access to school. The more time I was there the less conflicting with Nichelle and most importantly, no more run-ins with the stepfather. Bethanie had become the sister I'd always wanted. Nichelle might have been a great friend but she was a pissy sister P E R I O D!

"Growing up I definitely learned to pick and choose my battles. I didn't always pick wisely but maturity comes with experience right?"

"Not everyone will agree."

"Well, I've never cared what everybody else thought about before."

By the time high school came around I didn't care much about anything anymore if at all. My sanity was sketchy and I was barely hanging on. I wasn't eating or sleeping but barely walking and breathing. I'd become more secluded from the world with every passing day I spent with them in that townhome. Although my stepfather and I never spoke about the incident that happened when I was younger we carried on as if nothing happed. Except those awkward moments where we seemed to have an unspoken understanding.

"You were probably too old for him by this point."

"I could tell by the way he would lick his lips at me and glare at me with his eyes. I could tell that he still wanted to play those games we used to play when I was younger."

"So even when you were in high school he would…"

"Still have urges yes. He just knew better to act on them."

A few years later we ended up moving from Paddle Brook North into their first house. Nichelle was a hop skip and a jump from graduation and finally getting her own room. We still had locks on our doors but she was a still a bit obsessive when it came to hers. She had a chain, a latch, a slide latch and a bottom lock. *Sister wasn't playing!*

"I only had one lock and I didn't even use it."

"Why do you think that is?" Dr. Smith asked.

"It's almost like I was inviting him to come in. I used to keep this knife under my pillow. I named her Suzy. Sometimes I would lay there awake and think of all the different ways I could kill him. I'd watch television all night waiting up for him just in case he couldn't fight back his urge and decided to pay me a late night visit. Suzy and I would be ready! Any time I heard the smallest creek in the house my hand instantly went for Suzy. One day in passing when he was cutting his eyes at me I extended him an invitation to come into my room only so I can cut his dick off and put it in his mouth and see how he likes it."

"Is that how you still feel?"

"No not anymore"

"Did you ever ask him to stop?"

"Why should I have to?"

"You are right."

"I did tell him though, one day he will get his. There is nothing I can do to him that God can't do better and he has a plan for people like him."

I sat silent in reflection of that moment him and I stood starring each other down in the hallway after he had to digest my insolence. In how strong I felt the moment I let him know verbally that I was no longer scared of him anymore.

"You are so strong Vickie. I am proud of you and you should be proud for recognizing your strength. Good for you! That had to be a powerful moment. I'm curious how did he respond to your courageousness?"

"He nodded his head and walked on back into their bedroom."

"Not much else to say after that huh?"

"Nope, and it's all because of him that I tried everything I could to try in conceal my shape and for what?"

"Have you tried answering that question?"

"I mean, while other girls were busy developing and finding themselves. I was busy trying to hide myself behind anything I could."

I had already had very little hope growing up in this life. I didn't care about anything anymore. All the various forms of abuse clouded my perception sending me down a spiraling black hole. There would be times I would go to the block just to see if I'd be successful in never returning home.

"The block?"

"My aunt lived on this street called Kenwood. It was the house all the cousins would come to and the one everybody wanted to be at. My sister and I already hung out with my cousin Diana. She was always over our house or us hers. She was the second oldest to Sasha and Diana seemed to always get stuck watching us. Our parents were always gone doing something but there were so many of us we found ways to keep each other occupied whether we wanted to or not."

"How many of you guys could there be at a time?" .

"Sometimes there could be as many as 12 and we are all first cousins."

"Wow."

"There are more we are just the kids from 5 of the sisters and 1 of the brothers that are the tightest in the family."

Our family is large, crazy and we don't have the best of everything but we have each other and we make the best of what we have. Always have and always will. I love each and every one of you!

My aunt never really cared who was over as long as her house wasn't dirty when she got back to it. Her younger sons Michael and Peter were closer to my age so I hung tight with them and channeled my inner tomboy following them around the streets of the hood. Michael and I are only 4 months apart and we connected at the hip. *Once we got to our teens we were a complete trip.* "On the block I could let loose and not really worry if I was cute or if someone was going to touch me or if I was going to have to pretend to be something I wasn't. There I was able to release and let go of all the bullshit from up north and kick it with people that was cut from the same cloth as me. We were often left to fend for ourselves and lots of the times it resulted in us doing some pretty dumb shit to get by." *Of course we didn't think it was dumb at the time but in hindsight it was.*

Lots of shit went down on that block. I started smoking weed on that block, drinking alcohol on that block, I lost my virginity on that block.

"Ms. Night you had a lot of 'firsts' on that block?"

"Hell most of us did."

"I'm curious, with all you had experienced how did you react to losing your virginity if you don't mind me asking?"

"No, I don't mind. Over the years Mark and I grew close especially with him living next door to my cousin. Hugs grew into kisses and kisses into a weekend relationship. He wasn't the only boy buying for my affection. Michael and I had our fair share of pickings but he stuck to the neighbor Jasmine across the street while I teeter tottered between Mark and my cousin's best friend Stevie. I knew Stevie well before Mark but we never made a connection until his mom and my aunt moved onto Kenwood. Oddly enough Stevie seemed to live if not next door to my aunt then down the street from every house she has ever lived in. Mark and his sister Danielle had been on the block for a few years now and Stevie and I had become good at ignoring our chemistry. That is until Mark stepped up to claim me as his. Mark's actions triggered Stevie's dominant gene and that had sparked a silent feud between the two of them. Mark was the more outspoken one when it came to his feelings while Stevie was more secretive and reserved." *There is no wonder why Mark got to the cookie first.*

"I wasn't going to at first but eventually, I gave in to his advances but not because he worn me down but because I had something to prove to myself."

"What is that exactly?"

"I wanted to try and see if I could withstand the sight of a different penis."

"I see."

"I was 14 and the only penis I ever saw was my stepfathers. I was tired of envisioning his. I wanted to see if seeing another's would have the same effect if it was with someone I was attracted to. The boys at school would try and be slick and slide my hand down their pants but only a few was successful at getting a hand job. The first time

Michael and I tried to actually go all in, we were in Chris's bathroom. Chris lived at the end of the block with his mother, younger sister Rochelle and younger brother Brent. I tried so desperately to make this happen but every time he would get close to me with it hanging out I would run. He took it as a game while I was simply scared as hell. He laughing and I played it off. In the end he was a gentleman about it and we ended up not doing it that night and leaving the bathroom and rejoining the click over at Jasmine's crib. Plus, his ego had blown up so big that the three of us couldn't no longer fit. Thinking somebody was scared of his big ol' penis…"

Dr. Smith let out a slight giggle in light of my sarcasm.

Living in the same space as my molester, sex was the furthest thing from my mind. My concept of sex and love was skewed from the beginning. Outside of the games with my stepfather I only knew what Diana watched through the fuzz on the T.V from the Nasty channel. "I so badly wanted to imagine someone other them him being on top of me. So when Michael finally worked up the courage to ask me to do it again I said yes. This time we were over Jasmines in a dark room with the lights out."

I got quite. "It's okay Vickie." Dr. Smith reassured me.

I took a deep breath, "I felt nothing. Sadly, I just laid there reverting back to what I knew how to do best. Being quiet and being still until he finished. Listing to him having what sounded like the best time of his life. We kept that moment between the two of us but my self-curiosity eventually pushed me away from him and into the arms of Stevie."

All the touching and feeling just wasn't me. Plus my heart I thought was with Stevie so maybe this time would be different."

But who was I kidding? I still felt nothing I was just too empty. It was just too late for me. I wasn't going to go around screwing everybody just to fulfill some void I had darkening my heart. Therefore, when I got with Darrien I made it so he was all I needed. I learned to love him and I already knew how to given into what people wanted. When I met Darrien I was so over life he could do and say anything and it would be ok. Sex at this point was nothing to me. Darrian like it so I made sure he enjoyed it. *Where is this explosion everyone is talking about? Is this what my life is? Nothing… My life had become meaningless and I was running out of steam.*

Listen

Shhhh…
I'm trying to listen
Attentively.
To the sounds of my ACTUAL heart beating.
It's Cold in there I'm sure,
It's because my heart has always felt so lonely.
Oh but if only…
I could drift away like she.
Be like the great boxer known as Muhammad Ali
But instead it is she.
Who can float like a butterfly and leave me HERE to be stung by the bee!
Is that why here I now stand in awe?
With HER body lying in front of me?
Float away little girl its your time to go,
Who are u talking to…me?
Yes yes my sweet little girl you can
Now go
And be free.

A stomach full of pills and a glass of water
Is this really and truly the only way one's to end up to be?

To give up and sacrifice my soul
All Because of he?
Decides to demoralize my youth AND INNOCENSE,
And haunt me in my dreams.
Terrorize me in my sleep.
At night is when he started to come
You see.
And that Is why the little girl inside
Would run and hide.
Scared of what,
She'd really see.
Her pain, my pain I can no longer deny
It's over powering.

I can no longer cry and stand by.
Torturing my soul I'd rather give up and just die.
My Depression lies,
Pretty deep

Suicide.
Its real
So trust and believe
I've tried.
No lie.
That's my only defeat
It wasn't my time to go
And that's when he really carried me.
Go on back now little girl
Your struggles I know,
I've make them really steep.
I wouldn't put anything on you IN WHICH, your heart couldn't bear
So don't worry my child come now follow me.
Back to the body I lent to you
It is her that needs you
Not me.
Fear not my child, I will carry you
ESPECIALLY, in your time of need.

This Purrfect Accident,
I've created
Your soul YOU! shall forever keep.
I gave it to you and not to them,
Now stand on up and get on your feet!
Be Patience my child
Inside you are now to go.
But *I can't hear a single sound*
The silence is becoming deafening.
Give it time my child and you will EVENT-UAL-LY,
Hear the thumbing from HER HEART... beating.
There is one last thing I need you to remember
And you heard this directly from me.
It is I,
Who brought you into this world!
And it will

Be I who's listening.

Chapter 17

By the time I had entered high school I was on a whole other level of depression. I still wasn't sleeping and I was steadily trying to pretend to be something I wasn't. *Happy!* We lived so different from my aunts and them. When my stepfather moved us from the projects he took us from the roaches and rats. The family automatically assumed we thought we were better than them. I would hear them say stuff like ya'll think ya'll have everything or they would call Nichelle and I white girls for living out north. Money isn't everything, you see. It's brought me nothing but pain, it brought my stepdad 2 young girls and my mom a cataclysmically fucked up situation. So be careful in what it is you value because it may be more trouble than it's worth. If it were up to me I would have rather continued dodging bullets in the hood then being stared down like a piece of meat by the man who was supposed to be protecting us. Or better yet, looked down upon like a piece of trash by your own mother because her husband wants you and not her. My stepfather loved to put on a front especially in front of mother. It would look like he hated me like the rest of them but he really was mad that I wasn't feeling his antics any longer or could it have been he was jealous I was messing with boys right in front of his face. Either way, my hate was fueled by the lack of acknowledgement by her. Fueled by the aggression she bestowed upon me and fueled by the creepy actions of this man she was married to.

The fact she chose to stay with him after all that was said and done still bothered me to this day. With the amount of disrespect and anguish from my family, the touching at school, the pressure of my grades all increased my anxiety and my hate had surpassed just myself but had spilled out onto the world! I don't recall me ever being able to cry to my mom about the boy problems I was having or the aggression I spilled out at school or how other kids did or didn't bother me. Or the amount of energy I put towards my academics and into my sports. Her absence from every basketball game, and track meet, every performance, awards ceremonies and accomplishments I'd was recognized for, affected me. I made my own transportation arrangements to get back and forth from practices, trainings and meets. My coaches brought my supplies and equipment or I hustled up my own money to get what I needed. I lived my life and shared nothing with no one. I walked alone and had only myself to lean on and that I did for a really long time.

When I say I'd rather be anywhere else than be at home with them I literally meant anywhere. *How is it that he walks around free while I'm trapped in this maze of pain?* Being on the block allowed me the perfect platform to depress my emotions. I begin self -medicating to hide my obvious insanity, to numb my reality and to end my mortality. I began smoking marijuana, popping pills, drinking alcohol and behaving reckless while I was over there. I would sit around all day and binge on alcohol and drugs. So fuck love but at the same time if that meant pretending just to annoy the fuck out of my stepfather then I didn't mind pretending. Out of all the things I was good at I learned to perfect the skill of pretending. Pretending to be something other than who I was which was to be something I was not. I learned how to play so many different roles effortlessly that I wasn't sure how to be the person I was born to be. A few times once it got late enough I would go walking by myself in hopes someone would come along and take me out of my misery.

I prayed for death and welcomed it. Yes it is true I wanted to die. I was suffocating and it felt like time was running out for me in this life. Was I ever going to get away from this hell? I had even become frustrated with myself, "Maybe I can't do anything right? A whole bottle of pills and I still wake up in the morning?"

"Maybe I should have taken two bottles."

"Next time just take three!"

"Fuck!"

"Somebody is bound to take me on these streets."

"Patience Eden."

"I don't have no more!"

I wasn't sure how to be a daughter to a woman who hated me so much. I wasn't sure how to face myself any longer. My mother could easily turn on me with the blink of an eye. Nothing I'd seem to do was ever right except maybe make good grades. She could take away my phone, my television, my friends even my dignity but she couldn't take away my intelligence. Hell, I didn't want him to be attracted to me and I sure didn't ask for him to touch on me either. As a matter of fact, I didn't ask to be here. There was literally nothing I could do to change what happened. *Is there? Is this my fault?* It was clear that they all hated me but not more than I hated myself. It had gotten so bad that I couldn't even look myself in the mirror. I just remember looking past myself and focusing on the distance. I couldn't make eye contact with anyone scared of what they might see in me. I couldn't see myself. I had reached a level of hopelessness where there was no means to an end. *Where is this light that I hear is supposed to be at the end of the tunnel? When I look ahead I only see more darkness. So why would I want to put myself through this misery anymore? I hear people saying that suicide is a selfish way to go. Well so the fuck what! They don't care if I live or die. The only reason I can see them getting mad is because they will have to start cleaning up their own shit and find another punching bag.*

Even when I was away from the house I still was responsible for what went on at the house. How was I going to be gone all week and come back to a nasty house that should have been cleaned up by the ones who made the mess in the first place? What happened to picking up after yourself? I could have sworn that was a trade you picked up in preschool. *Who do they think they are?* With all this darkness I only have one option…I must try again. I can't take another day of this shit! Once upon a time, I had a mother. I was able to sit on her lap and stare up into her face and adore the creature I shared my DNA with. Look up to the woman who gave birth to me who fought to deliver me to my darkness; she couldn't have known that it would come to this. But now I hear her words play over and over in my head, "I am a good mother, I made a good home for ya."

It just pisses me off all over again. *Did you? Make a good home for us?*

"In her mind she did make a good home for you and your sister. You were no longer in the ghetto but now in a nicer neighborhood and with food to eat and toys to play with. She was able to afford you with better opportunities and she did all of this while working how many jobs?" Dr. Smith asked.

"My momma kept at least 2 to 3 jobs at a time."

"Ok see, before you all went to live with your stepfather you didn't have none of those things right?"

"So?"

"So in her mind she was making a good home for ya. You said your mother went through her own hardships?"

"Yes, that is what she says."

I can't bare to listen to her stories. It's not that I don't want to or that I don't care I am afraid of taking on her pain and I couldn't bare hers too.

"She didn't ask for any of this either Vickie. She was a victim just like you. Pedophiles tend to single out mothers with strong abusive histories. They prey on woman like your mother in order to fulfill their own needs. Your mother working allowed him the alone time he needed to maneuver his way in."

He did tell my mother that he will take care of her if she took care of us. Knowing she would go hard for her girls. Dr. Smith went onto explain, "Most pedophiles typically will find work in or around children unless they have access like your stepfather did. Most live alone and have very few friends in the same age range as them and if they do it's a rouge to hide behind."

Just as I suspected, he only married my mother to get to her kids. "They tend to provide everything that is missing in the woman's life and will make excuses to play with the kids instead of hanging with other adults."

"Well that will explain why he didn't have a problem babysitting me. I mean what grown ass man volunteers to watch a 1 year old in the 80's?"

"A pedophile will find any reason and put their interest in children because they are easiest to manipulate and they can't articulate well. There are different types with them having a specific liking but will they usually stick to children who haven't hit puberty. A pedophile needs to create a sense of confusion for the child to make their actions more successful."

"Now that I actually sit her with you talking about this out loud it all makes perfect sense. I saw him as my hero, as my protector and as my friend. He would always take me places and buy me all sorts of gifts. I became so infatuated with him that I would walk around using his last name as my own. I remember how thrilled I would get when people would approach us in public and say how I looked just like him." *He was my dad.*

We both sat in silence for a moment. Dr. Smith allowed me to wallow in my pity but it wasn't pity it was clarity validity understanding; an awaking.

"This is good Vickie!"

"I hate thinking about how much I cared for this man and with all the things he did to me and my mother..."

"Your heart is solid Vickie...I think your mother unconsciously saw him still wanting her kids not her."

"That could explain why she took out her aggression on me?"

"Could be, the only way we will ever know is if we invite her to a session."

"Well let's not get ahead of ourselves. We will just see about that!"

I can see why that would piss her off, but why not take it out on him, why me? I can't believe the sense of relief I felt leaving Dr. Smith's office. This woman I speak of, she is my mother and you only get one. I am finally starting to realize she is his victim too. She just hasn't learned to find her own strengths. I'm sure she has suppressed just as much to make it through her life herself. I felt sorry for my momma in that moment. It's only a matter of time before she reveals her evil self. I have to find a way to deal with her. She is my mother! I called my mom on the way home. I needed to hear her voice I needed to hear that she was ok.

There are times when the mind is dealt such a blow it hides itself in insanity. There are times where reality is nothing but pain and to escape that pain the mind must leave reality behind.

~Patrick Rothfuss

Chapter 18

These sessions were really opening up a can of worms for me. Mostly they weren't doing anything but pissing me off. Having to relive all of these memories was more painful than I thought but it has opened my eyes to some new truths. I have been seeing Dr. Smith for some time now and I must admit I am starting to look forward to our sessions. I strongly believe everything happens for a reason and I was meant to sit on his couch. I've tried sharing my thoughts with other people only to find out they think I'm lying to gain sympathy. I laugh at the thought of anyone making up shit like this to get sympathy. Is that how you see me? Am I so weak that I have to drudge up demeaning bullshit in order for someone to feel sorry for me? This is why I keep my life to myself. I have never opened up like this before and although it was hurtful it was nice to hear someone answer my questions besides myself. I'm starting to realize now, that I am stronger than what I thought I was. I don't think I would have been so open had Dr. Smith not been so real with me up front. He actually cares about my well-being and that I'm not sleeping. He offered me some sleeping pills but I can't make myself take them. I told him I'd rather just smoke some marijuana to keep my anxiety at bay. He laughed of course and prescribed me the pills anyway.

After I got mommy on the phone I shared some my session with her. "He told me that he admires how dedicated I am to my family."

"Vickie you have always been a sweetheart!" Momma sounded like a baby through the phone trying to fight her sleep.

"Mommy, why don't you go to bed and I'll call you tomorrow."

"Ok baby, peace."

"Bye."

I wonder if I'd still be her baby if she knew I was sitting out front of her house ready to take her life. I call my mother once a day and will do whatever she needed, I also pick up the phone for my sister when she calls, break my neck for my niece and nephew and still talk to my stepfather. I wasn't built to be what people expected. I only knew how to be how my god made me.

I sparked a beezy while I waited for Jerome to arrive. I finally agreed to meet with him here at the house. I had my buddy purchase me a dime sack since I had no connections here in the city. I hadn't really smoked last since before Darrius was born. Rolling and smoking was just like riding a bike. I was rolling them well before I was smoking them so I had no problems getting my blunt together. Darrius was spending the weekend over Darrien's parents' house so I was all clear of any interruption. Moments later Jerome was standing at my door looking exactly how I left him. He opened his arms inviting me in for a hug. I accepted and I was glad to be back in his arms. *Oh how I missed him*. I took advantage of the moment and laid into his chest. His hands slid from the middle of my back down to where his hands could rest on my ass. His face cradled my neck and I felt his lips pressing against my skin. He knew just how to touch me. We had six years to perfect our love life and it didn't hurt that he was sexy as hell. I pushed back from him and walked over to Mary and took a hit. He took the blunt from me and took a couple of hits. I offered him a seat but he stood there while I found my spot on the couch. He kneeled down in front of me and finagled his way in between my legs. He pulled me towards him and looked deep into my eyes, "You look good baby".

I smiled "So do you."

He whispered in my ear. "I've missed you."

"Mmm huh sure you did," and I gave him a hard one eye-wink.

"I did." He confessed whole heartily and started to rub his hands up my thighs and around to my backside. At the same time his nose was rubbing across my neck taking in my smells. "I've always loved the way you smell." He whispered.

I fell into his body welcoming his touch. He pulled at my waist and slid me down the back of the couch. He handed me the blunt and I continued smoking while he worked my leggings down from around my waist until they were completely off. I arched my back to allow him to do the same with the red laced panties that hugged my bottom so perfectly.

His lips found the birthmark on my inner thigh. He pressed his lips up against my skin giving me small kisses that sent chills to my throbbing cookie. His tongue trailed up my leg until he found his place in my jungle. His tongue danced around in my nectars. Sliding gracefully across my opening, he pulled me in closer to his face and became lost in my juices. His hands kept busy tracing my body, gliding across my skin, up and down my stomach until he reached the peaks of my mountains. My hands wrapped around his perfectly baldhead and buried his face even deeper. I had forgotten what he can do to me. Our eyes meant right as his tongue traced his lips. This man is so fucking sexy! Each touch brought me closer and closer to my climax. I am sure my moans told him how much I missed him… wanted him. I was helpless under his touch. I tried to contain myself but my body cried out for more. He didn't stop and I didn't want him to. All my emotions re-surfaced and in that moment I was in love with him all over again. I pulled his face up to mines and kissed his lips intensely.

"I love you Vickie and I will always love you!"

I kissed him again but slower with more passion this time. I needed him know that the love was mutual. I didn't have to say it he knew I loved him. Our tongues reuniting lit a fire in the both of us. I locked my thighs around his waist just as he stood up. He supported me with one arm and snatched off the rest of what I had on with the other. I aligned vibrant kisses down his strong chest until he pulled me into him. He pressed my breast firmly against his pecks while he lowered us back down to the couch. He stood there taking off his clothes one article at a time. I watched his every movement thanks to the light from the kitchen accentuating his muscular physic. His hard oversized penis sprang from his boxers standing fully at attention. I put my foot up to his chest stopping him from getting any closer. I started playing with my pussy teasing him becoming wetter with the anticipation of his entrance into my warm cave. He walked out the pile of clothes to kneel in front of me only to grab my legs and forcefully pull me into him. I straddled his lap and allowed every inch of him to slide inside of me. We made music! You know that hot, sweaty, super intense, passionate, nasty, raw R & B kind of love.

After what felt like hours, we laid naked and exhausted in each other's arms. I nestled in on top of him keeping my head on his chest. He kept his arms tightly wrapped around my waist keeping our energy connected. I begin to drift into a conscience sleep. Jerome always made me feel safe. It took a while, *6 mouths but who was counting*, for my anxiety to finally subside enough to finally allow us a chance to fully appreciate the sexual nature of our relationship. He was patient and understanding throughout my process. I knew he wouldn't let any harm come to me nor my son and for that I trusted him. It didn't hurt that he was active army and equipped with all sorts of trainings. I saw how he was with his sister and mother and I knew I was good. He was however closer to his grandmother and she wasn't your average grandmother neither. She stayed up all hours of the night and was all about her wits honey. Whenever I would call over to their house, she would pick up the phone before it could even ring and have an excuse for me every time, "He's not here" or "I'm on the phone." She would say.

At 11:00 o'clock in the pm? Most grandparents who are that late in age would be in the bed by 7:00 pm but noooooo not Jerome's grandmother. She would be up on the phone almost like she was staying up just to tell me he wasn't home when 95% of the time he would be right there in his room. If he didn't pick the phone up and hear my voice I would never catch him. I would have to just wait until he called back or if too much time passed that meant she never relayed the message and I would have to call back and face her all over again. Eventually, I learned to appreciate her love for her grandson. It was his lack of maturity that got in our way.

His breathing deepened so I was expecting to hear the sounds of a roaring train going across an uneven track but instead I heard his deep voice soften. "I'm sorry. I'm sorry we lost our baby. I'm sorry I acted the way I did when you told me and I'm sorry I let you get away."

A tear dripped off my nose onto his chest. "I'm sorry about our baby too Jerome."

I got up and started looking for my clothes around the living room. He gave a small smack on my backside and rose to look for his.

Our clothes were scattered all about the living room. We got dressed in silence. I let his words play over and over in my head. *I'm sorry we lost our baby. I'm sorry I acted the way I did when you told me and I'm sorry I let you get away. I'm sorry we lost our baby...It was for the best. I was in no condition to be a single mother of 2.*

"So, when you start smoking again?"

I didn't want him to think I was nervous about seeing him so I lied, "Right before I moved back to Nap."

He starred at me for a moment doing the LL Cool J thang with his lip. I could have mounted him again! "Why you didn't call me, when u got back?" He asked

"How did you know I was back?"

"Dustin said he saw you riding down the street. He wasn't positive if it was you or not so I did my research and here you are."

The last time I saw Dustin I had bumped into him at Wal-Mart. He had been the first to discover I was still pregnant with his best friend's baby. He called Jerome right there on the spot while I was standing there in front of him. Jerome wasn't aware I was still pregnant until Dustin opened his big mouth. *Always blowing my cover...* I chuckled at the memory.

"You did your research, huh?" I smiled at the thought of him searching for me.

"Yeah I did my research," he smiled back.

"Ok but aren't you married?"

His smile disappeared from his face as he looked down at his empty finger and whispered, "Yeah I am."

The sarcasm elevated in my voice, "So then, that should answer your question as to why I didn't call you when I got back."

I knew how hard it was going to be to resist him and I didn't want to interfere. "She is who you chose. What was I going to say,

Hey Jerome, congratulations on the marriage and oh by the way I'm back… I do my research too boo boo!"

He chose he words wisely and allowed the next sentence to drag on, "If you know about her then you k-n-o-w about…"

"Yes I know!"

My heart weakened briefly but I showed him no emotion. "Boy or girl?" I asked abruptly.

"Boy."

"What is his name?"

"He's a junior."

"I can see that, how old is he?"

"Three."

"Hold up…a *female is pregnant for 9 mouths technically 10 but whatever. I've only been gone for 2 years*…so you telling me you had her knocked up before I left? Wait wait wait better yet we were knocked up together? So once you found out I was pregnant, you dipped out what to go make sure your other baby momma was good?"

"This dude wonders why I lied about still being pregnant. I knew he wasn't up to no good." I said to myself.

"I told you my feelings about being a single mother and yet you just leave me while I'm pregnant. There is no wonder why I lost the baby." I screamed at him.

"Everything happens for a reason." I tried telling myself to calm my nerves.

"Who is she?" I demand.

He didn't want to respond. Who is she Jerome?"

It took him a minute to respond, "You remember Stephanie?"

"You mean *young* Stephanie the one that use to play on my damn phone. The one who use to have a crush on you, you mean the one who was too damn young for you to even be entertaining her emotions…that Stephanie?"

He hung his head in shame. He didn't have to answer I knew from his body language. I laughed hysterically, "Yeah you sorry alright… that bitch!"

I didn't feel bad at all that I just fucked her husband." I laughed again and shook my head in disgust. "Look, we had our moment but I think it's time for you to go."

He stood there in silence not moving. *What could he say?* I held back all the emotions that was teetering the edge of my nerves. *I dare not give him the satisfaction of knowing I'm hurt by any of this.* "Jerome I'm really happy for you and I sincerely wish you and your new family all the best."

I couldn't bring myself to hug him even though I knew I would never see him again. Before he got to the door, he turned and said, "Whether you choose to believe me or not, what we had Vickie was special. When I asked you to marry me it was because I wanted to spend the rest of my life with you. Stephanie just happened. I know I fucked up but you will always be the one that I let get away."

For the last time I stood back and watched him walk away from me, my house and my life.

…But will he ever be gone forever?

Chapter 19

My decision to move to North Carolina was risky but it was my decision and mines alone. I had been working for my company for roughly three years at that time. I picked up on the training rather easily which allowed me opportunity for advancement straight out of training. In the time I was there at the Indianapolis location I advanced to 3 separate departments before realizing my opportunities were very standard at this office. Being a young black woman in corporate America wasn't as easy as it should probably be. When you add in strength and intelligent along with independence; you have ingredients for an intimidating specimen that I am. It wasn't nothing for me to be instructed on how to do something once and be able to replicate immediately. This skill allowed me to stand out within my peers and rapidly excel in my positions. I was born to lead and as it is known any good leader has good followers. The treatment and lack of disrespect here at my company had to be because they felt threatened by me. Although I was excelling, the leaders all decided it was time to knock me down a couple notches and place me back to an entry-level position. I didn't argue. It hadn't bothered me especially since

I was going to a position that held less responsibility and therefore less stress for me.

They all were surprised by my reaction to the demotion. I supposed my track record with my attitude would justify their actions. The one thing I can definitely agree with my mother was when she says, "You don't care who it is you will speak your mind to no matter the cost."

This is true I probably should have been a lawyer but don't get it wrong, I will admit to being wrong when I am wrong unless I don't think I am wrong and then you will have to prove that you are not wrong in order for me to consider changing my perspective to no longer being "wrong". Now, the only reason I didn't click off was because I was able to keep my pay. They could have put me wherever they wanted to in that joker, didn't matter none to me as long as my dollars still rain supreme. I knew I wasn't being demoted because of the lack of effort in my performance but because I had gained too much education and power and they tried me and tried me often. I'm smart enough to not give them the benefit of seeing me sweat. All I'm saying is that you better be ready when you do come for me because I will always have my ducks in a row before letting them off to swim.

One of two things was happening, they were trying to get me to quit but when they saw that wasn't happening they were trying to get me fired. The big boss over my department once I went back to inbounding tried all sorts of little tricks to get at me. See when you are on an inbound unit everything you do can be seen by big brother and for me big brother was the big boss over my department. He was always trying to find some reason to write me up or call me into his office. It was almost like he got some kind of freaky ass kick from holding authority over me. He would do stuff like call me all the way into his office just to ask me if I was late from a break or if I using the Internet or would ask me why I was scheduling days off when I wasn't supposed to using to schedule time off or going into my calendar asking why do I need the days I requested off? Most of which he can find on a report the rest was simply none of his business.

It took everything I had to come into that office daily and be on my best behavior. I've never been interested what so ever in arguing with a person to the point of escalation. I'd walk away first before I'd allow a person to take me to that point. My attitude only can become a problem when a mother fucka wants to get jumpy. So I always say if you feeling froggish then leap. However, if you do decide to take that leap then my friend we have a whole different situation in its entirety. I am known from going from 0 to 1000 in the blink of an eye and will simply just black out on your ass. Dude took things too far one day and he saw a whole side of me that he wasn't ready for. I was in the copy room trying to fax out an estimate for a customer and he came in screaming at the top of his lungs, "Where have you been, I've been looking all over for you?"

"Really? You have been looking all over this office for little ol' me? Okay, well now you found me so what is it that you want? But first, why are you yelling at me like you're crazy?"

At that point, I didn't to hear what he was talking about and decided to walk away from him. He didn't like that and decided to grab me by my arm like I was his child? *Now why did he do that?*

In response to his actions, at the top of my lungs might I add I screamed, "Who the fuck do you think you are grabbing on me. You are not my daddy so you might want to keep your motherfuckin hands to yo motherfuckin self."

Before I could do or say anything else my supervisor was in the copy room trying to stand in between him and this ass whooping he had coming. Instead I paraded through the office looking for the exit.

Talking too loudly to myself, "What the fuck? I am out of here! He is going to wish he never put his hands on me! He got me fucked up!"

I had already been in communication with my supervisor to start looking for another position within the company because I was already at the end of my rope. I was invested in this company at this point and didn't just want to simply quit but this incident had put the icing on the cake for me. Of course they were scared of a lawsuit so everything was put into motion and my transfer was magically approved.

A day or so after the copy room incident my supervisor came back to me and told me there were no other locations available for me in the city but if I was willing to relocate she could get me into one of the locations out of state. There wasn't much to think about. Although it was a risky move, I was always up for a challenge. All I had to do was pick the location and she would do the rest. *Where would I want to go and start over?* I wanted a place where I could still enjoy all four season and allow my son to flourish to his potential. The west coast was out for that reason alone. The east coast was too fast paced for a single mother with a 9 year old so down south it was. *What did I have to lose?* Granted I would have very little support and be alone there but I didn't see much different than what I had here in nap. Here I had everybody and still had nothing. *Yeah it was time to leave!* My biggest regret would be leaving behind Bethanie. We never really had the chance to experience life like our peers. We were one of the few to have babies first in our class. While everyone else was off taking spring break vacations and traveling away to college, Bethanie and I were stuck at home being mothers. I've been here my whole life and there has been so much to go on here. I could use this break to start over. Get away from my family, put some distance in between me and Darrien plus use this time to get over Jerome.

Then there was Nathan; he was the other man in my life. He and I weren't headed in any one direction but we hit it off from day one. Nathan and I had worked for the same company and in the same office. Like any call center, there is a very limited amount of men working there so eye candy was at a minimum. So yeah I had noticed him around the office standing right at 6'2 with a lean muscular tone to his body. He was of caramel complexion, wore designer glasses and kept a fade. He didn't make a lot of ruckus around the office and pretty much kept to himself and the few buddies he associated with there at work. I learned through the grapevine that he used to be a fat boy in his younger days. You'd never know by just looking at him. His veins would protrude from his large forearms and his pictorials sat perfectly in place in the center of his chest. We would bump into one another in the break room and engage in short conversations but that's about it. Until…

One day at work I was sitting at my desk during down time and my neighbor come running back to her desk telling me how she was just coming from placing a note she wrote on the desk of her secret crush. She had gotten all giddy and was nervous with anticipation of his response. *Really… a note at your age?* She was all, "I have no other way to tell him."

I didn't care that much so I just went straight to the point.

"What did the note say?"

I wasn't asking out of curiosity just being straight nosey plus she was too geeked to direct the c conversation. Her tone became bubbly, "I told him how cute he was and how he made me feel when we passed each other in the office and how I wanted to get to know him better…"

She was the kind of chick that would smack her lips together after every other word. She had bright auburn blonde hair that did nothing for her skin tone wore glasses that was too little for her face and she thought was the bomb. She carried this rump that wasn't one too gawk at but you can't help but stare. She literally looked like she had 2 pigs of different sizes hanging off the tail of her back. She clearly perceived herself in a different manor than what we actually saw. Her ass was deformed and nasty not big and sexy like she thought. Otherwise she would stop wearing those skin tight pants that highlighted that cottage cheese…*but u aint heard that from me.*

Just when she was wrapping up her story she began fidgeting at her clothes and hair.

"Here he comes", she said whispering over to me. I looked up and saw his broad shoulders turning the corner headed in our direction. He looked particularly sexy for some reason that day. He was wearing his glasses and was serving us a freshly cut fade. He had on a butterscotch and white stripped button down shirt with just a little hit of blue. His shirt was tucked into to his slacks to show off his huge boss belt wrapped perfectly around his waist. *Did I start salivating and biting my lip?* His swag made me wonder what else he had hiding underneath those clothes. As he got closer I could see his shoes squared off at the tip and matched his fit perfectly. *Why hadn't I noticed this swag before?* He started down our isle and she turned to meet his approach but was passed by when he walked directly up to me. I watched the excitement melt from her face when he waved her note in mines. *Damn!* He thought it was me. I looked over at her with the, *you didn't put your name on it?*" look…really? *You thought this brother was just going to trout right on up to you huh?* How do I rectify this situation? But before I could try she had whisked herself away. I couldn't help smirking as her gigantic ass cheeks wrestled with each other with each step she took. The faster she walked the harder they fought. I went ahead and spilled the Tea.

"I'm flattered but when I received the note I suppose I wanted it to be you."

I giggled, "Yeah well, I am a little past the note passing stage…"

I tried to keep serious but I was still laughing at her walk off. That all changed when he started writing his number on the back of her note.

"Call me, maybe you let me see what stage you are at."

I smiled, and gave him my one eye wink, "Sounds good."

"I was now intrigued."

Nathan was quite the gentleman; after a few conversations we decided to meet outside of work for some drinks. I arrive at his apartment to him standing at the door dressed to perfection. He fit nicely in his soft orange and yellow-stripped tan button down, which hung over his denim Levi's. "Hello sexy, Come on in, you look beautiful"

"Not bad yourself Mr. Harris."

Sir you swag! He opened the door and I walked into a mixed aroma of chicken, herbs and countless spices.\

"Oh and you cook too?"

"I hope you're hungry."

"It smells delicious!"

"Thank you. Can I get you something to drink?"

"Yes, please."

"Absolutely."

I could see his muscles contracting when he reached for the wine glasses. He poured our drinks and left them on the counter. Walking back over to me he asked for my hand. Luther's voice sprang from his speakers while he pulled me over into him. We waltzed over to the counter where our drinks awaited us. He fed me fillet mignon with a balsamic glazed sauce, red potatoes and some sauté asparagus.

"Dinner was delicious."

I wasn't expecting all of this. I offered to help clean up afterwards to assure we made the movie on time but he wouldn't hear of it. I leaned against the counter sipping on my drink while he gathered dishes. I was standing there keeping him company and there he was standing right in front of me. *I must be feeling my drink.* I was ready for him but instead he reached over my head to put a dish away. What can I say, his cologne tickled my senses and he became more and more inviting. We stood there drawing each other in to where our bodies became so close I could feel his heart pulsating down to his growing penis. I knew where this was headed. He had drinks, the dinner, music and dancing *I mean really... he had me at hello.*

"I'm going to kiss you now", he whispered.

I bit my lip and nodded my head extending my lips with permission. He planted his lips softly up against mines and I was instantly in his arms. His hands wrapped my waist to secure our position. He slid them down to my ass and lifted me onto the counter. I wrapped my legs around his waist. His lips trailed my neck and his hands explored my curves. He pulled me from the counter, twirled me around, pulled up my dress and bent me over the counter top in what felt like one motion. I felt a sticky substance trickling down my backside and then the smell of caramel hit my nose. His tongue followed the trail until I felt his tongue teasing there at my girl. I bit my lip wanting more and I never had to ask, he went right in for the kill. He pulled off my skirt completely, hoisted me off the ground and walked me over to the couch. This man and his strength had my mind swarming with lust. He laid me down so that my back was on the seat of the cushions. His strong hands went up under my backside and brought this buffet back up to his face. I was weak, he didn't know but I was completely under his control. *Or did he know?*

I suppose he got full because he backed up from me licking his lips. "Take off your clothes," I demanded.

I needed to see what he had going on under them clothes. He stepped out of his pants not fully complying with my demands and dead lifted me from the couch. In a matter of moments I was back in the air with my legs wrapped firmly around his waist. "I can't wait to get back in between them thighs."

He started for the bedroom and I started for his shirt. "I'm going to fuck you first and then I'm going to make love to you. Maybe let you rest before I fuck you again. Are you ready?"

I had no arguments *hell yeah I'm ready.* One by one, he unbuttoned the rest of his shirt revealing his chest and then his stomach and there he was... all this man standing stark naked before me. I was right his body was even better than I had imagined. His chiseled stomach matched the rest of what he had to offer. *Thank you pig in a blanket!* Needless to say we never made it to our movie. He did exactly what he said he was going to do. Taking his time being attentive to me and assuring all and when I say all, baby I do mean all of my needs were met.

Nathan had me spoiled cooking me dinner, personal massages incredible sex, all a girl could want but upon our meeting we were in two different places. His spontaneous nature didn't mix too well with my structured organized single mother life. We began hanging out with the same crowds and doing a lot of things together, but no we were no couple. We worked in the same office so he knew immediately about my plans to move to the south. We discussed it over drinks and of course some wild sex until we came to great understanding. Nothing would change between us except he would stay here and I would be there. He made it a point to come visit me and I assured him I would stop in on him when I came into town. The "friends with benefits" thing worked for us.

Now, Darrien on the other hand, he was the one I'm most concerned with when it's time to inform him of the news. Whenever he thought there was an opening for us to try again he would jump at the chance with both feet first. Him and I went to the same school but didn't meet until we both started working for Kroger. Darrien and I developed a love and a bond that was unbreakable. During the start of our relationship we were inseparable. I was a grade higher than him but our age difference didn't stop us from growing in our relationship. As tight as we were we still ran into our fair share of issues. He was dominant and I was no longer submissive as I had been which caused us to butt heads. Darrien wasn't really used to me saying no to him and would feel a certain kind of way when I did. He thought no matter what happened in life I would always be his. After we grew up in age I realized our personalities were too strong for each other and we would be better off as friends. Every now and then when he saw an opportunity he would try and jump back into the old us like nothing ever changed. Darrien will always have a special place in my heart. He is the father of my child and my first tangible love. I wasn't sure what his reaction would be when I tell him I was moving six hundred miles away to Charlotte North Carolina. I had to tell him in order to get the permission I needed since we shared custody of Darrius.

Once I broke the news he reacted much better than I expected. He hit me with a 101 questions but finally agreed to give up some of his time for Darrius and me to make the move. This move hopefully will allow Darrien the space he needs to move on from us completely. His reconnection attempts for us getting back together were wearing on me, our friendship and any relationship he was attempting. Darrien didn't care who he was with or in front of. If he wanted to make a pass at me he would, if he wanted to smack my ass he would, if he wanted to play with my ears then he would. His nonchalant attitude got me nowhere with his other baby momma or interested females. They just didn't know I didn't want him like that. I suppose every now and then I'd throw my power as a reminder that they're not me and they never will be. If I wanted him to get in this wetness then so be it. He wasn't going to turn down what I had. Plus he was baby daddy slash best friend slash my first love. So Yeah, I let him hit it every now and then especially if he caught me in the right mood. It was hard to say no to him knowing what I know he can do to me. I was cautious and carful to not allow my emotions creep back up. It took me a long while to get over Darrien but I was eventually able to detach myself from him and move on romantically in my life.

Life is like riding a bicycle, in order to maintain balance you got to keep moving.

-Albert Einstein

Chapter 20

The last few weeks at work were interesting nonetheless. I could have slacked off but it wasn't in my nature. Nathan and I spent as much time together as possible before my departure. In that time we spent together made me realize how good of a man Nathan was. It's a little too late to do the could of should of would of's. The plan was for me to transfer into an inbound team there at the Charlotte office taking property calls. The center was preparing to transition into a larger entity within the organization meaning a better change for upward mobility. This center is 24 hours servicing property and soon to introduce the auto piece of the industry. Since I was being considered a transfer my shift and pay would all stay the same as they were at the Indy office. The only down side was that I would be responsible for all the fees associated with the move since I was transferring into the same position. The only downfall was that the company would not pay for the relocation. The move would be completely on my shoulders. I wasn't worried about that as long as the opportunity was there I'd be good. I knew my capabilities and was not worried about the stipulations. I instantly went to work on looking for apartments and schools best suited for Darrius and me. Eventually all that was left to do was for me to tie up a few loose ends here in the city and I would be all set for the Carolinas.

I knew my move would affect a small number of people but I wasn't expecting the reaction I received when I did finally break the news. It wasn't as easy as I first anticipated but my decision to move showed me who indeed my real friends were. The last few days in Indianapolis became down right eventful. Nichelle called me to come over to one of my oldest cousin's house. They had rented a bounce house for all the kids and she thought it was a good ideal for me to swing by since so many of us were at one spot. I agreed mainly because I was about to move 600 miles away and although we've been through a lot with each other, we were still family. As I got older I grew more and more distance however, only coming around on a few special occasions or out of respect for the elders. Everybody has that one person in their family that attends every function and knows every person from the first cousin to the last. Well Nichelle is that person in our family. Being liked by many allowed her to easily keep track of the bloodline. She once discovered our family genes trace back to European and Indian decent with very little African American embedded in our DNA. My grandmother was mixed with Indian, Angelo and African American. My great grandmother was Angelo and Indian. While the men going from my grandfather and back were all either Indian or African American. Our genes and our heritage had endured a great many triumphs and all of the apples fell from the same a withered tree. There is a reason we all don't be in attendance all at the same damn time. It is rather easy for tempers to flare and for a fight to break out. Don't get me wrong, there are some that are cooler and more relaxed than others but for the most part something is bound to happen. *I had my reservations, but what the hell. I tend to stay in the background ...most of the time so I should be cool right?* Wrong! When first arriving, everybody was spread about clustered up into small groups. Before I could reach the back yard I had to walk past a table of aunties. Naturally I went around giving hugs, kisses and hellos. I couldn't even sit down good before my aunt Pam started going in on me. She began questioning me about me finding a new church home and this and that. I tried to explain to her that today in my current stage I am leaning more towards a spiritual reckoning than that of the more traditional religion she values. I tried to be respectful as possible she is an elder but she was compelled to read me my rights. I went from her niece to a straight demon. I was going to hell and this and that. *First red flag* and I should have left then but instead I educated her on the difference between religion and spirituality. Christianity is what I've always knew and I felt that I fit in best with the Baptist Growing up, I struggled with my faith often because of all I went through. Gratefully, I seem to always be able to talk myself into believing he was there. It wasn't until I went to college and was given the opinion to study other religions did I truly begin to understand there is a difference between religion and spirituality. Once I begin to expand my heart to other cultural values did my religious contributions decrease and my spiritually strengthened. I don't like putting a name to the higher power. I just put my faith in it. I try not to judge people and love everyone. Just because I don't attend church every day of the week doesn't mean I am going to hell. "Auntie, it is your bible that discourages judgment and yet you sit here and judge me. I believe it is the same god you serve that once said put your faith and men and they will deceive you, put your faith and me and I will lead you to salvation. I suppose it's a good thing that I don't have my faith in you. My god knows my heart and because of that I don't have to explain myself to you. Let's just say based off your belief and what you just said, I guess I'll see you down there."

I gave her my hard one eye-wink, dropped the mic and went straight to the back yard. That didn't shut her up of course but it brought me enough time to get away from the table so I didn't have to hear her going off about it anymore.

I made my rounds to the ones lounging in the back yard. We were catching up, snapping pictures and enjoying the scene. Some of us were over by the side of the bounce house when my eldest cousin Henry broke out into a full out snap off on the kids. We weren't surprised to hear him yelling at the top of his lungs but we were surprised that he was projecting it onto the kids. I don't play when it comes to the babies and especially when my child is evolved. It wasn't anything for me to over speak the others and ask him if he was out his rabbit ass mind. My cousin stood 6'3 and weighed 200 plus pounds. He was ex-military and assumed everybody was scared of him. He had the wrong assumption since this girl feared nothing but my god; red flag number two. It was time for me to gather my child and exit stage left. Unfortunately, my mouth wouldn't stop running and in doing so I only agitated him further. I assumed because he called me a bitch and pushed me so hard in my chest that I slid back at least three feet. *Okay, so you know shit get real when everything slows down around you Right?* In my mind during the time I was sliding backwards I was able to have a full conversation with myself. I said, "Self, if you hit his big ass back you better make it count!"

"*You better motherfucking believe it.*"

I mentally prepared myself to defend at all coast even if that meant breaking out my black belt skills. "Seven years of Saturday mornings and 4 nights a week practices."

"*I better whip his ass!*" *I said to myself.*

Next thing I knew my fist connected square dead in the middle of his eye. The family must have started their retreat at the push because as soon as my punch landed they were all over us like white on rice. I was ready to connect my round house to the side of his face when Double K came up behind me and yanked me backwards out reach of Henry's fist.

I landed on my back and in a matter of seconds Henry was standing over me ready to drive his fist through my face. Luckily Michael, Double K, Mean Money, Dollar Billz and some others where there to keep him away from connecting. Good thing because when I feel had the wind knocked out of me. *That's why I hate when people interfere when I fight but in this case I'm glad they did.* I couldn't imagine what would have happened had the males not been there to tame his wild ass. After I caught my breath, I got up off my back and took a second to observe the chaos around us. It looked like a scene from a Texas saloon brawl. Children were crying and running amuck. Family members were screaming and running all over the yard. I saw momma trying to get at Henry with a beer bottle. Diana ran past momma knocking it out of her hand. Nichelle was rounding up kids. Stacha was in shock. I was right in Momma and Diana's path. I went to swoop up the bottle and here come LaTanya begging me to drop the bottle. I'm trying to crack it on the cement and she chasing after me with her hands flaring in front of her. "You want to put your hands on somebody?" I screamed out towards the raging hulk.

"It's not worth it Little Vickie…Don't do it!" LaTanya got closer.

Even now LaTanya was calm and collected. I don't know in all the years she has hung around my cousin have I ever seen her upset outside of losing someone to the heavens. Even when we worked at the hospital and it looked like Tanya was getting close to her breaking point. She would brush it off and keep it moving. She got to me before I could get to the patio slab to break the bottle. She pulled me in the opposite direction of the chaos and around the side of the house. The scene was complete madness and I still was in pursuit of my puck ass cousin. "Oh I got something for his ass aight." I screamed out ignoring LaTanya and her calm ass demeanor.

"Little Vickie he just aint worth it." She said following me towards my car.

And that's when I popped my trunk. "Lucy, where is Lucy?" I screamed frantically.

Throwing the few things I had around in my trunk. "Who is Lucy LaTanya asked?"

"Never mind, don't worry about it. Tell my sister to bring me my child. I better go before I kill some damn body."

He was lucky Lucy wasn't in the trunk and was packed up for the trip or I don't know what might have happened. He should have never put his damn hands on me. I had two big ass paw prints on my chest to remind me of my last days in my city. *Thanks to him!* Of course my phone was blowing up from the aftermath and the running gossip from those who weren't in attendance. I dismissed majority of the calls and picked up very few. My Aunt Vicky also known as channel 6, 8, 13 and 59 was the first to call and check on me. She was my ace, is my favorite auntie and is one of the more tolerable ones of the bunch. She and I even share the same nickname for crying out loud. I know I can call on my aunt Vicky and not only will she keep it real with me but she will have my back completely.

"Girl, you should have seen his eye little Vickie." She screamed through my receiver,

"Whaaaat?"

"Girl yeah! He just left from over here visiting daddy. He tried to hide it behind his sunglasses but when he took them off it was as plain as day baby. I couldn't believe it. Double K and Keisha was sitting here and we was like damn little Vickie did that?"

You could tell she was trying to contain her laughter. After all he was her nephew too. "But baby you got him good…do you hear me?"

"Well that's what he gets Auntie! I had to. He was too big not to hit with the one time."

"Girl if you aint like yo momma."

We broke out into laughter together. I couldn't help but to get a sense of fulfillment knowing I gave that punk a dose of his own medicine. "Auntie can you believe this foo had the audacity to walk up into the middle of my party."

"No!"

"I guess he thought this was the best time to come and apologize but it caught me off guard."

"Well, see."

"Somebody should have warned me."

"Okay, so then what happed?"

"Auntie I was all turnt up you know feeling myself and him walking in just killed my entire vibe. I was like really? After you put your hands on me? So I had them cut the music. Then Stacha tried to explain for him. I couldn't even do it. I told them that I was going to go upstairs and when I come back down if he wasn't gone then I'd hate to be him when I get back."

"Damn Little Vickie!"

"I saw him and Stacha heading for the door before I could even make it to the steps."

"Look too soon?"

"Okay!"

We both broke out in laughter

"Other than that was the party jumping?"

"Other than that yes mam the party was hype. There were a lot of people that came and turned up and turned it out with me. We had bottles popping, blunts in the air, music cracking."

"Oh yeah, ya was having a good time."

"Let's just say they sent me off right."

"Girl, come on over here and give yo auntie a dollar."

We laughed again.

"Imma get ready to get off of here. But before I go I wanted to tell you he did call me later to apologize. I accepted, we squashed it and that was that."

"Good, I am so proud of ya."

"Right on."

"Well, ok then baby. You be safe. Call us when you get there and I will talk to you later baby… I love you."

"I love you too auntie."

Like I said if you see a lot of us together all in one space, it is almost guaranteed somebody bound to act a damn fool.

Chapter 21

Aside of the fiasco that occurred at my cousin's house I was in a good place. The turnout for the party ended up being off the chain. I really felt the love from every person that showed up for my send off. The emotions were raw, the love was strong and the hype was real; it was everything I expected and more. Of course I was the life of the party in my black and gold studded cotton cross neck tunic that tied right under the breast line exposing all my cleavage in all of the land. I had on some black leather shorts with some black sandals that laced up to my knees. And *No none of it was name brand but with thighs like these who needs labels.* This girl is a single mother and don't have time to spend money just because. Technically don't all clothes… have labels? *I'm just saying.* If it's cute, my son is straight and I got the money then I'll buy it. The night was still a bit fuzzy from the turn-up but I remember everybody looking quite dapper in there get-ups. Edward came in the house floating like he was in a Spike Lee flick. He was wearing a green top with a butterscotch belt to hold up his denim jeans. He had a butterscotch fedora that had blue trim with a green and blue feather. I didn't know what was accenting what. He had on a vest to match his squared off shoes and he eyes had all three of the colors bringing the entire fit together. *When I say the boy was clean, the boy was clean!" Tonight I will call you the godfather...* Bryson was no better with his piercing green eyes peering from under his black Kanfol that of course only highlighted his all black fit. These two are the only male friends in my life that have stuck around from my childhood. I cherish their loyalty, respect and most of all their friendship. I am just another one of the guys when I with them. *They bring out my inner clown and keep me hella active.*

A fly better not had land on none of my guest. The amount of swag under one roof was electrifying. The ladies stole the show. There was more skin being shown at my spot then the law should allow. Speaking of law... they showed up showed up too. Nichelle tried to get them to strip for us but they weren't having it. Instead of locking me up for drunken and disorderly conduct they decided to stick around and "monitor" the scene. Once they had a feeling everything was under control they left the party under the control of the homeowner...ME and we party all night long. Everybody was in attendance except for the one person who matters the most to me outside of my kid. There are so many different layers to our friendship; it truly is unexplainable. It's almost like we drifted down from heaven at separate times, floating in and out of each other's space side by side until we landed here on solid ground. After it was all said and done I felt horrible for not inviting her. Bethanie isn't as outgoing as I am. She was more of a homebody and didn't care to come around large crowds. I couldn't bear to hear her tell me she couldn't make it so I opted not say anything to her at all. The morning of, was quite the emotional one. Bryson, Edward and I had just finished packing up the truck while Tacoya, Ramona, Nichelle and Diana sat around waiting for the rest of the brigade so we can roll out. I was up in the house chopping it up with Edward when Bethanie walked in. That was my queue; I jumped into Edward's arms giving him a hug for the gods. "I'm nothing but a phone call away baby girl." He said to me hugging me even tighter.

I walked him and Bryson to the car shedding a few tears not knowing how to say bye to Bryson. Bryson was by boy this was harder than I thought. The feelings must have been mutual because he kept it short and silly, "Don't worry Edith, you will be back and my number won't change."

"Understood."

"See you later?"

"Duh!"

We hugged and I watched them drive away down the street until they were out of sight. Bethanie and I sat there for what seemed like hours spilling our guts, crying, and laughing down the minutes. She begged me not to go but the arrangements were already set into place. "Promise you will keep an eye out for my baby." I said to her.

"Of course."

Darrien and I agreed that Darrius would be with me for all school days and he would return Indy for all holidays, breaks and special occasions. My mother was going to keep him for the last week of school. 1 week would be enough for her since I couldn't trust her to commit to anything longer than a day even though she didn't work and everyone else did. Darrius would most likely be with Darrien dad since that is where he would stay unless he was at his girlfriends. At the end of the summer Darrius was then to come back down with me in time to start the school year. Time had run out and it was time for me to get on the road. Bethanie and I cried, hugged and cried a little more before she handed me a note. "Read this after I leave", she said before driving away in her truck. It felt like I was losing a piece of my heart. Nathan and B9 finally drove up just as Bethanie was pulling off. I am sure their tardiness was all Nathans doing. He is one of the biggest procrastinators I've ever met. Nathan will be that guy who is late to their own wedding because he was still at the shop still picking out his fit. B9 was a super light skinned black essay from the bay area. He was a big boy with a big heart and an even bigger personality. He had thee longest and thee waviest hair I've ever seen on a man. His swag was off the charts and he was just simply sexy for no reason. B9 jumped out the car trying to tell us something but he was laughing so hard that nobody couldn't make out what he was saying until finally Nathan let us all in on the hysterics. "He found out DeWayne is going to be transferring down to Charlotte too."

"What the hell…"

B9 busted out laughing again. He was damn near rolling on the ground. We all joined in. His laugh was contagious.

"I can't right now with you B9." I said trying to find my breath.

I had other things on my mind. I went inside the house leaving them outside in the yard. Her note was burning a hole in my pocket.

Dear Best friend

I am writing this as I feel so lost right now. First let me start off by saying…please don't go! I know how dedicated you are and this won't stop you from going but I had to try one last time. Call me selfish but if I have to choose one time in my life to do so, I choose now. I don't want you to go and since I know you are, I need you to know…I'm your person and you are my person. That means no matter what, we're there for each other; it may be delayed (mainly on my part) but we're here. The truth is, we've always been good friends…BEST friends; but I don't believe it was until the day you told me you were moving to North Carolina and all of our secrets came out for the first time, did I realize you are my person. It was like looking in a mirror yet not quite sure what was looking back at me. It was then that I knew we were always meant to be! We were placed in perfect time for one another, destined for greatness through our individual stories that unknowingly link us emotionally together on the path designed for us in our lives! We are life partners and our strengths radiate when the others is weak and uncertain. The understanding of our common struggles sooths the ravage beast within; no words needed. We are each other's person because Adam, Darrien, Sara or Nichelle; our moms', no one will ever know the depth of our paths with the respect and applause it deserves like the two of us. That is why in any relationship we commit to you must ALWAYS understand that no one will have the full capabilities to understand who we are as the successful individuals we are today as a result of our survival and triumphs through the horrific circumstances. Never expect anyone to appreciate if for what it really is…That's why we are each other's person. I hate that you are leaving me here but I understand you have to go. It doesn't matter how far you go or where you are in the world I will always be by your side.

I love you
Always!
Bethanie

She can't understand how much she means to me. I just don't know how to express that to her. *Damit!* I got myself together and went back outside where Nichelle and Diana were getting packed up into the rental. Nathan and B9 took their position in the U-Haul with B9 behind the wheel. Tacoya waited for me outside of my vehicle while I said goodbye to Ramona. She couldn't be there for the party since she works like a Jamaican but she wouldn't dare miss out on saying goodbye. What can I say? Ramona is the best! She is part of the work family and is my Sunday brunch buddy. She is the more reserved one out the bunch but is has more stamps in her passport. *If that tells you anything.*

Ramona sped off in her sleek grey Hyundai Elantra. I turned to the crew, "Does anyone have to use the bathroom before I lock up and we get on the road?"

Tacoya ran up to the house screaming and dancing, "I better!"

I decided to try and call Heather one last time while I had a second to myself. Of course she didn't pick up the phone. She rarely ever does. She's been distance since the last conversation we had. *What did she expect from me?* We had two different perspectives on life and she should, of all people understand that. At least that is what she said when we first met but her actions are proving otherwise. I've been so confused in life that my emotions are fragile and I can't allow myself to be exposed right now in the way that she wants. *She can't understand where I am coming from? Hell, I don't even understand where I'm coming from.* I just need her to pick up the damn phone!

Please leave a message after the tone…"

Hey it's me. I knew you weren't going to pick up the phone but I thought you would want to know that I am on my way out to Charlotte North Carolina. I've found me an apartment and my job is transferring. This is not how I wanted to tell you but you have been doing a good job at ignoring me. Hopefully you call me back sooner than later otherwise I guess I'll talk to you later or… whenever Bye, Oh and Uhmm… I do too. Bye.

Tacoya jumped into the passenger seat just as I was hanging up. "Okay let me go lock up and we can ride out.

Just as I suspected when I ran to the door she called me right back.

Chapter 22

We had been on the road for at least 10 hours. I drove the entire time from Indianapolis to Charlotte stopping only in Tennessee and South Carolina before actually making it to the queen city. Tacoya kept me company for majority of the time. She only fell asleep for a few hours of entire drive. I appreciate her coming down to help me with this transition. She was going through her own shit but this trip would be good for her to take the time she needed to reflect on what was best for her. Regardless of what she decides for her future I will always be there to back her all the way. I'll have her back no matter what. That's my girl and we will ride til we die! Toy and I met at work back in 2004 and we instantly clicked. She has a big personality like me but she is not scared to be in her skin. She one hundred all day and that's all I can mess with. Nichelle and Diana led the pack while we stayed in the middle and the men trailed behind us in the U-Haul We all had walkie-talkies to make sure our abilities to keep open communication were efficient since we was moving through mountains. Reception out there sucked making our cell phones pretty much useless. I could see a lot of movement up in the rental. It was guarantees that those two were clowning, gossiping and dancing to their choice of music.

There was no telling what the men were doing outside of pranking and spitting lyrics through the walkie-talkies.

Nathan made beats in his spear time while B9 laid down lyrics on the beats Nathan made. Knowing them they probably done wrote a couple songs on the way down here. Toy and I stayed busy dancing and singing along to all the best hits of that summer. We had our drank and our 2 step, we walked it out to Lil' Boosie's I N D E P E N D A N T and listened to Jeezy put on for his city. I enjoy the way music took my mind off of things. I firmly believe music is like food to the soul (in my boys to men voice). We had arrived in Charlotte slightly ahead of schedule, which was perfect since we had been driving for what seemed like forever. We had some time to spare before the apartment complex opened. We pulled into The Waffle House to grab a bite to eat. The scenery was such a sight to see on the way down. The mountains alongside the winding roads, the hidden waterfalls drizzling down the sides of the rocks and the clear sky with the stars trailing in the darkness… *It was quite captivating!* It made me want to pull out my pencil and pad to capture the moment. I discovered my artistic talents the day my little cousin tried to commit suicide. She liked the Minnie mouse I had on my pants the day I went to visit her at the hospital. I didn't have any money to go to the gift shop to buy her anything symbolic. I just started drawing what I saw on my pants. Amazingly it was a direct replica allowing me to make her a fly ass get well soon card She loved it bringing a bit of light in her hour of darkness and I've been drawing ever since. It as just before the start of summer and the weather down here was just perfect for the move. The temperature was about 88 degrees with a breeze that would hit your skin right as the heat settled against it. It was only 8:00 am and the forecast predicted the mid 90's by midafternoon. We definitely wanted to beat that heat and being a head of schedule would give us that chance. We settled into our booth and tore into some good ol' southern chicken and waffles, bacon, eggs, biscuits and gravy and some fruit with some fresh squeezed orange juice. I ate enough for the gods while listening to my people crack jokes about the various characters surrounding us. B9 went in on some of the managers at the Indy office while Nathan impersonated a couple of the male managers. Diana couldn't help but be loud and couldn't stop laughing. Tacoya was present giving soft giggles but was really lost in her thoughts. Nichelle asked, "So what about DeWayne?" *I had totally forgotten all about that.* Removing my face from my food, "Yeah what about DeWayne?"

The table got quiet. B9 filled us all in about how the day after I left the office, DeWayne started bragging about her transferring to the Charlotte's office also. *Aint that a bitch...!* We finished breakfast and pulled up to the office at the apartment complex to pick up my keys and guess who we see? DeWayne. Okay, Ok, I knew she was moving down here to the same city and transferring to the same job but what are the odds that DeWayne would move to the same side of the same city to the same apartments? *Well damn.*

Everybody had the funny look when we both walked out the office chatting it up. When I got into the car Tacoya looked at me and before she could say anything I was just like... "I know I know I know"

What can I do? DeWayne is free to do and go where ever DeWayne pleases but damn...Really! This is definitely going to be interesting. Everybody followed me through the complex to my new apartment. DeWayne pulled up into the same parking lot just two buildings down. "I mean are you for real?" Tacoya said and just started laughing again and shaking her head.

"You got to be shitting me!" I said.

I could see the others cutting up from the side of my eye. While the men wrestled with unloading items from the truck the women tried to arrange the apartment by putting items in their place. Half way with unloading the truck, Edub and his friend Willie pulled up talking about "Surprise!" Edub jumped out his ride.

"Hell yeah" B9 got hype and started dancing in the parking lot.

"We didn't think you were going to be able to make the trip." Nathan said giving E some love. Edub worked with us back down in Indy and wrote music with the boys on the side also. Over the years we all became rather close and established our little work family. "The more the merrier." I said.

We were ready to get the manual labor on and up out the way so we can turn up in the queen city.

There was so many of us that it didn't take any time to get business handled. We finally sat down to talk about the elephant cluttering the room. No one really wanted to break the ice but I knew they all had something to say. "Alright don't everybody start talking all at once." Edub was a little confused until Nathan went in about DeWayne being my new neighbor. Everybody looked at each other and just started laughing. "We know you will have plenty of stories for us to cut up about later", Nichelle said.

We all busted out into laughter again and disbursed from the table to get ready for the night.

We drove around just checking out their down town before finding a club to slide into. We all was dead tired but was determined to get it in and get our clown on. We danced a few songs, had a couple of shots and that was all she wrote. B9, Edub and his friend was Willie was ready to go in. They hopped in the rental and decided to drive down to Greenville to visit B9's sister. They would meet back up with us sometime tomorrow. The rest of us jumped in the Nissan and headed back to the apartment. I got Nichelle, Diana and Tacoya all settled in the living room. I sat and gossiped with the girls for second before leaving them to go to my room. I was just a shower away from crawling into my bed.

I was exhausted and not to mention tipsy. I heard the water running as soon as I entered the room. Nathan was completely naked extending his arm to me. I walked over to him examining the body that stood before me. He lifted my shirt from over my head and tossed it to the side. His warm soft hands slid across my back releasing my bra. *Dude knew exactly what he was doing.* I felt the wetness stirring in between my legs with anticipation. I knew what was about to go down and there was nothing I was going to be able to do about it. He had that smoking aces look in his eyes the, I'm about to blow you back out addition. "You ready?" He asked.

*My mind telling me noooooooo.....but my body, my body is telling me yesssss baby....*R Kelly rang from his iPod at the right time. He slid into the shower behind me pulling me closer to his erection. I stood there letting the water fall in between us while he poured soup down my back. His nasty ass stepped back to watch it slide down to my ass where his hands were waiting. I stood under the water while he washed my body and we switched positions while I returned the favor. I had no problem running my hands up and down his chiseled chest. He massaged my shoulders and placed kisses all over the back my neck. Even under this hot water he was still sending chills down my spine and into my jungle. His hands slid down to my stomach pressing me back against his body. He crested my thickness until he found the entrance to my cave. All I wanted was for him to bend me over, fill me up with every inch and simply make me cum. But nooooooooo, not tonight I could tell he was taking his time with me. He was holding me hostage with one hand while taking advantage of my body with the other. Caressing my breast and massaged my clit to now the smooth grooves of Jodeci…Forever my lady. He had all the perfect songs for that moment. Nathan and I had spent so much time together that when we went into the studio for a session we made magic happen in one take. He continuously teased me knowing how I wanted more by the way I'd bit my lip. He slowly harassed my nipples causing my head to fall back onto his chest and my ass against his dick. He had every inch of my body stimulated by just his touch. He knew I was ready for him. I wasn't sure how much longer I can hold out. *How much more of this torture I could withstand?* I tried taking him into my hands but he quickly secured me pressing my back against the shower wall. "This is all about you tonight baby! Not me so keep still, if you can." He instructed.

He got down on his knees and buried his face in between my legs wrapping draping them over his shoulders. All I could do was lean back and let him take the wheel because he was straight driving me to the high heavens. I begged him, "Fuck me! *Please* Nathan please!"

Finally he released his grip from my ass, twirled me around, bent me over like I wanted and pulled my waist into him. I felt the warmth of the water hitting my back at the same time he was pushing himself up and through my jungle. The combination of the two was overwhelming and I came instantly. "You ready for round two?"

Did I have a choice? I was his all night!

Chapter 23

I woke up to everybody sitting around in the living room eating breakfast. B9, Edub and Willie had made it back from Greenville already. I was the last to get up of course; none of them had experienced the night as I had. I could barely walk but I couldn't let them know that. Nathan smiled at my entrance and they all greeted me with a sarcastic good morning as if they were a witness to all the nastiness that took place in that room. We shared a few more laughs before they all decided to get back on the road. They have a long drive ahead and were trying to get back before dark. They all piled into the rentals and I watched them disappear one after the other making a left back towards the highway. I could see DeWayne's car parked outside of the building. The U-Haul truck was gone so I assumed she was all settled in. I didn't care to go check since I wasn't ready to confront that beast yet. The apartment complex was small in comparison to some of the apartments we had back home. The neighborhood seemed quiet for it to be sitting so close to a gas station. There was one other apartment complex centered at the end of the street blocking all thru traffic making our street a dead end street. The apartment was in close proximity of Darrius's new school and only 15 minutes from the job.

I had my route all planned out from the house. All I had to do was make a right onto Albemarle and make a left onto Wt. Harris. Take that up to Tryon and I was there at the job.

I was ready to start this new chapter of my life. I was due to report to work at 8:00 am giving me a short amount of time to handle business around the apartment. There would be plenty of time for other stuff but right now it was time to turn on my mp3 and allow my OCD to take on over. I was grooving to the cold beats of little Wayne's Lollipop when I heard a knock at the door. "Who is it?"

I looked out the peep hole and seen DeWayne standing on the other side. "Do you have a minute to talk?"

"*Here we go.*"

I opened the door, "of course, come in."

I wasn't ready for whatever it was we needed to discuss but I pulled down a couple of glasses and poured us some wine. DeWayne found a seat at the table and began explaining her reasoning for coming to Charlotte. She wanted to establish her new self here in Charlotte. I'm not here to place judgment on anyone or knock their hustle. "*Too each is own!*"

Three glasses later we were laughing and planning our goals for the Charlotte office. She wanted to become an adjuster and I wanted to run the corporation. I've always been ambitious and why not? Dream big and big things will happen. "I need to get back to my cleaning but I'll be seeing her around."

Clearly, she was here and not going nowhere. She agreed and she trotted off back to her apartment. "See ya at work tomorrow." She said.

"*Yes you will.*"

It was 7:15 in the morning and the sun was already blazing and coloring the sky. The temperature was up around 80 degrees reminding me I was no longer in the Midwest. It was time to shave off a few of these pounds, tone up this body and see who was awaiting the new me from up under this shell. It was time to stop hiding behind the layers of clothes, the sweaters and pants. It was time to replace my old gear with shorts, tank tops and flip flops. I wasn't going to be able cover up like I did back at home. I had become self-conscious of my body and of my mind since taking slack from when I had grown up in the hell back at home. I had to remember I was in a new state and in a new city where nobody knew me. I should have been able to begin with a fresh start. I was curious how the DeWayne thing was going to play out. I took my planned rout cruising up Wt. Harris listening to Ne-Yo singing about how he is not Addicted to sex. This man's vocals really can do something to me. I stopped at the McDonalds to grab my large coffee with 4 creams and 8 sugars before going into the office. I was gathering my belongings out the car when DeWayne pulled up in the parking lot in the spot next to mine. We walked into the building together full of curiosity and questions. We reported to Human resources and from there we were directed to the training room. We both had to go through orientation since it was our first day at this office. There were only five of us in the training room. The trainer asked us to go around one at a time and tell a little bit about ourselves and what brought us here to the company. Next thing I hear is DeWayne introducing herself as Malaysha.

Who?!?

"Now I see what she meant by her new beginnings."

You see, Malaysha was born a man and everyone back at home and at the Indy office knew this. She slowly began transitioning from a boy to a girl starting with the spelling of her birth name. Those before me, saw her as a full out man who was of a homosexual nature. By the time I met her she was dressing, walking, talking and looking like a woman. She went from a fade to wearing micro braids, makeup, lashes and altering her voice. Although she still sounded like a man we all accepted her as what she saw herself as. The only challenge was her using the woman's bathroom. She hadn't fully transitioned so the office gave her two options, use the men's bathroom or go off site. I commend her; she opted to go off site every time she had to use the bathroom truly identifying with the woman she saw herself as. She would be the silent challenge of all the newbies from training. Who could spot out the woman who was really a man? She looked so much like a woman that most couldn't figure it out. I had to give it to her; she did make a beautiful woman. I'm not sure what her intentions were at the Charlotte office. She didn't bring up none of this name stuff or any other specifics about her acting as a full out woman in conversation with me the other day at my apartment. "I suppose it's none of my business as long as I'm not pulled into the okie doke."

"My name is Bennett and I not in it." I said to myself.

She was really a cool person and I had nothing against her, her dreams or her ambitions. I understood all too well about the struggle of identifying with who you are or aren't. Malaysha and I both connected with the only other black girl in the training class. Latoya was from the east coast and just moved down south with her younger brother. She had a strong Jersey accent and seemed like somebody I could get down with. After a long boring day of repetitive information I learned Latoya also lived in the same apartments as now Malaysha and I. Latoya was all about us all hooking up and kicking it after work. I didn't have a problem with that but I knew deep down in my gut something was going to blow up. I didn't come down here to get involved with anyone's drama. I came down here to handle business and establish new roots. I just knew Malaysha was going to come by later and talk about the bombshell she dropped in training but she never did. She didn't say anything to me about it and I choose not to bring it up to her.

Now that I was inside the building, this office was completely different than the Indy office. The building itself was 10x larger; it had five different floors all allocated for the company, a full cafeteria and a gym. My desk was down in lower part of the building near the gym in an area they called the basement. Our department had a few pieces of eye candy but nothing compared to what the sales department had going on. I told myself here in Charlotte I would not be mixing any business with any pleasure. All the eye candy in all the land was not going to deter me from my goals. I'd see Malaysha had a different outlook than I did considering all the traffic of men she was drawing to her desk. There were men coming from all different floors trying to halla at her. Latoya and I would sit at lunch and listen to the different stories she had about this guy and that guy. It seemed that Malaysha had all them fooled. *None of these dudes were questioning her sexuality?* By the way she was talking, it sounded like they had no idea she is a man. It also sounded like she was referring to herself as being born a woman. I just sat there and listened to the conversation and made sure I did not put any of my two cents into anything she was saying. Honestly, I was more concerned about promoting and passing by this inbounding role. Slowly but surely, I begin noticing some of the same guys from the office parked out in front of her crib. "Oh shit, what is she doing? Is she trying to get fucked up? You know what Vickie, this aint none of your business." I would say to myself.

Back at home she wouldn't be able to pull this shit because everybody knew what she really was. Down here she had been lying about her gender, flirting with what I assume were straight men and now she was dancing in the eye of danger.

Chapter 24

Here I was back at Dr. Smith's office where I sat in the same seat for every visit. We have been making a lot of lead way with my dreams and uncovering a lot of hidden memories. Moving to North Carolina was definitely a breakthrough moment for me. I was able to learn a lot about myself, spiritually, physically and mentally. I threw myself into my work concentrating solely on advancing my career and building new relationships. I had changed the way I ate, began working out more extensively at the gym and discovering who I was personality wise. After moving to Charlotte I also learned to appreciate my beauty and discovered my worth. The newly attracted attention I was receiving motivated me to push myself harder than I've ever done before. "Sounds like you were starting to connect with the little girl linger back in the distance? Are you beginning to see her?" Dr. Smith asked.

"I am and she is no blur but a figure now."

"I am so elated. Your growth is astounding. Keep using that anger, power and drive her home."

While I was down there, I ended up losing roughly 60 lbs. and turned my Midwest figure into a down south bombshell. My career was gaining momentum and I was learning a lot about who I once was and developing into who I was trying to become.

"Vickie you have come a long way and if nothing more than in the way you view yourself. I hear the change in your tone. I see the pep in your step and the confidence in you stature.

Your weight lost, 60 lbs. amazing."

"Thank you. I've lost another 20 since then Dr. Smith. Not sure if that was on purpose but it came off and the new me is committed to keeping it off."

"Wow that is fantastic! Did you feel accomplished once you started recognizing your transformation?"

"I did, with every pound I shed I felt like I was shedding away a layer of the pain."

I also was able to finally break free of my mother's grip when I moved. Once I got my son away from her she had nothing else to hang over my head. It's like she means well but it feels so intentional.

"Dr. Smith, do you know she called me after the second day I was down there demanding that I come all the way back to Indianapolis and pick up my son?"

"After she agreed to watch him for the week?"

"Right!"

"What was it this time?"

"She doesn't have to have one but on this day she said it was because she was supposed to have visitors in her apartment longer than a day."

"Did she know this before she agreed?"

"If the ruled had applied I am sure she would have known so no, I don't know why she would have agreed to have done it in the first place. Either way, why wait until everybody gets good and away for the damn state to start flipping out. She went as far as to say the office threatened to evict her."

"*Really...?*"

He is not a bad kid at all. He wouldn't have caused any commotion to draw any attention to himself. What is she talking about? He is quiet and keeps to himself. He has no siblings and has had to learn how to become self-sufficient really early in life. Meaning my mother only had to supervise him, cook his food and get him back and forth to school for 5 days and that's it.

How they even know my son was there like that?"

I was a young mother determined to make something for us. That required me to work and go to school. I've been grinding since I was 12 years old. I started off babysitting to eventually turning getting my foot into the door of corporate America to start building my earnings. I've never been unemployed, worked for every single thing I own and never looking to anyone for assistance. "*There wasn't anybody if I prayed for it.*"

The Collins did enough; I would ask them for anything more than what they had already done. My mother was never available for me and too busy taking care of Nichelle to see that I needed her. Let Nichelle tell it, momma didn't do anything for her. *Where in the hell do you turn when you can't even turn to your own mother?*

Instead of momma calling me to figure out a plan she called throwing out unreasonable requests and threatening to call cps on me. Screaming I was neglecting my son by leaving him there in Indy while I was in North Carolina. "If you don't come and get him by midnight and not his father or godmother or grandma or papa but YOU! That's it Eden." She said.

Then hung up the phone and decided not to pick back up and just stopped answering my calls all together. She was literally acting like

I was down the fucking street or around the corner. I was 600 miles away in a whole other city in an entirely different state and she tried to pull this shit on me? The entire phone call, I couldn't get anything accomplished. Hell I could barely get out a word for her constantly reminding me how she wasn't about to get evicted over me. "This is where I have to lay my head", she said.

I knew I shouldn't have trusted her but I figured because I was so far away she couldn't pull a stunt. *Apparently not!* Dr. Smith sat quietly shaking his head while I spat out my feelings.

I franticly went for my backups to see who I could get to rescue him away from her before she really does something stupid and turn my child over to cps. Before I could call Bethanie, Jordan was calling me. At some point mother had called Jordan and she was calling me to see what was up, "Hey Vickie what's your mom talking about?"

"You would like to know that too!???

"I mean what's really going on? She talking about cps and you left Darrius."

"Girl your guess is as good as mines. Jordan will you go get my baby?"

"Vickie, yes. I am off tonight and the next two days. I have to work the next two days then I'm off again if you need me."

"Jay, I will have somebody over there tomorrow."

"Well why don't you just let me keep him my two days off and then whoever you have I'll make sure he gets to them or whatever."

I learned to always have a plan B and sometimes a plan C when it came to my mother. There were times my mother would agree to watch my son and the next day when we'd show up she wouldn't open the door. My mother like to do things like get on my nerves about not seeing my son, get him all the way over to her house, wait until I'm good and close to home and call me back to get him. The problem with that is that she would ask for all the kids to go home just my son. She would intentionally keep my niece and nephew there. She began doing my baby the same way she had done me growing up with Nichelle.

Jordan was my plan C and Bethanie was my plan B but Jordan was all over it. Jordan told me, momma wasn't playing when she said she wasn't trying to give D to anybody but me. When Jordan arrived she wouldn't even let her in the building. I had to call the police to have Jordan escorted into her building. The police had to go to her door and make her bring Darrius down to Jordan.

"Who does shit like that?"

I understand my mother isn't perfect. I understand she went through a lot of things when she was young herself. I'm not a licensed psychiatrist but I know there is something wrong with her. She could call me 1 minute flipping out, being harsh, sounding all evil and calling me out of my name. We'd hang up and she would call me right back with her soft angelic voice acting as if she didn't just call me a bitch a second ago. *Just oblivious.* My momma had to have a couple of different personalities in there.

"Do you really believe that?" Dr. Smith asked;

"Yeah I do."

"A crazy person doesn't recognize they are crazy."

"She doesn't seem to have a clue that she is even the least bit crazy beyond our normal crazy."

"Real talk, Doc after I knew Jordan had my son and he was safe I had a meltdown in my new apartment. I slept in my closet that night trying to figure how I got here with her. Why do I still allow her to do these things to me? And not just her but all of them, my stepfather and Nichelle included."

"Because you love them but you don't have to punish yourself to show your love to them."

"What do you mean?"

"Removing yourself and love them from a distance."

"I hear you."

Even though Jordan started out as Nichelle's friend we had become really close over the years. Outside of Bethanie, Jordan was the only other friend that had consistently witnessed firsthand how my mother favored and babied Nichelle over me. She was the only other friend that witnessed firsthand how cruel my own sister could be towards me. Jordan was more available with an open ear for me than anybody else. She always encouraged me to stay strong and stray away from the bull. To use my intelligence and shine as she knew I could. Jordan was more like a sister to me than my own sister was. Jordan and I just had more in common with each other than Nichelle and I did or even than Nichelle and Jordan. Jordan was the one who got me interested in watching and playing tennis. We were no Venus or Serena but we got a workout in, which was the point. I got Jordan into riding bikes and we would go on the Monon trail to ride for miles. She shared the same passion towards animals and science. Jordan is now a successful Respiratory Therapist with the ability to explore whatever she wants. She has a beautiful soul and tends to see the good in people. I admire her care free spirit and I am grateful for the compassion she extends not only to me but my son as well. Not that I'm trying to put one against the other but Jordan has done far more for us in the time she has known me than Nichelle has ever done. What can I expect; Nichelle hasn't really ever been able help herself without her mommy in her corner. I can't ever nor have I ever expected her to extend a hand to me but when momma kicked us out of their apartment, after being there for only 8 days…we had no choice. "*Do you think I was able to call on Nichelle?*"

Nope, she was already living there with them with and had no job, no car, no money to contribute and a whole kid. In those eight days I had already given my mother three hundred and fifty dollars, hadn't eaten any of their food and slept on mattress in the living room. Now you know I had to be desperate! And I was and still nothing! As a matter of fact, Nichelle was standing right next to my mother while she called me all sorts of bitches and pointed at the door for me to go. Instead of her taking up for me she simply walked away and went into her room, shutting and locking her door behind her.

"Her and her damn locks."

I had to listen to her unlatch and unlock every lock every time she decided to leave her room. There were plenty of nights my sleep was interrupted by her and her damn locks. My insomnia was even heightened because of them damn locks. I couldn't even relax until I heard every single one of her locks click than clack. At that point, I was more concerned about him going into her room because I already knew what was going to go down if he came into.

Thankfully Jordan was available to open her door to Darrius and I yet again. We were able to stay with her for a couple of weeks until I found somewhere more permanent for us to stay.

Growing up with Nichelle was no picnic and you would have thought by now she would have matured and learned to treat me better than she had. Nichelle always carried that 'I'm prettier than you' complex and it wasn't even necessary. I wasn't materialist or even secure in myself to care what she looked like to be honest. She really had nothing to worry about but apparently she though different and didn't see life in the same way I did. She felt accomplished every time she called me fat or ugly assuming it would hurt my feelings. Little did she know I wanted to be fat and I wanted to be ugly; the less attractive to my stepfather the better. I hadn't realized how much her actions actually did affect me until now. I'm not going to sit here and say it didn't irritate the hell out of but back then her actions didn't faze me in the way she wanted them to. She was, even then too naive to see that much. I am sure Nichelle had her own struggles and her own pains better yet, I know she did. However, I had just about run out of steam with her and her shenanigans as well.

Outside of the obvious I've done a lot for Nichelle and her children. If she still chooses not to recognize me as the sister that I am then that is just too bad for her. Whenever she is in a real bind, I am about the only one she can call on and I actually deliver. I've watched her place everybody on pedestals my entire life and quite frankly I'm tired of it. My mother doesn't work, lives off of one paycheck a mouth and still Nichelle will take and take and take and take from her. She thinks because my mother offers it that it is ok to accept it. "My mother is always trying to offer us something. I think she feels guilty about a lot of stuff from our past and tries to make up for it but she just goes about it all wrong."

"That could be." Dr. Smith said.

"I never accept it if I can help it. Momma likes to throw that shit back in your face and I didn't have time for it."

I got use to taking a back seat to my sister whether I wanted to or not. It eventually became routine. When we would go shopping Nichelle always came out with just a few more outfits than me. She was the one who got the brand new this and the brand new that and I was handed down the fits even though out body types didn't match at all. Momma even took out a loan to get Nichelle a car, paid off Nichelle's outstanding school balance and all her tickets and fees she ran up being young and dumb. There was nothing momma wouldn't do for her Nichelle.

"After all isn't that what a mother supposed to do? Go hard for their children."

"Absolutely but a mother is supposed to teach the child so they can grow and learn from their mistakes. Not pamper them into making the same ones. My sister knew what she was doing and took full advantage of my mother. The sad part is I had to sit back and watched Nichelle be glorified for that shit while I was beat on for just being born."

Shits pathetic!

"You do make point. But if I can play devil advocate, do you really think Nichelle knew what she was doing?"

"Okay to be fair, in the beginning no she didn't but our life changed in cycles and I can tell you when we were in our teens she had to know what the fuck she was doing? She might have been lost in other categories I don't know because I didn't care to learn but when it came to her behavior at home and all that she knew what she was doing What burns me up the most is how Nichelle and I mostly fought because she always had something to say about how me and my mother interacted. I hated how she would always interfere but would leave when then shit got real. 8 times out of the 10, Nichelle would be the root of my problem with my mother."

I swear! She had no fucking ideal how much bullshit she caused for me.

"Dr. Smith can I ask you a question?"

"Sure?"

"Does it sound like I am jealous of my sister?"

"Why do you ask?"

"People used to always tell my mother that I was just jealous of Nichelle."

"Jealous of what?"

"Momma said it was because she smaller than me, lighter than me, taller than me and prettier than me. Momma said that to me a lot too that I was just jealous of Nichelle and that I needed to stop worrying about her and she gets to do and get to get and blah blah blah."

"Well when you play one against the other. It can become quite evident to the other and being that you are observant and as attentive as you are I can only imagine how you viewed things your surrounding growing up. I wouldn't say you were jealous more like you were no dummy."

"You get it! It's like being told when you are a kid by your parent… do this 'because I said so', I hated being told 'because I said so', but why because I really wanted to know the why to everything. Plain in simple"

"Like you said you loved to learn."

"That and I didn't want to make the same mistake again. Not like it would have matter in my childhood but that's the premise behind it."

"So let me ask you Vickie were you jealous?"

"I was jealous of her but not because of the physical things like they thought but because she was loved. My entire life that is all that I ever wanted was to be loved and it didn't have to be by everybody just my mommy, just my daddy, just my sister you know."

My family.

"Sounds like you have it figured out?"

"Somewhat but it I did would I really be here?"

"Everybody needs a little help every now and then Vickie. You are not exempt Vickie and neither is Nichelle."

"What you going to invite her to a session?"

"Is that what you would like?" Dr. Smith asked with excitement.

"She wouldn't go for it. She never wants to confront any of her issues. She thinks that if you put them behind you then they are left in your past and that is all you have to do. Just keep moving."

"Out of sight out of mind?"

"Right, but you and I both know that all the baggage you carry will slow you down and eventually your past will catch up to you."

"She is stubborn and will mostly have to figure this out for herself and she will sooner than later."

"I agree."

"You know Vickie, Your strength and intelligence has been what has guided you along through your pain. You've been able to recognize a great deal a lot earlier than most and that has allowed you to be able to sustain and maneuver through these obstacles. Where do you see yourself in a year, in three or even five? But don't answer that now, I would like for you to take that thought with you. Really reflect on your past, your present and thing about your future. We will come back to revisit these thoughts a little later."

"Okay, I can do that."

"Where do you see your relationship going with your mother from here?"

"I can't answer that. She is too unpredictable with her moods but if we continue on this route I will have to cut her off."

"It's obvious that you have love for her and you have a yearning to rekindle the connection you two once had."

"You know doc, I do. I want to have a relationship with my mother. She is my mother. I see the struggles she has in her world, with her kids, more importantly with herself. It breaks my heart. I'd like to think that one day we really could have a real mother daughter relationship."

"I think it is a good thing to be optimistic and open to the possibilities. Does your mother seek any form of counseling or therapy?"

"Nope, let her tell it, can't nobody help her. They don't know what they're talking about… blah blah blah but I think she would benefit in seeing someone for sure."

"Do you share your progress with her from our sessions?"

"I try but then she always seems to make the conversation about her and her past instead of concentrating on us."

"Do you think she would be open to coming to one of your sessions with you?"

"Her too! I'm not sure I'm ready for that but let's just leave that open for right now."

"Why are you not ready for that?"

"She really wants to know what happened to me as child and I can see that being the priority and I'm not sure I'm ready to open her up to that hurt."

"How do you know what she can handle?"

"I think my mother has to deal with her own demons before she tries to understand mines."

"That makes sense."

"I would like you to think back to our very first session. Do you remember?"

"Of course I remember."

"Do you recognize any differences?"

"Like what?"

"How you control your attitude, your relationship with your mom, how you handle your day to day activities?"

"Yes I have actually. I have more patience with my mother. I don't seem as short with her nor as anger but I can feel my anxiety at times reeving up so I just maybe will get off the phone or leave with as little confrontation as possible."

"Good."

"I've been using the breathing techniques you suggested and counting as a form of relaxing and distraction."

"Progression we might be done sooner than you think."

Chapter 25

My life was going as I had planned there in Charlotte. I had been recruited to be on this special unit. I was one of two people down there familiar with the auto piece of the business with the other person being Malaysha. Management began leaning on me for my expertise on all projects and decisions. What can I say; I became the go to girl. Recruiting Malaysha to the unit knowing how she wanted opportunities plus the girl had skills at her job I won't deny her that. I picked up their expectations for my new role and in doing so discovered glitches within the programs we were using. I became part of the design team in charge of discovering patterns and creating workarounds until the team in production could straighten out all the bugs and present a more permanent procedure. One thing led to another and I was training all new hires, the new comers to the new unit and even some of the big wigs. Once the company began expanding they turned to me to get those centers up to speed and train all employees for every new site. I went for sitting in a cubicle to having a corner office next to the big man of the office. I became responsible for 2 different units, 30 employees, and an entire company relaying on my every opinion in order to ensure continued success of the organization. I was a young 26-year-old vibrant black female, strong, independent, smart and courageous. Those kinds of attributes drew a lot of unwanted attention. People were looking at me like who the hell does she think she is and where did she come from? I went from being most of their equals to an associate to now their manager. I had only been there a year started from the bottom and now I'm here. I've never questioned my abilities and what I was capable of. I came down to Charlotte with the intentions of bettering myself and I am a woman of my word. Therefore I do what I say and say what I mean. Latoya and I had become real tight and it didn't hurt that her brother Maurice was sexy as hell. He was only 19 but he stood at 6'1 and had this confidence that would cause me to roll my eyes up into the back of my head when I saw him. It was something about that little boy that told me to stay away from him 1. He was really too damn young and 2. He was the younger brother of my home girl. It was a little hard to avoid Maurice. He was everywhere, the trash receptacle, the gas station, and then he began coming over to the house with his sister all the damn time. It became a routine for Latoya to stop over to the apartment after work to cook dinner for us. On Tuesdays, we would go to Bw3's for their wings and well the other nights we would just play it by ear. Dinner usually turned into a card game which led to music, drinks and every now and then an extra guest or two at the table.

My spot became the spot for everything regardless of what it was, *my house was it.* One Saturday we were all at my table me, Latoya, her dude, Maurice and his cousin. The four of us was chilling listening to music and play cards. Maurice was on his high horse talking about how he handles his woman. I couldn't help but to comment, "Boy please your little young ass swear you be doing something and probably don't be doing shit!"

We all laughed except for Maurice who was quick with the comeback; "I'd work your ass."

This started a rebuttal session between the two of us. The other two sat there cosigning for their family member.

"'Boy please!"

Waving him off like I just knew what I was talking about. Maurice pulled out his wallet and started popping gold magnum packs onto the table.

"Is that an invitation?"

"Anybody can carry them Maurice, but can't everybody wear them."

Latoya looked at me with the "okay" face and we laughed. The boys didn't find the humor in my comment and the conversation turned into a girl verses boy thing until the conversation finally faded. My phone rang and it was my mother. I took me a minute to decide if I wanted to pick up the phone. I was having fun and didn't want to give her the chance to spoil it. I decided to let the call go to voicemail. If it's an emergency she will call back or I would start getting multiple calls from different numbers. *"I'll just check on her later."* *I said to myself.*

That was the joy of being down there. I had the option of not picking up her calls without the worry of her popping up at my house. Momma doesn't do the interstate or airplanes so the chances of that occurring were very slim. But I found myself thinking back on some of them comments Maurice was jabbing at me. I must say he talked a lot of game. He had me a little curious, but those who talk about it usually can't be about it. *"Naw no need to waste my time…But what if it really is big?"* *I thought to myself.*

My phone buzzed on the table alerting me to a new text message. A number I didn't recognize.

Unknown Number: U should go out with us!
Me: Who is this?
Unknown Number: Me.
Me: Who is me?
Unknown Number: I'm in your house.
Me: Oh yeah?

I begin looking around the table to see who this was playing on my phone. Everybody was doing something with their phone but I know it wasn't LaToya and it couldn't be her dude. That left Maurice and his cousin Tray.

"How did either one of them get my number?"

Tray had been trying to get at me all night but I don't remember giving him my number. Come to think about it, I don't remember giving Maurice me number either. *Why would I?* When I did deal with Maurice which wasn't often it was always through his sister.

Me: Ok so who is this?
Unknown Number: r u cumin or no?
Me: Ha. Thanks for the invite Tray but I think Imma pass tonight
Unknown Number: This aint Tray

I heard Latoya say her and Tyrel was getting ready to go and head back to her spot. Tray was super hype about going out and Maurice was still all in his phone.

Me: No
Unknown Number: Why not?
Me: It's already late I'm in for the evening.

The boys got up and left to go get dressed for the queen's city nightlife. I sat there with Latoya and Tyrel shooting the shit until they finished their drinks.

Unknown Number: Last chance

Me: Go have fun.

Unknown Number: Oh I plan too.

Me: ☺

Unknown Number: You going to wait up for me?

Latoya and Tyrel finally left to go to her spot. I started cleaning up a bit. After turning off all the lights, checking the locks, I retreated to my room. *"Am I going to wait up for him?"*

I laid across my bed confused in how to answer him. "What kind of games is he really trying to play?"

Unknown Number: ?

Me: Stop Playing?

Unknown Number: Wasn't never playing?

Me: Oh is that right?

Unknown Number: U don't have to be scared

Me: And just what am I supposed to scared of?

Unknown Number: Exactly, so u going to wait up for me?

Me: No I am not.

Unknown Number: Yes you are

Me: Boi bye, I'm about to get in the shower

Unknown Number: C, I told ya…

Me: Whatever…

He knew exactly what he was doing.

This equation...MAGNUMS + SWAG + CONFIDENCE - SISTER and X =? Uhmmmmm. He really had me thinking! I strongly considered solving that equation but instead I decided against it. It just wasn't a good ideal. "Do I really want to get involved with this? *But on the other hand…I'm just saying.NO!* This could definitely get messy."

"Awh, decision decisions?"

Unknown Number: U ready?

Me: Y don't u stop texting me and pay attention to what's in front of u.

Unknown Number: Ok I will.

Me: Have fun and b safe.

He went silent after that last text message. I didn't think any more about it and rolled over to settle into my sheets. Just as I got good and comfortable I heard the alert from a text message.

Unknown Number: Open the door

Chapter 26

"I know this little boy is not at my door at some 2:oo in the am"

I went to go peek out the peep hole and there he was standing just on the other side of my door. So many things began racing through my mind all the way up until I opened the door.

"What are you doing here?"

"Can I come in?"

I stepped to the side to allow him entrance back into my spot. He didn't say anything else from there. He locked up the door, grabbed my hand and walked me into my room. I wasn't sure what was about to happen but I was done trying to avoid it.

"Lead the way."

"You ready?"

He whispered in my ear. I nodded my head and put my hands up over my head; giving him permission to take off my shirt. Maurice sat me on the bed. I watched him take of his clothes one piece at a time. I wasn't ready for what all he had underneath those clothes.

I wasn't ready for what he had in between his legs. This 19 year old wasn't playing. *Was he right?* My nerves became heightened as I sat in amazement. I was about to be in for one fabulous night.

"Can I handle that thang?"

There was only one way to find out.

Maurice walked over to me and laid me down on my back. His hands traced my body until he reached my panties. He pulled them down my thighs and off to the floor they went. He crawled on top of me and I felt his dick at the entrance to my cave. The heat from his body radiated through mines and I took him in my hand to lead him to his salvation. He placed his weight down on me and made his way into her. It was the complete opposite of what I expected. Feeling him inside me was nice. It had been a while since I last had some. I hadn't been comfortable enough to add anyone on my team down here so masturbation it was. He took his time at first, going slow until I was able to match his rhythm and then we were all over my bed. We rolled around switching back in forth between all sorts of positions. I couldn't let him know that he was indeed working the hell out me. In a sense I'm sure he knew by the sounds coming from my mouth and the way by body reacted to his touch. It was damn near impossible to keep quite. Each stroke brought out a different yet louder noise.

There was no time for cuddling after wards, I immediately showed him to the door and went straight to bed. *Talking about being worn out.* Knowing Maurice, I could hear him singing J. holiday's Imma put you to bed all the way home… and that he did. Needless to say I slept like a baby.

A couple of days went by and there he was back at my table eating dinner with me, his sister and her boyfriend. Nothing was said between the two of us about the other night. I figured it was a one-time thing and that he was just trying to prove a point. He threw out settle hints all night that only he and I knew about. I thought it would be awkward but it was quite the opposite. *I wonder if anybody outside of Maurice noticed the giant grin across my face.* Once dinner was over, they all departed and I went to watch television on the sofa.

> Maurice: Can I come see u later?
> Me: I thought that was just a 1 time thing…
> Maurice: Nope… say yes.
> Me: You a mess
> Maurice: You like it…
> Me: Whatever.
> Maurice" Say you like it.
> Me: But u r little brother, too messy
> Maurice: Only if she find out.

Maurice did have a point. I really hadn't found anybody that was worthy to take control of my box while I was here. Maybe he could be that boy toy I needed to come and scratch this inch every now and then. I couldn't stop thinking about how hard he made me cum. Maurice started sneaking back over to my apartment after everybody was well into their own lives. Our late night sessions became regular night events. He would sometimes act like he left something over to my house. Giving him reason to come right back over, knock it out and return home as if nothing ever happened. Most of the time we didn't even get a chance to make it to the bedroom. The heat was on as soon **as our eyes met**. His dominance was electrifying. He would text me with special instructions like: be naked by the time I get there or unlock the door and have that ass up for me when I get there or my favorite…start the shower…I'm on my way over

"*The boy had swag.*"

"Who would have known I would be so submissive to a 19 year old."

"…but the way he handles me in the bed."

"I know right?"

"Just think I almost passed that up."

Latoya would ask, "Who got you walking bow legged today?"

"Your brother…" Is what I wanted to say but instead I made up some random name to avoid the truth. While she drilled me about my sex life and rambled on about hers and Tyrel's, I thought about the other secret relationship I had once upon a time and the rush I used to get from nobody knowing about us. There is nothing more exciting than *be engaging at an event with all your friends and colleagues having drinks one minute and then sneaking off to share an organism with your secret lover the next.*

Nobody thought any different to our secret relationship, which only intensified each session. While nobody noticed Maurice's and my behavior, I did notice Latoya and Malaysha becoming quite chummy. They had been hanging out together a lot more lately. Malaysha hanging out over to Latoya's, the two of them going out clubbing together, and even double dating. The club scene has never really been a thing of mines so I would never be included in majority of they're outings. Plus it gave me an excuse to stay back and kick it with Maurice. Down here in the queen city, the club scene was a bit young for my taste. It felt like it a group of under aged children bunched up all together in a little whole in the wall. Latoya and Malaysha was right in the bunch, lined up to see every known rapper with the word "little" in front of their name. I didn't mind it every now and then but I was the oldest in the "clique" and was more into the chill grown up spots. Now while Latoya and Malaysha is being all buddy buddy with each other, I wonder if Latoya knows that Malaysha is really DeWayne? I have to assume she doesn't because Latoya is the type that would have addressed the matter with me well before now if she had known. *No harm no fowl.* Except I found out Malaysha was still up to her little tricks. I overhead some people talking about her and what I was hearing was different than what I knew to be true. I decided it was time to pull Malaysha to the side to get some clarification on what was actually being said and basically what she called herself doing.

She was now going around telling people that our relationship was something more than what it was. I simply just worked at the same office in Indy with her. Of course I was cordial but as far as us hanging out? *That wasn't happening!* We weren't sisters first of all she wasn't a woman so that was impossible. Our hanging didn't exceed past eating lunch in the break room. The activities her and I had going on down here had been the most active we had been with each other outside of anything work related. She could thank Latoya for that because I had no intentions on going out with her if she was being untruthful about her situation. Where I am from, that is how people get killed. From what I was hearing, it sounded like she was implying that she was born this way… a woman? *BULLSHIT.* Deception is a very powerful tool. I was well aware of the type of company she was keeping and none of it was my business until now.

I know all about being guilty by association. Being that of a leader it is not hard to emerge and stand out from the rest of the flock. I was always getting in trouble in school especially for something somebody else was doing. *Now how does that work?*

My sophomore year in high school my English teacher Ms. Jackson tried to expel me from her class. *You were wondering why too?* Apparently she wasn't liked by many of her students, well at least the students in my class. Out of us all I think Phenyx couldn't stand her the most. At some point, Ms. Jackson had pissed her off so much that she had to write me a letter telling me all about it. The letter was cutting Ms. Jackson up so bad I almost felt sorry for her. The stuff Phenyx was saying about her was so mean it wasn't even funny but I laughed anyway. Nosey ass Monica decided she wanted to read the note before passing it back to Phenyx. Her loud self couldn't contain her laughter and drew unwanted attention right over in our direction. Ms. Jackson walked on over to Monica and demanded the letter. I couldn't let her get her hands on that letter so I spoke up, "you better not give her that letter plus it isn't yours to give away!"

They both looked at me confused by my statement. She turned back to Monica asking for it again but before she could get out her second demand I had already snatched it out of Monica's hand. "I said NO."

Of course the entire class started cosigning with the ooooo's and the awhhhh's. Ms. Jackson and I went back and forth a few more times before she snatched the letter out of my hand. *What, was I supposed to do wrestle her for the note?* She read it and I knew immediately this wasn't going to end up good. *I mean there were pictures and everything.*

"Vickie and Phenyx get out of my class!"

"Just Vickie and Phenyx? *What about Monica she read the note too?"*

It probably didn't help any that we were snickering at her while she read the note. I mean, her facial expressions were priceless. Ms. Jackson personally walked us down to the dean. When we get there his door was shut so we sat in the waiting area still giggling about the letter. Ms. Jackson was about to pop her top when Mrs. Bandage finally emerged from Mr. Russell's office. Ms. Bandage was headed out until she spotted me sitting there. "What are you doing down here?" She asked.

"It's a long story, stick around and I'm sure you'll see what's up Mrs. Bandage."

Mrs. Bandage was my gym teacher and I was her pet. I didn't have to do anything required of the other students unless I wanted to. As a matter of fact, I skipped swimming all together. *"You weren't about to have me walking around school looking crazy all day, Giving me gym first period. Negative!"*

This hair was too laid to be getting wet on a daily. *If I didn't care about shit else I cared about my hair.*

All the favoritism in the world wasn't going to help Phenyx. She ended up getting expelled from the class and having to repeat it. Me on the other hand, I was told to go sit back down out in the waiting area and wait while Mr. Russell made his decision. Ms. Jackson went back to her class, Phenyx went to the holding cell and Ms. Bandage went back into Mr. Russell's office shutting the door behind her. I sat there in limbo trying to figure out what in the hell was going on. Twenty minutes later the bell rang right as Ms. Bandage came back out of his office, "Go on to class and Il see you bright and early tomorrow in the gym."

I didn't ask no question I already knew what that meant. I had been getting my punishments substituted for workouts since the 7th grade. *When you hold records and put your school on the map you'd be surprised what you can get away with.* Then I'm sitting at home just arrived home from school, watching television when

BREAKING NEWS... Gym teacher caught in sexual relations with the sophomore dean just as the School year was coming to an end.

"Did she say my school?"

Really Mrs. Bandage, *in the janitor's closet? On the last day of school? When this foo had a whole office? So much for being the teacher's pet next year!*

Most people would look at being intimidating as a weakness. I considered intimation a form of flattery opposed to weapon. Unfortunate for me, I was even intimidating to adults as a child. My family was about the only ones who could get over on me; everybody else was fair game to my wrath. I was too smart to be toyed with and I was nothing to go against. Before my son came along I had nothing to lose and unfortunately my attitude carried over into my adult life. History has proven how an individual whom inhabits natural intelligence threatens society. I will take this opportunity to speak on behalf of all of us geniuses and intelligent people when I say don't make your insecurities our problem because you mad we smarter. *Honestly, not our problem.* I didn't have time for the shit Malaysha was bringing here to this office. I didn't come down here to be associated with the drama. I was in a good place and was trying intensely to not have anything mess that up. She was pulling some of the sexiest men too but they were all from our office. *Now how messy is that?* She wasn't an ugly girl and on top of it all she was a true sweetheart and like anyone else on this planet she too is well deserving of love. *Couldn't you look outside the office for your boy toys though?* I would always wonder what would go on with these office men behind closed doors. *Who wouldn't though?*

They say curiosity kills the cat I personally am not that curious to be killed. There was this one dude she hung out with who was so sexy that when he would walk through the office he would make the woman stutter. He could easily turn heads and distract you from whatever it was you were doing. If he wasn't visiting Malaysha he was on our floor to go to the gym. He had fine hair to go along with his dark chocolate skinned tone. You didn't have to see him going into the gym to know he worked out. You could tell his body was ripped up just by the way he walked…*Swag honey!* He had tattoos that peeked out from up under his shirt collar and sleeves. He dressed very appropriate for the office but with suave nonetheless. I couldn't believe I was witnessing this monstrosity unfolding before me. He looked good and all but he also looked like he would take shit to a whole other level if the shit got real. *I'm just saying. Like I said, it was none of my business and I would have continued minding my own business had she not start involving people that I had in my circle into her bullshit.* I could see something unfolding and I didn't want any parts of it. No one had a clue that Maurice and I had this secret relationship brewing meanwhile Malaysha is kissing and spooning with Latoya's dude's cousin. *Are you fucking kidding me? What is wrong with this chick?*

Identity disorder is real and I just couldn't imagine battling that struggle. *Like I said everybody has a story.*

My son was back and forth from Charlotte and Indy a lot of the time therefore was clear of a lot of what was going on down here. That didn't mean he couldn't be exposed to it later. If I was nothing else I was a mother first. We were down here all by ourselves and it was my job to ensure our safety. I wasn't about to be liable for her bullshit too. Lord knows I have enough on my plate to worry about without her adding on unnecessary bullshit. Some of the shit Malaysha was doing could get her and everybody this way shot the fuck up. *No sir not this one!* Before I could get the chance to talk at her about my feelings I received that call every child dreads. It was my mother, I almost didn't pick up but something told me to.

"Hello?"

"Eden you need to get home as soon as possible." Momma's voice rang through the phone

"Wait wait wait…what's going on? What are you saying?"

"The doctors are saying they don't expect your dad to make it past the weekend. His cancer has progressed and he is getting weaker by the minute."

"Oh my goodness, Mom will I make it before he passes? Can he talk?"

"I don't know Eden; you might just want to get here as soon as possible."

"Let me talk to him."

"He can't baby, he's just too weak."

I could hear Nichelle in the background crying hysterically. Even then I was concerned for my sister. She was really attached to him, unlike me. I was surprised by the overwhelming emotions I was experiencing from the news. I contained them all the way until I reached the first set of double doors to exit the building. My knees instantly became weak and tears just flooded my eyes. Latoya witnessed me breaking down on the way to the doors and was able to catch me before I hit the floor. The man who gave me his DNA, the man who beat me senseless is dying and I don't know how to feel about that.

Chapter 27

Darrius and I had arrived back in Charlotte mid-day Sunday afternoon. Good thing I decided to leave as early as I did since when we arrived to the apartment the door was literally hanging off the hinges.

Darrius stood confused while I called the police. I hung up with them to call Maurice and Latoya. My nerves were already on edge from the funeral and to turn around to come home to this. We stayed standing outside of the apartment waiting to see who would pull up first. Latoya and Maurice rushed right over parking next to the Mecklenburg police.

"Are you and D okay?"

"Girl, do you see this shit?

"I can't believe this!

I could tell Maurice wanted to wrap me up in his arms but resisted, as did I. The police didn't seem as concerned since nothing was actually taken from the apartment. Latoya, Maurice and I came up with our own theories while the police officers went door to door in search of witnesses. "Remember me telling ya how me and the maintenance man had been beefin ever since I reported him for misconduct. First, don't just walk in my apartment without so much as a knock like you live here. Then when I call you out for throwing passes at me you wanna get mad because you got caught up lying because you screwing the ugly chick in the office."

"Right, first the fish takes a so called suicide leap out of his bowl and now your door is hanging off the hinges."

"My point exactly!"

The police came back over to where we were standing to provide an update. Of course nobody saw anything but heard some banging. With that information we were able to pinpoint the day this could have occurred. They provided me with a case number and went back to whatever it was they were doing before getting this call. Now before I left to go home, I called the apartments to explain the situation. I wasn't going to be around to pay the rent and didn't want them putting any notices on my door. The whole point in me calling them was to reduce the chance of this very same thing occurring. So why is it when I came home, there was a notice sticking in the corner of the broken door. In my mind one of two thing occurred, you broke my door exposing my home on purpose or you saw my door broken and didn't give a dam still putting the note in my door like you didn't notice this mother fucka hanging off the hinges. Latoya took Darrius back to her new apartment in order for me to handle this situation here. "What kind of thief takes a whole door off the hinges and takes nothing."

Needless to say I was beyond pissed and headed straight for the office. A phone call later, I was out my lease and the apartments were down a maintenance man.

Latoya had been generous enough to allow us to stay with her until we could get another place. Latoya has recently moved into a bigger apartment in order to accommodate her, Maurice and now her boyfriend. Oh how Maurice and I took advantage of those two weeks we stayed with them. There were so many of us in the house the probability of us getting caught was highly favorable. That didn't stop Maurice he would wait until everybody was asleep and come to wherever I was laying usually in the living room on the air mattress. He would kneel down to my ear and always say, "Are you awake?"

We quietly tip toe back into his room, no music and no television just deep breathing and smothered moans. Now that everything had a chance to blow over it was time for me to handle this Malaysha situation. In the time I was back at home, Malaysha and the cousin had become even more involved with each other than before I left. Does this dude really not know she is a he? I'm conflicted but real talk this is getting out of hand. I sent her a text:

Me: let's meet up at the Starbucks in an hour
Malaysha: cool text you when I'm leaving out
Me: Bet

We arrived at the Starbucks ordered some drinks and found some seats. She had no clue as to why I invited her here. "Sorry to hear about your father." She said giving me hug.

"Thank you, I appreciate that."

"Other than the obvious how are you doing?"

"Glad you asked actually, I am quit conflicted by some of your actions."

"What do you mean?" She was confused by my statement.

"I've noticed some of the company you've been keeping and frankly it is none of my business. However, I understand that you are now dating Latoya's boyfriend's cousin?"

"I wouldn't call it dating but yeah we are getting close." She said while rolling her eyes.

"Okay so does he know the deal?"

"What deal?" she asked like she didn't know what I was referring to.

"Really?" I asked her with my question mark face.

"No!"

"And you don't find that to be messy?"

"Nope."

"Obviously!"

"What business is it of yours Vickie?"

"If you must know, I'm fucking with Maurice and what you are doing is starting to hit too close to my home. You dig?"

"Oh really?"

"Yes, and why are you walking around the office exaggerating our relationship? Telling people we sisters, and this and that...what is wrong with you?"

She became all defensive about her life and choices and I jumped back in defense to my life and my choices.

"You are right, Malaysha Who you fuck don't make me cum (in my J. Cole voice) so that is none of my business and is the main reasons I haven't said anything to you before now but you are starting to get real selfish considering only you in this situation. Have you even thought about Latoya at all?"

Fuck the guys back at the office. You messing with her dude's cousin could be jeopardizing both her and my relationships and in extension your life. You know as well as I, people get killed for a lot less. What are you going to do when he realizes you are a fucking man?

We ended the conversation with no love lost but I did present her with an ultimatum. "One week Malaysha, one week to tell them or I will."

Could you imagine? I can hear them now you knew and didn't tell us. Oh hell naw, this bitch is doing the most. She from Indy, I'm from Indy we transferred from the same company. She moved to the same side of town as me into the same fucking apartments. I couldn't play it off if I wanted to.

On top of my burying my father, my spot being jacked with, this Malaysha thing Work had started getting intense. Since being promoted, haters started popping out of the woodwork. This was expected like I said I was once they peer and now I had all the authority over their job and money. The older employees weren't too enthused about taking orders from a younger woman such as myself. The younger ones would say I was feeling myself and was letting my new role go to my head. They all started to question my every decision as if I was unqualified to handle my job. It didn't bother me that they were feeling this way about me but what I wasn't about to allow was their insecurities and jealousy to bring down me nor my accomplishments. It was time for a meeting! "I have gathered you all here today because it has been brought to my attention that some of you are unhappy in your current roles. You all come to work to collect a paycheck and I am no different. Like each and every one of you report to me, I too have a boss and contrary to popular belief I don't make the rules, I only enforce them. It has also been brought to my attention that there is a petition going around to what I assume is to get me fired. Well, let me save you some time and energy because that is not going to happen. Anybody that is not happy reporting to me I suggest you fill out the proper paperwork so we can get you placed on a different unit. I am not here to make friends nor am I here to make problems with or for you. The bottom line is this, get on board because at the end of the day if it came down to me or you, it will not be me. Now, does anyone have any questions?"

I didn't think so. "Let's get back to work."

I went home that night full of tension. Maurice was usually the one making all of the moves but tonight I needed him. I was a bit concerned that Malaysha was going to tell Latoya about Maurice and our little secret. *One week, if you don't tell them I will.* I am so pissed at her for bringing this dumb shit down here. All I did to avoid the drama and here it is staring me in the face. I just know they are going to feel a certain kind of way for me not telling them. *It is not my story to tell I am merely trying to avoid the obvious.* As much as I wanted to see him I tried everything to avoid him during that week; working late, spending time with other friends just straight avoiding him.

Maurice: Where you at

Me: What's up?

Maurice: I'm at your door, your car here and you not

Me: U stalking me

Maurice: Girl stop playing where u at

Me: At the movies

Maurice: Wit who?

Me: What's up Maurice?

Maurice: I wanna c u…who you wit?

Me: Give me an hour and I'll be home

Maurice: bet

I secretly sat fidgeting for the rest of the movie. I couldn't wait to get out of the seat and back to my apartment. What can I say I couldn't resist him? I knew what I had waiting for me and I couldn't wait to get there to get a taste. Marilynn took her time driving me back to the apartment. My mind drifted off picturing the things that were about to occur while she talked my head off. Maurice was standing off in the distance when we pulled up. Marilynn drove away and he walked on over to me, "An hour huh?"

"I didn't know the movie was going to last that long."

Or maybe I did and self-consciously I was hoping he would get tired and go home. *Since when do we just start popping up?*

I felt his warm breath on the back of my neck while I attempted to unlock the door. I felt the heat rising between the two of us and couldn't wait to get in the house. This might be the last time since the cat was about to be out of the bag, who knows what his reaction will be. There was no talking between the two of us, he merely pushed me in the direction to the bedroom and went in. Maurice was powerful in the bedroom, all I am going to say is his deliverance of pain was definitely accepted and all my pleasure. The deadline had come and gone with no conversation from anybody about what I knew. *This bitch is really going to force my hand.*

Toya drove us to work on that particular day and on the way home I decided it was time.

"I have something very important to talk to you about"

"What's up V?"

"Listen, before I tell you. I need you to understand the severity of what it is I am about to tell you. I'm not telling you this for you to go back and run your mouth or to even change your feelings about this person. I am telling you this in order for you to be more aware and cautions of what is going on around you. But before I tell you, you need to know how serious I am. If what I tell you will get back to the office then there will be no question in who went running they mouth. I will automatically know it was you who said something. There will be no questions or conversation the shit will just get real. Point blank period..."

"I get it what sup?"

"No I don't think you do. This is so serious Toya that if it were to get back to the office I would have to bust your ass over it. That is how serious it is, you feel me?"

She was taken aback by my comment but I didn't care. I needed her to understand that I was not playing.

"V, I get it and I understand… I'm not going to say nothing. So what's up?"

"Okay, so you hadn't noticed anything peculiar about Malaysha?"

"Huh?"

"For real Toya nothing…?"

"What do you mean?"

"Oh my god Toya, let's just say Malaysha was born DeWayne"

"What?!?!?"

"You heard me."

"No fucking way, Vickie are you telling me this bitch is a really a man?"

Now the cat was out the bag!

Chapter 28

It wasn't even the next day before my phone was blowing up. *I wonder why?* I knew as soon as I told her that this kind of shit was going to happen. I already knew the amount of attention this topic would attract. Rumors began spreading the office like a wildfire in California. People actually thought it was ok to walk up to me and flat out ask if she was really a man. I had no reason to discuss her situation any further than the conversation I had with Latoya. Every time I was confronted I responded in the same manner, "Why are you asking me? If you are so curious, why not go directly to the source?" The problem with that is everybody knows when you avoid answering a question the answer is generally implied. I wasn't trying to give anybody the chance to say I even commented on the situation. I could have lied for her but just because I spilled the tea doesn't mean I was going to clean it up. Do I feel bad? Of course this was not my intention at all but at the same time, I wasn't ready to take no bullet for her. I had a child to protect! Maurice popped up at my door knocking like he was the police. I had been trying to avoid him, his calls and his text messages along with everybody else. I wasn't ready to confront whatever emotions or behavior he had for me. I opened the door and his response was completely unexpected. He pulled me into his arms to whisper in my ear, "I just wanted to make sure you were ok."

"No I am not; I just can't believe your sister did that. It's one thing to tell the people in our circle but to go running her mouth at work. What the fuck was she thinking yo? Malaysha went running to the big boss accusing me of slander and discrimination. Now my job is in jeopardy and my reputation. This is some bullshit."

"It's going to be ok."

"No it's not Maurice. I'm not just some entry-level rep I am a manager. I have a certain level of ethical obligations to uphold and this is not acceptable. The turmoil you sister has caused it is irreversible."

Maurice kept quite while I stood there with my arms folded shaking my head in disgust. "Fuck her Maurice. I owe her an ass whooping".

I turned my back to him so he couldn't see my angry tears streaming down my face. "Our friendship was over! There was no coming back from this. I told her what I was going to do if the information got back to the workplace."

Maurice came up behind me and wrapped his long arms around my waist. He twisted me around and wiped the tears from my face. "I'm not mad at you. I understand why you kept quiet and I understand why you told Toya. You were trying to look out for her and she did nothing but stab you in the back. I know that is my sister but she wrong for that shit."

I walked him backwards towards the couch until he couldn't go any further. I pushed him down, tore off my clothes and climbed onto his lap. His hands slid up my back until they were in my hair. He made a fist and pulled my head back exposing my entire neck. He softly kissed my spot transmitting tingles down to my box. He took his time exploring my body with his tongue. His free hand found its way in between my legs teasing and playing with my clit. He purposely wouldn't allow me to touch him but moved my hips along with his rhythm. For the first time I wanted to kiss him but I altered my course and went for his neck. I felt his manhood rising to the occasion in preparation to what was about to happen next. He lifted us from the couch and into the bedroom we went.

A couple of days later I was called into a meeting as I expected. I walked into the room and there sat my boss, his secretary and some woman from Human resource. "Good morning Victoria, have a seat." Larry said.

"No that is ok, I think I will stand, I don't plan on being here long Larry so why don't we cut to the chase. What can I do for you?"

I tried to contain my temper but it was slowly seeping into the atmosphere. "As you are aware, there has been a situation brought to our attention that cannot be ignored. One of your employees has reported some serious accusation against you. We wanted to allow you the opportunity to shed some light on the ordeal."

"Who are we talking about here?" *Lori, the bitch that tried to sabotage my job, or maybe its Ms. Karen, the one who mad because I pulled her in the office and told her if she didn't like what I had to say she could quite since she wants to challenge my authority. Naw, let me guess...is it Malaysha, the one who is mad because somebody else came to work and ran their mouth about her little secret.* The HR rep looked at Larry for confirmation and took over the conversation. "I can't tell you the employee's name due to confidentiality but what I can tell you is the list of accusations which were brought against you."

"And what exactly are those?"

"A short list to include: sexual harassment, discrimination and defamations of character. All which are unacceptable for anyone but especially for someone in your position within our company."

I couldn't wait until she was finished bumping her gums. The first breath she took I used to go head and jump right in. "Okay are you done?" I said as calmly as I could.

Holding my hand up to indicate she was even if she wasn't. Larry spoke up abruptly, "Victoria, hold on…"

My finger went to him, "Naw Larry, see you hold on! I need you all to listen very carefully to what it is I'm about to say. I don't know what was said to you and I frankly don't care. I know exactly who it is you are talking about. My involvement in this matter does not extend pass the four walls of my home. I did not bring this situation to the work place and if you thing for one second I am going to allow anybody to stop my grind you all have another thing coming."

They all sat there dumbfounded while I continued my rant. "I personally spoke directly to her to let her know how I was uncomfortable in the way she was flinging my name around this office, uncomfortable in how she was giving off an unrealistic truth and how her antics were beginning to interfere with my personal life. I am a single mother and have a whole entire life in which I am responsible for. She is playing with fire and the smoke is causing trouble in my life. Respectfully, every other involved party is single and without child EXCEPT me. Soooo when it comes to mine, any and everybody can kiss my ass! I gave her amble amount of time and plenty of opportunity to set the record straight. She chose not to. I told one person…ONE! I told them in confidence and for their safety since miss girl wanted to do the unimaginable. I have done a lot for this company and if you want to talk about my role and how I conduct myself here at work please go ahead but my personal life is none of your business. If you want clarification as to what is going on then maybe you should talk to the ones stirring the pot. I don't talk about this with the pondering minds out there on the floor and I won't talk about it with you all either. What I will say is this, do what you feel you have to do but this conversation right here is over."

I left them all sitting there with their mouths to the floor. I went back to my office to finish what I had left on my schedule and quickly cut out for the rest of the day. I drove around Charlotte listening to music in attempts to clear my mind. Maurice was sitting on my steps when I arrived at home. He looked up from his phone, "Long day?"

Like my face didn't reveal the amount of bullshit currently on my mind. I told him all about it over dinner and drinks. I sat Indian style on the floor across from him while he fed me bits and pieces of what he knew about his sister and the status of the situation. I still haven't talked to her since she started all this shit and I had no intentions on ever speaking to her ass again. She'd better be lucky we haven't crossed each other's paths outside of work, considering we live in the same apartments yet again. I still owe her that ass whooping I so explicitly warned her about. "I am so pissed right now; I swear I can't even see straight but at this point, it is what it is!

He noticed my mood changing and summoned me towards him. It was like I was his rattlesnake and he was my snake charmer. I crawled over towards him hypnotized by his overly sized erect penis. I starred directly into his hazel green eyes while he removed the rest of his clothing. I ran my hands up his long lean muscular thighs. I enjoyed listening to him pant and struggle to stand under my touch. His muscles contracted to me sliding my nails down his skin after I gripped his butt. I massaged his meat stimulating every pore within his body. I knew the minute I had him and it was well before I took him all in. He wasn't ready…my actions were quite surprising, tantalizing; I think he is now realizing. I'm usually so submissive to his every touch but uh uh not tonight baby; he wasn't about to put up a fuss. Tonight I wanted to have all of the control. Watch him throw his head back while I drain his energy until he firmly curls those toes. I know my shit is just that good to have you all open exposing your weaknesses. I'm the queen and you're my pond in this here game, just wait its bout to get heated. I've kept quiet for far too long it is now it's time to reveal some of Victoria's secrets.

With all that was going on it felt like what little control I had left was being snatched directly away from me and I wanted it back! Tonight I will be the dominant one and he will be submissive to me. After further investigation into the matter, management came to the same understanding as me. I was released from all responsibility, Malaysha had to deal with the new rumors and well Latoya was assed out. *Ya girl got fired!* Like anyone in corporate American, they had to find some kind of way to distinguish these flames. Coincidentally, Larry came to me boasting about all my accomplishments and how collectively they were in agreement. He came to inform me that I would be transferring to the main office to assist with various projects. Something about I had outgrown my role in this office…blah blah blah… you do such a great job… blah blah…*Oh really?* Like a boss, I accepted it with grace. *What the hell, the building was just next door to this one.* There will be even bigger opportunities for growth and more money. *Why not? I suppose* they needed some kind of way to cut the tension in the building. I said my goodbyes to my teams and off I went on next door to begin yet another chapter in my life.

Chapter 29

Me going over to the other building was supposed to be temporary. "Don't look at this as a punishment but as a learning opportunity", Management said.

I actually use this idealism in my everyday life therefore it wasn't going to be a problem, so I thought. What was supposed to be a fresh new start was turning into more of a divergent. I had a lot on my plate at the moment and wasn't too interested in arranging that current shit just to add more bullshit. Despite all that was occurring, my mind was more focused on how my son was feeling abandoned by me. "Mommy you work too much", Darrius said.

I didn't pull him away from all his people just to be left down here alone. Yeah I'm here with my interests prioritized but my attention is misdirected; this is why I was not prepared for what I was walking into when I reported to work that Monday morning. He was a mirror image of my Stepfather. Same built, height, width, style, face and all except he just wore glasses. He eye-balled me the moment I walked into his office. The Introduction was awkward especially since he couldn't stop drooling over my arrival. He personally walked me to my desk and even sat down to chat for a while, "trying to get to know me better". He was showing clear signs of interest in me. The way he leaned in when he talked to me, his constant smiling, licking of the lips and fidgeting. The conversation was moving in an unclear direction and was beginning to make me uncomfortable. My new neighbor had also noticed his inappropriate behavior and interjected herself into our discussion. I was grateful because he was so full of himself he had forgotten we were at work. *Sir your professionalism…*

According to my neighbor, he had a thing for showing interest in the younger girls in the office. He has even had a few close runs with former employees because of the misconduct towards others. *Oh really?*

"Girl you had better watch out for him!"

"What you mean…watch out for him?"

"Girl he is a closet freak! Walk around here flat out flirting with these girls."

"And nobody says nothing?"

"He still here aint he? Last year he was pulled into the office for flirting with Denise. I don't know what ever come of the situation but she quit soon after. He done run another one outta here too uhmmm huh, I see the way he look atcha girl…"

She was an older dark-skinned woman, born and bred in the south. Originally from Mississippi but has been living in the Carolinas for over the last 30 years. Outside of talking about the love for her grandchild she also enjoyed pouring that tea and spreading that office gossip baby… but you aint heard that from me. "Yeah he looking at you in the same way he was looking at them other ones."

"Is he always this friendly?"

"He only come out of that office when he see something he likes and he done seen something he like alright."

This was all too familiar and she was right. He became very aggressive very fast asking me personal questions like... do I like woman, do I have any other piercings outside of my obvious ones, if I'd ever had a threesome and would I consider one with him and his wife? I tired ignoring his advances but his curiosity escalated to a point of fear. My neighbor wasn't the only one noticing his unprofessional behavior towards me. He was real obvious with his actions constantly visiting my workstations, asking me out to lunch and calling me into his office for basically nothing. He would try and pile work on my desk to keep me working late every night but it never worked.

Until, one evening I was so engulfed into my work I hadn't noticed everyone else had left for the office for the evening. Of course he was still in his office with the door cracked open. I tried gathering my items to beat him out of the building before he could notice. He met me right as the elevator had approached the floor with this tired grin on his face. *Damit!*

"Ready for the weekend?"

"Yep."

"Any plans?"

"Yep."

"I see how you are, never got time for me..."

"Oh my god, I am so ready to get away from this man. Can this elevator go any slower? If I just ignore him maybe he would just shut up and leave me alone. I probably should have just taken the steps and maybe I wouldn't be stuck in this elevator with his overly aggressive ass."

He began invading my personal space reminding me of my stepfather and the day he went berserk on me in the bathroom. I wasn't sure what he was going to do moving in so close. I prepared myself for the worst but he stopped shy of my face and started whispering, "send me a picture of your..." but the elevator doors sprang open and

I ran out before he could finish his request. He was definitely going too far with this!

Sexual harassment can occur in several different ways and should be taken as serious as any other form of abuse. When a person of power abuses their authority in turn placing an individual and or the work environment in a position of discomfort these actions are defined as sexual harassment. Women are easy targets for workplace discrimination and are regularly harassed if not cohosted with sexual advances in exchange to further their careers. Even to this day, it remains a struggle for the workingwoman to receive the same benefits and equality as the workingman. It is sad to still be viewed as intimidating all because of our natural inhabitants as women. To be part of the minority within a corporate society where we are clearly the ones capable of embodying the realistic attributes of the roles we are so often denied. I once heard somewhere that power is intimidation and those of power are often the ones enslaved due to the insecurities of others. Makes sense, hints slavery, hints men always being placed in positions of power, hints pedophiles taking advantage of little children and serial killers practicing their impulses on defenseless animals.

After the Malaysha thing, I decided to stop involving myself with so many coworkers outside of work. I had been at the MCO for only 3 months and it was not going as expected. My performance was quite staler but the harassment was getting out of hand. I wasn't looking for a repeat in advertising my drama and jeopardizing my livelihood yet again. I knew I was going to have to confront this situation but needed time to contemplate the approach. The plan was to use the weekend to completely relax and maybe try to depress from the week; leaving all the buffoonery back at the office. Outside of Latoya, I only kicked with two other females Marilynn being one and Tameka being the other. Out of all the mayhem they were the only two outside of Maurice who stood by my side throughout it all. I had gained close relationships with these people but was starting to second-guess it all…even the Maurice thing. Tameka wasn't about to let me sulk around the apartment trying to be in my feelings. She came by to help distract my mind baring presents. She brought us something to drink on and a sack to smoke on. I wasn't even bout to turn it down with the week I had been through. *Let's go!*

She kept me up to date with the latest gossip at the office. I didn't tell her everything that was going on but she knew I definitely was bothered about something. She was thinking I was still upset about the Malaysha thing. The only thing I was shitty about still was that I haven't been able to follow through with passing off this ass whooping. Apart of me wanted to just let it go mainly because of Maurice but me being who I am, I just couldn't. *Oh she got it coming!* We were sitting at the crib when Tameka started confessing, "Okay look, check it out right. It's this honey down at the job, right. She got this nice figure you know V, hitting it in all the right places. I don't think she gay but I think she get down… you know what I'm saying?"

More than you know.

Tameka has this Brooklyn accident mixed with a southern twang. She talked with her hands and will get hype when she is really feeling the moment. She got a girlfriend who has her ass on a tight leash so it was almost like she was whispering like her girl was hiding behind the corner or something. "I gots to have that V, I gots too!"

"Is it like that, Tameka?"

"Oh it's like that and she smoke too V. Uhmm, you think I can invite her over here?"

"What the hell, I kinda wanna see what all the fuss is about."

"Naw go head…she going to bring a sac too?"

"I'm sure she will, she drive an old school BMW."

"And what that mean…but ok."

A little bit later, in walks this light-skinned chick. She was thick alright but in my opinion a tad bit ill-built even standing at 5"9. She was taller than I expected but her torso didn't match her lower body, her hair was rugged and it screamed for moisture. I almost laughed when she bounced with her tittles leading the way but she wasn't alone. *Did I say they can come or did I say she could come over?* Tameka was just as surprised as me but I couldn't tell if it was because her crushed walked in with a man or if it was who she walked in with in general? I saw his tattoos before I saw him. *Oh my, you got to be kidding me?* He was just as fine as I last remembered. I saw him a few times outside of work but it was always from a distance. I remember his tats being well hidden the few times I saw him walking through the office to her desk but it's a little hard to hide them away when you are working out shirtless. I was always in the gym every free chance I got and would bump into him from time to time. I've been avoiding this dude since the day I found out he was kicking it with Malaysha. I never heard any bad rumors about their dealings nor did she ever elaborate pass them having drinks and him being cool. Malaysha would have easily bragged if they would had taken it there even in the slightest bit. She talked about her dudes at lunch table like we talked about ours. The only difference was our dudes knew we were women, her dudes… well *your guess is as good as mine.* I didn't want any dealing with him. Whether he knew or not, he was kicking it with a man and he didn't strike me as the type to be ok with something like that.

Now, here he was standing in my living room with this beater on, khaki shorts and some all-white air force ones exposing his tats and rocking his shades. *Is he really here with this whack ass fake valley girl Barbie?* Tameka's and I looked at each other confirming it wasn't her walking in with a man it was who she walked in with. "Hiiieee, I'm Lauryn, nice to meet you." She came bouncing over with her arm linked into his.

"Hey what's up?" He said.

"And this is boo, Anthony." Lauryn said showing all of her pearly whites.

"Oh yeah, your boo?" I said to myself

"What's up boo Anthony, I'm Victoria."

I extended back my hand to greet him. "What's up Victoria, do I know you?"

Oh shit!

"Naw, not really. We might have bumped into each other a few times at the gym there at the office maybe but I think that's about it."

Lauryn was already looking confused. "Yeah, that's it, I haven't seen you in there lately. Where you been?"

"Yeah, I'm over at the other office so I've been using that gym."

"Oh, okay, looking good girl...looking good!"

"Right on."

Lauryn tightened her face in response to his compliment towards me. Tameka was still dazed by her crush walking in the door with Malaysha's old boo. "Anthony baby, this is my friend Tameka." She hurried to introduce him to Tameka I'm sure to distract him from looking at me.

"How you doing Tameka? You're one of Malaysha's friends right?"

"Yeah."

Tameka was a little stuck from the question but pulled it together before anyone couldn't notice. "How is she by the way?" Anthony asked.

And there it is...I'm going to definitely need that drink.

"Can somebody go ahead and pop that bottle?"

Chapter 30

We all sat around smoking, talking and drinking on some patron. I sat there sipping on my drink looking at the current scene unfolding at my pad. Tameka had a crush on Lauryn who was infatuated with Anthony who thought I looked good but was linked to Malaysha who I exposed to Latoya who ran her mouth to the office and is why I'm questioning my secret relationship with her brother Maurice ...*you with me so far.* After a few shots, I didn't care who was linked to who. I was buzzed and feeling myself. Anthony was just as I expected, well-rounded, like-minded and intelligence with some street sense. I started getting the feeling that Lauryn wasn't at all too happy about the connection Anthony and I had developing right in front of her very eyes. I guess she thought she was going to be able to stay the center of attention once she got around me. I quickly gathered that she was a quick fix for him and that she was reading more into them than he was. *Obviously look at her and then look at him.* She struggled to keep up with our conversation and that too was making her mad. I can't help miss girl that you are nothing but booty because you show aint got the brains and quite frankly I have yet to see the beauty. We hung out the rest of the weekend shooting the shit and kicking the breeze. The charlotte air was brisk and the sun was beaming just the way we liked. It was perfect weather to go down to the park and kick it outside the house. We'd end up back at my house afterwards anyways so why not? Here I met this sexy tall drank of water named Terrence. Him and Anthony were friends and baby when I say birds of a feather… he had the tats and the muscles but he didn't have the level of intellect he did but what can I say; you can't have it all right? Thankfully, him entering the picture took some of the tension away from Lauryn's little ol' insecure heart.

Monday morning rolled back around and I was back at work barley able to get seated at my desk before my desk phone was ringing.

"Hello, this is Victoria."

"Ms. Night this is Jane from Human Resources can you come down to my office at your earliest convenience?"

"Uhm sure, where u located…?"

I got up immediately and headed up to RM 504. I honestly was dumb founded not sure to what they could possibly want. There had been so much going on I just wasn't sure about anything anymore. "Hello…uhmm Jane?"

"Yes, Victoria please come in and have a seat."

I kept quite locating my chair and allowing her to lead the conversation. "Please don't be alarmed, you are not in trouble however, we have been made aware of a serious allegation and need to inform you that a formal investigation has been launched on your behalf. We take sexual harassment serious here at our company and we are committed in assuring your safety and comfort from the beginning to the end of this."

She went on about policies and procedure, asked a few questions and instructed me on my next steps. "You are to leave from my office and go home for the rest of the day with pay. Tomorrow you will report back to Larry and return back to the other office. He will instruct you on your new assignment from there."

"*Seriously?!?*"

"Do you have any questions?"

I wasn't sure what to say, "No I don't have any questions."

What could I say she just told me what it was. I left her office and my items were already waiting for me at her secretary's desk. I didn't tear up until I was far away from the building and sitting isolated in my car. This wasn't close to the drama I was experiencing back at home but it was still enough to have me seriously considering moving back there.

"How in the hell did they find out?"

I had only told Jonathan all the details she was confronting me with...but why would he go to HR before I had the chance? Jonathan and I had established a great working relationship. We were placed on many projects together and in my absence he monitored my team and vice versa. I confided in him and he confided in me many times before. Did I go running off and telling his business? I swore I told him I would handle it. Being young and a woman of color our opportunities were far more limited. I wanted to make sure I had a plan in place; to not only secure my safety and comfort but also my job. "Now what's going to happen?"

I know how these things go! Maybe he thought he was protecting me?"

There was only one way to find out. Go directly to the source.

Hanging at my spot had for sure become the new thing. I didn't mind except I was becoming a little uneasy about how Lauryn had started acting towards me. What she didn't realize was how I didn't want Anthony, had I known she was bringing him to my crib with her the first time she wouldn't came through then. I didn't want to get close enough to Anthony to risk the chance of him asking me anything about Malaysha. Luckily, she hadn't come up in conversation since he first asked Tameka about her day one. Tameka hadn't been socializing with her anymore since she tried to blame me for the whole blow up and apparently Anthony hasn't been fucking with her either. As we all hung around each other more I started noticing Miss Lauryn lightweight getting messy with mouth. She was already loud but now she was snapping and becoming very opinionated towards a lot of what I had to say. Add in the fact that she is flighty, it just makes for one bad combination. I talked my suspicions over with Tameka just to see if I was crazy but she wasn't trying to hear what I was saying. She had an excuse ready to give me for little Miss Priss. "Nuh uh V, that's just how she is yo!"

"Bullshit!"

I guess she still thought she was going to get piece of that. *Bless her heart. I really wasn't feeling the* shade Lauryn had been throwing my way. When I brought up the change to Anthony about his little girlfriend's attitude he had noticed it to. How she was becoming very defensive and straight rude, lightweight disrespectful. It was almost like that was the only way she could include herself into the conversation is if she came at me. She wasn't sure how to articulate on our level but don't get mad at me because I have more in common with your man...I'm just saying. I brushed her off like she should have been brushing her hair. I no longer gave her my energy and directed my attention to everybody but her. She took noticed right away desperately trying to pull all of Anthony's attention away from the group and me especially. *However, when I was around...She couldn't keep his direct attention if she was naked and sucking his dick at the same damn time. And that is some real shit for yo ass.* I wasn't going to be sticking around too much longer so let her ass act up if she wants to. I found her behavior although irritating quite hilarious, immature and somewhat entertaining. I wasn't going to allow myself to drop to her level. That is…

Until that one Saturday night we all decided to go to hang out with Anthony and Terrence down at the courts. *I was always down for watching some basketball especially when the men looked like some of these southern Mandingos…Baby!* Lauryn was more interested in finding a seat than surveying these bodies or even watching the game. I wasn't trying to be disrespectful in front of Terrence so I brushed off the few that came my way. Lauryn on the other hand, was attracting them like flies. I guess so, the girl's skirt was so short I thought her pubic hair was going get caught in the wood from the bench she found to sit on super far away from the action…by the way. *What in the hell? I came to see some men not run from them.*

"Why you wanna sit all the way over here?" I asked.

"Girl, I'm tired of standing!"

"Okay, well you can sit over here but Imma go on back over by the courts and finish watching them play."

"You just wanna be over there by Anthony."

"And there it is…Is she giving me attitude? Victoria…don't do it."

"Girl, please…what I look like trying for Anthony and I'm talking to his homie Terrance."

"I see the way you look at him, the way you talk to him like aint nobody else around."

"Is that your observation? Well observe this, there is a park full of men, sweating and wrestling over balls with their shirts off, playing the game that I love and you think Imma bout to be over here arguing with you over some nigga that I don't even want. Girl you can have him and this conversation."

I walked away from her trying not to blow my complete top. "We not done with this conversation Victoria!"

She yelled in my direction. "Shhhhiiiit, *you wanna bet?*"

Their game must have ended while we were busy arguing. The men were headed in our direction by the time I made it back under the lights near the courts. Lauryn came rushing over trying to prevent contact between Anthony and I. She wasn't quick enough; he was already wrapping his arms around me pulling me in for a sweaty hug. We laughed while he wiping the sweat from my face. I went over to Terrence to show him some love and that's when I heard her loud annoying ass voice slanging words at me...*again!* "What are you doing hugging up on my man?"

Okay this bitch is really asking for it!

"You got to be fucking kidding me right? OK! I think it is time to go before THIS situation goes N-E further. For whatever reason, this broad has it in her mind that I want you Anthony and I think we all understand that not to be true... but her empty headed ass."

I'm not going to **A.** keep repeating myself and **B.** continue on with this bullshit. No no no no no no! And with that being said I don't want your man. Terrence Imma call you later and Anthony, I'll see you around...I'm done with this shit right here."

I walked off in the direction of my car and left them to discuss it amongst themselves. I heard them muttering behind me but they was fading. I was too steamed to care. Anthony yelled to me, "V, calm down baby girl, we were going to ride back with you remember, if that's still was okay." He jumped in front of me slowing my stride.

"Look, she just going to need to keep her mouth shut so I can get ya to where ever it is with no complications you feel me?"

He grinned and winked at me then fell back to wait on Lauryn who was struggling to keep up in the shoes she was wearing. *Who wears stilettos to an outside basketball court?*

Terrence and I exchange a few more words before hugging it out. He came down to lift me off my feet and I accepted his embrace. *Sweat and all.* He kissed my neck took in my smells before putting me back on the ground. We heard Anthony and Lauryn approaching the car where we were standing, "Damn, I can't even leave you alone for one minute." Anthony was spitting to to Lauryn.

"I just don't like the way ya interact with each other." She said in her defense.

Anthony jumped in the back seat and Lauryn bounced into the front passenger side.

No sooner than we can get out of the parking lot she had started running her damn mouth I turned up the music drown her out. *"Just get her to her car…" I kept saying to myself.*

I got halfway to our destination and I noticed her saying some whole other shit. I heard fake, I heard liar… "Wait Whaaat?!?"

Then this hussy turned my radio down before I could. I guess so I can hear her loud ass even better. She screaming, "You fake, you make up stuff up just so you can be able to talk to Anthony, you act like you have stuff in common with him. You aint no real friend… you're a liar! I heard what you did at the office before I got there."

And that did it. I just snapped, "YOU DUMB BITCH! You just can't leave well enough alone. Can you? CAN YOU!!!!! I asked you to SHUT the WHAT? FUCK UP talking to me, so I can get your dry ass back to your car and YOU can get the fuck on. BUT NO! no! You wanna keep RUNNING YO mouth. What is about to happen is you about to get put out of my ride, or worse I'll let you decide just keep on!"

She was really shocked by the demeanor. "You really going to put me out?" She asked.

See that's the shit I'm talking about. After all of that and 6 words is all she had to say. She really isn't worth the energy.

"And you call yourself my friend." She huffed.

"Friend of foe…you keep talking sideways you can get the fuck out."

"I just can't believe you."

"Oh but I thought you knew me. Let me ask you something friend how long you been feeling this way? About me being all fake and such? By the way that wasn't meant for you to answer so don't hurt yourself trying to think of an answer but check it… if I'm so fake and all that… then why you hanging out with me? Coming over to my shit, wanting to be in my presence? I'm confused. Anthony, would you keep fucking with somebody, coming around them, pretty much trying to be relevant in their life if you didn't like the way they got down?"

"On a serious tip? Personally I wouldn't."

"Oh, oh oh so you're going to take her side?"

"There is no side. I was merely answering her question."

The man is right there is no side. Listen, let me help you out. Don't come back to my crib, don't look for me in the office and don't call my phone. If I'm soooooo fake leave me the fuck alone, how about you do that! THE END."

She continued to try and salvage our relationship. *Too late for that miss girl.* "All I was trying to say…"

"What you trying to say don't matter and girl you no longer matter! And don't touch my radio again."

I turned the radio back up to and ignored her the rest of the way. I hit the gas rushing to get this girl on away from me before I black out on her ass. I can't be going to jail over no bullshit. We pulled up to the house and I patiently waited for her to remove herself from my car but as I suspected she wasn't done. "We need to talk about this!"

"Girl, if you don't get out of my car, you going to wish you had."

"You being petty, I mean… for real."

"Hold up, I think you may need some help because I'm not sure why you aren't moving? I've told you, there is nothing else we need to talk about. You said all you had to say and I don't care to hear shit else from you. DO YOU UNDERSTAND? NOW DO I NEED TO HELP YOU GET OUT MY CAR?"

Anthony stayed quite in the back seat observing the scene. She had realized how serious the situation done escalated. If she thought for one more moment that I was going to sit back and actually hear her out after she called me fake while riding in my car…oh hell no! I got out of my car mumbling under my breath. I had to keep talking myself down so I wouldn't snatch this chick up by her roots. I opened the passenger car door, "Lauryn please listen. This will be the last time I'm going to ask you to get the out my car, now do you need some assistance because the next time there won't be a question pumpkin."

She hurried up and unsnapped her seat belt recognizing my crazy. She steadily was trying to plead her case but this time she was multitasking. "See stupid. I knew you had it in ya."

I shut the passenger door and walked back over to my side of the car ready to pull off. I almost forgot Anthony was in the backseat. "What you going to do because I'm ready to bounce?"

"Yeah, uhmmm V, do you think you can give me a ride back to my crib? I think I'm through with this situation."

"I heard that!"

Anthony jumped in the passenger side of my ride and we left her whack ass standing next to her car with her still running. "*Stupid bitch!*"

"Damn, V was you going to whip her ass?"

"It was just about to that point. She was really trying my patience and pushing me close to the edge. Plus she touched my radio."

We broke out into laugher and kept talking like she never happened. He rolled up another blunt and kicked it a little longer before calling it a night.

All of this madness that had happened while in Charlotte had my mind swirling. Darrius has been riding my back and rightfully so. My career was tarnished but not deflated, the Latoya thing, the Maurice thing, the Malaysha thing and now the Lauryn and Anthony thing... not to mention burring my father, my car being stolen, the attempted burglary and all the wasted money...this was no longer worth it. At least back at home Darrius would have his dad, their family, my mother despite her shenanigans, my family, his god mom and his friends. I understand that with great success come large sacrifices but not enough for me to sacrifice my son. The decision was final, it was time to say my goodbyes and head back to the Midwest.

Saying goodbye was harder than I thought it was going to be. At this point, I literally only had a few people to say anything to. I sat down with Larry and broke the news to him. He understood where I was coming from and didn't put up too much of a fight. Larry called in a few favors to secure me a job for when I returned back to Indy. He also put me on to something I was unaware about. "You know Jonathan was trying to sabotage your career here at the company."

"What do you mean?"

"All the projects you two worked on together. He was trying to put his name on it and take full credit for the work and then some."

"Really?"

I bet that's why that motherfucka ran to HR. Sad ass excuse for a man.

"We don't tolerate plagiarism and in the manner in which he as conducting business was not going to be tolerated. We knew from the beginning that he was stealing your work. I wanted to see how far he was going to take it and he tried running a marathon. In the long run…no point intended. He ended up burying himself. He took advance of his role and that was on him."

"Wow."

"On the other hand, I'm sorry we sent you over to that office just for you to be placed in that situation. I wish things would have gone better for you, for us but just know you will always have a position here at this office if you ever decide to come back to this city. I appreciate everything you did for us and your accomplishments haven't gone unnoticed."

He handed me a farewell card with a nicely loaded gift card inside. "Larry you really didn't have to."

"This was the least I can do Victoria…you have truly been a tremendous asset to our team and you will be missed."

"I really appreciate the kind words and all the opportunities afforded to while I was here Larry."

"If you're ever in the area, please make sure you stop by and say hi."

"Of course!"

I took the rest of the day saying goodbye to everybody in the office. Some of the ladies collected farewells and placed them on a large banner, some provided cards and gift cards but Marilynn gave me a fit. She was that person I would normally not be bothered with but she grew on me the first day I met her and I haven't wanted to get rid of her since. She has the softest soul and the biggest heart and I wasn't sure how I was going to say goodbye to her. Regardless, of where I lived I knew her and I would remain friends. The way her compassion radiated from her soul could have lit up a dark room. I am pleasured to have met her and she really helped me stay concentrated and focused on the positive. I will always and forever value our friendship. *Thank you for being my friend.*

After arriving home, I sat down struggling to text Maurice the news. I waited until the very last moment before telling him I was moving back to Indy.

Me: I got something to tell you?

Maurice: You not pregnant are you?

Me: Boy naw, I'm moving back to Indy.

Maurice: Why u wanna go and do that for?

Maurice: When?

Me: I'm leaving Friday.

Maurice: Next Friday?

Me: No, tomorrow Friday.

Maurice: Why u just now telling me?

Me: Thought it was easier this way.

Maurice: Open the door.

He must have already been in route to my house because when I had looked out the peephole, there he was standing on the other side of my door just like the very first time he came knocking. I opened the door and he quickly pulled me into his arms.

"I don't want you to go."

"And that's why I didn't want to say anything to you."

"What you mean, we could have been getting it in."

We both snickered with it both being filled with emotion. "We've already been getting it in…"

"You know what I mean."

He picked me up off the floor; I wrapped my legs around his waist and my arms around his neck. He turned to shut the door using my back for assistance. He didn't remove his eyes from mines the entire time. His hazel-green eyes pierced through my soul and I became lost in him. Our emotions were obviously elevated because for the first time ever I allowed him to press his lips against mine. He was hesitant, I am sure from remembering my reaction the last time he tried to kiss me but this time I wanted it. Our energy was kinetic and our tongues danced around searching for a lost end. We stood there taking each other in for what seemed like hours. His hands cupped my ass while we danced towards the entrance of my bedroom. I refused to loosen my grip from around him and he couldn't get enough of my taste. The heat became unbearable and clothes started flying off. We started kissing again this time less passion and more intensity. He laid me on my back while trailing kisses from my mouth, down the middle of my chest pass my stomach and onto my thighs. He buried his head into all of my sweet nectars over flooding my cave with moisture. He used his fingers to explore the inside of her depth finessing my g-spot. I wasn't ready to cum but I didn't have much to say in that matter. He did everything to me in that one night than he has the entire 2 years we've been carrying on our secrete relationship. I begged him to stop teasing me, "Please baby, just give it to me!"

"Tell me what you need?"

"Maurice please you know what I need."

"I wanna hear you say it."

"You…I need you!"

He pushed deep inside my cave right the moment I answered him and my body pulsated in reaction to his arrival. I stammered out soft moans and tears fell from my eyes… *it felt so good.*

"Is this what you want baby?"

He continued stroking my box, kissing my neck, touching my body. *I was putty in his hands and like I said, he had me at hello.* My orgasms had me paralyzed giving him free rein over my body. He could have done whatever he wanted to do to me and I would have let him. This was our last night and he was going to make it count. We made love, fucked, had sex, fucked some more, and made love until I had no more energy left. When I woke up from our sexapade Maurice was gone.

Chapter 31

Since arriving back home I could tell the vibe was all different than what it had been before I left. Nichelle had finally seen the multiple sides of momma and could now understand why I chose to stray away. Momma was now lashing out her frustrations onto Nichelle since I was no longer in striking distance. Nichelle wasn't use to our mother being this way let alone towards her. She wasn't sure how to react to momma's actions. She began calling me for more than just material things. "Little Vickie, what do I do when momma does… or why is she so… or why does she do… or your mother…" she would say.

Unlike Nichelle, I tried not to interfere with their relationship since it was always estrange to me. Nichelle was just selective in her actions and always picked and chose what she was willing to deal with. I was fed up with always coming to her rescue. It was time for her to grow on up and accept responsibility for some of her own actions. I had been trying to tell her for the last, I don't know twenty plus years that momma was not herself. I guess some people just have to bump their head against a brick wall before they actually learn the hard knocks of life.

Darrius sure was happy to be back in Indy. He still had the entire summer before starting the fifth grade. Fortunately, I was able to come back home to a nice set up with a different insurance company thanks to Larry hooking me up before I left Charlotte. I was able to find a house in the same neighborhood as Darrius's grandfather and best friend Donald. Donald stayed with his grandparents who lived directly across the street from Darrius grandfather. Darrius and Donald have been playing together since Darrius was born. Donald is a few years older than D and oddly they look exactly alike. It was hard to tell the two apart when they were out playing in the neighborhood together. I'm not sure how excited I was to be living so close to Darrien's dad since Darrien was always over there. We had been getting along fairly well lately so me living around the corner shouldn't cause too much of a rift in our co-parenting abilities. He is very territorial even though we are no longer together and I think he has a girlfriend. *Like that has eve stopped him before.* I can see him becoming jealous of my company now that he can witness the comings and goings from his street. *He has never been ok with me flaunting another man in his face regardless of our status. Out of sight out of mind right? Well I guess we will see.*

I was real secretive about telling people I was back in town. I wasn't ready to jump back into old relationships or circumstances. Not that they were all bad, I just needed some time to get settled in before the drama started to reveal itself. Very few outside of my family knew I was back in town. Those few told some others and those people told some more people and before you knew it, there was a bunch of us parting at my spot. *This is what I was talking about…but these are my people. Did I really expect them to act like I wasn't home after being gone so long?* There weren't as many people at this party as there was at my going away party. Papa Collins had fired up the grill and prepared the deep fryer for some of his good ol' fish. We had spaghetti, French fries, coleslaw; all sorts of meats from hotdogs, hamburgers, ribs and of course plenty of alcohol. Surprisingly, no body popped off especially with some of the people that were there in attendance. Clearly, we were all there to live it up and have a great time. The party seemed like it had went on forever. By the end of it all there were only a few people lingering around the house before the crowed completely dissipated. I told Nathan I would meet him back at my house once I finished up my conversation with Darrien. Nathan wasn't too fawn of the ideal and Darrien got a kick out of it since they didn't get along. Darrien didn't like me kicking it with Nathan and Nathan did like Darrien because Darrien didn't like him.

Darrius had already went across the street to spend the night at Donald's grandparents and Darrien's roommate sat in the car waiting on him to finish his conversation with me. Darrien has always been a talker and tried everything to keep me from getting back home to meet Nathan. After an hour of talking to I decided to send Nathan a quick text message letting him know I would be a while and not to wait up. I made up some kind of excuse so he wouldn't be mad. He wasn't sweating it and said he would just catch up with me tomorrow. Darrien and I started reminiscing about old times and before you knew it we were standing there locking lips like we never parted. Kissing like we 14 again inside of the janitors closet in the front of Kroger's. His roommate became impatient after hour number two and finally got out of the car. "Darrien I'm tired, let's go!" She yelled from the car.

Darrien wasn't too concerned about her and brushed her off like she wasn't there. "Hold up, I'll be there in one minute." He barked back.

She never argued the point and simply got back into the car and waited for him to finish his conversation. Darrien and I hadn't done much of anything outside of hugging since we separated my senior year. We might have had sex a couple of times right after but nothing too serious that would indicate we were considering rekindling a relationship. Another 30 minutes of kissing and groping and the heat between us was getting too intense.

"I think I better go." I said pulling away from him.

"Why baby? We are just getting started."

He was always good to run some game but I couldn't fall for it this time. "Yeah but do we really want to do this again? Plus hasn't your roommate already been sitting there waiting on you for what like 2 ½ hours now."

"I can send her home and just stay the night with you."

I kissed him again, allowing his hands to feel all over my goodies but decided against the temptation and sent him to the car. "You sure?" He asked.

"No, but I think we both are drunk and probably will regret this tomorrow."

"I won't regret anything but I get what you saying."

"Plus, I thought you had a girlfriend?"

"Nope, so if you change your mind, you know my number."

"Indeed I do baby daddy."

I watched him stumble over to the car where his roommate sat impatiently waiting for him. They were engaged in a heated conversation when I walked past to go to my house. I was more concerned about getting into my bed and less about what they were talking about.

I was finally getting settled back home from the move. I was putting things away listening to Darrius, Donald and Diesel wrestling around in the living room. I thought about that last night I had with Maurice. He was nowhere to be found when I woke up but I did find a note he left for me on the refrigerator it read:

> *I can't believe your leaving me like this!*
> *Hope to see you again one day*
> *Sooner than later!*
>
> *I love you V,*
> *Maurice*

I can't believe he said it, *"He loved me!"*

"I thought I heard him whisper those words during our last session together but I was so caught up in the moment that he could have said anything and it would not have mattered. I tried getting a hold of him before I took off but he was nowhere to be found. "I wonder will I ever see him again?"

I was amazed at all the crap I'd held onto. It was time to clear out some of this old stuff, maybe sale some, collect a few dollars and donate whatever else we no longer had a need for. I was trying to conserve money since I had wasted so much of it relocating back home. I needed to switch my service back to the 317 from the 704, but I didn't want to waste money buying a new phone. I decided to use the phone I had right before I left for Charlotte. It was the only one out of the bunch still working properly and it was in better condition than the one I was using now. I charged the phone to get it ready for the transition while I finished separating the clothes into piles. Right on cue, the boys were ready to eat and Diesel was ready for his walk. I had a pizza already in the oven cooking while they were busy playing. Diesel monitored the boys while they ate and then they took him out for his walk. After the boys settled in over to papa Collins's, I grabbed the phone and headed for Sprint. I didn't notice the pending voicemail until I was headed back home from running errands. *"Did I get a call and didn't hear it? I don't have any missed calls..."*

I entered my code: You have one new message, Message received June 26ᵗʰ at 11:56 pm from 317. 555. 0169. Message marked urgent.

Hey baby...uhm I just got your message and I guess you are already gone? I'm heartbroken and at a loss for words. I guess that's what I get for avoiding... but I couldn't bare it anymore, I couldn't hear you tell me no ever again...now your are gone and I didn't get a chance to say goodbye... All I ever wanted was for you to be happy. We just can't leave it like this...please call me back. I love you...I'm soooo sorry! If only I could have just one more night.

End of message.

Acknowledgments

As humans we are faced with tumultuous and unbearable yet continuous and unfortunate situations in life. I started writing back when I was 13 Years old and I never knew how to fully express my feelings. I have a lot of unresolved feelings that I am still trying to work through but I am thankful for all the drama and yes necessary bull..... to which occurred in my life because without it I wouldn't be half the person I am today. In a way I was forced to find myself and for that I am very grateful. To my son, Demonte you inspired me before you were even implanted into my world but it was you my son, who inspired the growth within my life, my maturity and Siiiirrrr my heart! ☺ You have forever changed my world and will continue to do so beyond and into the next for eternity.

I want to thank all the individuals in my life (the goo the bad and especially the ugly) that saw my potential and who fought for me and didn't give up on me. For that I thank you, *grin* My friends... there are so many yet so few. Every single one of you already knows you much you warm my heart. You all are my family! The impact you've had on my life is beyond measure. Thank you for putting up with me, crying with me, and picking me up when I was at my lowest. Thank you for making me laugh and letting me know it will all be ok. Thank you for praying for me and Thank you 4 displaying and exchanging the same respect as I share with you. Angelina...I'd go to hell and back for you, what can I say I can go on and on but at the end of the day you are my person. *wink*

Lastly, and most importantly, my Savior. There is sooo much to say directly to you as you and the greatest part is that you already know. My heart is yours and I am. *at peace* you have literally turn nights into day. You allowed me to walk under your protection no matter how bleak as I am still here. My love, my heart, my dedication, and determination...my will...my purpose is because if you. And for that I'm grateful. My love is unconditional and I leave you with these thoughts Life is truly unpredictable and the one thing we are most certain of is that we are born to die...in our lives we all have choices and with those choices come consequences good or bad so ensure you choose wisely.

Peace and Love

E. Victoria

P.S. - I was watching American Top Model while closing up this book and I heard Tyra and her mother talking to the candidates about knowing yourself and building your worth. I was really in awe of Ms. Tyra Banks in that moment. Her journey is inspirational and if you don't know about Ms. Banks outside of her fashion and TV then you don't know Tyra. Her hustle is serious on and off scene. Her alongside of a few others... Michelle Obama, Queen Latifah, Oprah Winfrey, Ellen DeGeneres, Beyoncé, and Whoopi Goldberg are my people who drive me to do what I do...motivation. These ladies have passion, humility, heart, drive, will, determination, and endurance. I see this because one is married to the president of the United States.

Another owns her **own** network. I was listening to one when she said "I punched him dead in his eye and said who you calling a bitch"… U.N.I.T.Y (Queen, that is still my jam!). Another is keeping it 100 on the airways and grabbed my attention the moment she stared in my favorite movies *The Color Purple*. Another lifts my soul through airwaves with her bright sprint and smooth moves. While the last one is spilling love into our hearts through song and dance. Listen, these ladies have found what works for them in order for them to do what they love and do and they do it so well. I continue to work on my inner beast to be better than I know I can be. So thank you for showing us your hustle and sharing your struggle weather you choose to or not. Thank you.

With that being said, Tyra hit me with some words during this particular segment that really resonated and was so on point I had to share.

"Know your Plan for the end at the beginning."

~Tyra Banks & Carolyn London

I am

I was born, I was loved, I was blessed
From the time the connection was made and
his sperm entered into her egg.
However your perception, the true definition of conception, I say it to be
when the time the sperm enters the egg and in that very moment is when
we become to be. What a lesson and this my hidden confession
I am
Alive
The first month of the year the 19th day, fourth day of the week in
the early part of the 80's is the day my momma gave birth to me.
See, my heart began to beat but shortly after it began
to weep. Yes, my soul entered into this life challenged
but not alone my journey a never ending defeat.
But it was he who walked with me spiritually yet
emotionally in my head I grew to be.
Yes I was beaten
Yes I was abused
Yes I was molested
Yes I was misused
Yes I was stepped on, overlooked and accused.
I was…**I am**… exposed.
An open book, just look! At the many speed bumps in life
I've hurtled over and yet my heart is pure. That is one of
the reasons I stand here before you humbled, no longer
the victim but a mother, a mentor an entrepreneur.
Yes, I stand proud to say **I am** an artist, an author, a poet. Yes
I can sing, yes I played ball and broke records, yes I survived
and became a queen. Put my faith in he and my god has given
me the strength to endure and prevail within my calling.
Yes I am intelligent, grounded, ambitious, determined,
loyal, energetic and tenacious. Warm hearted and
simplistic with a sense of beauty and a love for life.
And yet, I still don't know how to open up fully as I am tired.
Of holding back my strengths because others are scared
to walk in their light. Fight! For what you want and open
your heart to understand the power of your mind.
It was he who created me to use all my senses to do and be anything…Is
that why I now hold 3 degrees and working on a fourth in psychology?

To live, to breathe, to love, to foresee, to witness and become
who/what it is exactly that he wanted me to be.
Even with all my 50 shades that lay deep inside of me. I
know he is the only one who accepts me for me.
I am all thee above,
A glamma, a teacher and a student. The woman who you all see.
For every day and every minute of this life, world Sir Mam…

I am who **I am**

Coming Soon

Sessions

Becoming a Grown Woman